JUST

An imperial stepped toward the gate. Hansen spread the thumb and forefinger of his right hand. His arc leaped out between the gateposts and the imperial staggered. "Now!" he shouted. They raced toward the gap in the fence as the first two imperial warriors struggled out of the flames, sweeping their arcs widely in order to drive back opponents for the instant they were blinded by the inferno of their own making.

Hansen thrust like a surgeon lancing a boil. His arc ripped the inside knee of the left man of the pair. The second warrior stumbled over the toppling body of his companion. Hansen stabbed through his backplate, where the neck joined the shoulders. Thirty meters to go . . .

≡ *Northworld* ≡

From the bestselling author of the classic *Hammer's Slammers* comes the riveting new future war series. Read all of the electrifying NORTHWORLD adventures in *Northworld*, *Vengeance*, and the gripping final battle of *Justice*!

Ace Books by David Drake

HAMMER'S SLAMMERS
DAGGER
SURFACE ACTION
NORTHWORLD
NORTHWORLD 2: VENGEANCE
NORTHWORLD 3: JUSTICE

Ace Books by David Drake and Janet Morris

KILL RATIO
TARGET

Ace Books Edited by David Drake and Bill Fawcett

The Fleet Series

THE FLEET
THE FLEET: COUNTERATTACK
THE FLEET: BREAKTHROUGH
THE FLEET: SWORN ALLIES
THE FLEET: TOTAL WAR
THE FLEET: CRISIS

NORTHWORLD
JUSTICE

DAVID DRAKE

ACE BOOKS, NEW YORK

This book is an Ace original edition,
and has never been previously published.

NORTHWORLD 3: JUSTICE

An Ace Book / published by arrangement with
the author

PRINTING HISTORY
Ace edition / April 1992

All rights reserved.
Copyright © 1992 by David Drake.
Cover art by Roger Loveless.
Author photo by Beth Gwinn.
This book may not be reproduced in whole or in part,
by mimeograph or any other means, without permission.
For information address: The Berkley Publishing Group,
200 Madison Avenue, New York, NY 10016.

ISBN: 0-441-58616-3

Ace Books are published by The Berkley Publishing Group,
200 Madison Avenue, New York, New York 10016.
The name "ACE" and the "A" logo
are trademarks belonging to Charter Communications, Inc.

PRINTED IN THE UNITED STATES OF AMERICA

10 9 8 7 6 5 4 3 2 1

To Beth Fleisher
My once and future editor

≡1≡

THE GUARD STANDING beside the four steps to King Venkatna's throne was probably bored beneath the smooth faceplate of his battlesuit. The armor's black-and-yellow striping made the soldier look like a giant bumblebee.

Memory danced in the mind of Nils Hansen: *Shill, Hansen's sideman in battered armor with black and yellow stripes, strikes home and crows his triumph. A hostile warrior turns. The arc springing from the enemy's right gauntlet rips Shill's legs off at the knees.*

Shill topples. The air is full of the stench of burned meat. Hansen screams as his own arc lashes out in a deadly curve. . . .

To the folk here in the Open Lands of Northworld, that event had occurred more than a century ago. Duration no longer mattered to Nils Hansen. The dead of ages crowded in on him, and he shivered in the warm hall.

The craggy trader who stood before the throne claimed his name was Grey. "Your majesty," he said, "the device I offer you—the *Web,* the folk who sold it to me called it—can change the whole course of your reign."

Venkatna's father had built a new palace on the outskirts of Frekka. Rooms surrounding courtyards within the palace complex provided space for the West Kingdom's growing bureaucracy. Previously, the court offices had been scattered

within the Old City over a number of buildings which dated
from long before Frekka became the kingdom's capital.

Before Nils Hansen made Frekka the capital of the West
Kingdom.

The city continued to expand. Already shanties and a stockyard lapped the exterior walls of the palace, and the king was
erecting additional barracks for his army nearby.

"We are not displeased with the present course of our reign,
Grey," King Venkatna said. The coolness of his voice left
uncertain whether he believed the trader's statement was merely unfortunately worded—or was a subtle curse.

Venkatna was a tall man, but willowy rather than massive.
His dark eyes glinted with a determination just short of fanati-
cism. His father had replaced the old linen diadem of the West
Kingdom with a circlet of gold, but Venkatna himself affected
a jeweled platinum helix which added timeless majesty to his
thirty-two years.

"Forgive me, your majesty," said Grey. He bowed so low
that his forehead almost touched the ground. "The course of
your reign is already splendid. This device, this Web, has the
capacity to build from that splendor into an era which will live
in memory for all time."

The petitioner who crowded against Hansen's right side
appeared to be a rural lordling. He wore imported finery
for this court appearance: hose, a jerkin, and a peaked cap.
The garments were dyed three shades of green which should
have been mutually exclusive. His belt was of aurochs leather,
while his boots were cut from the hide of giant peccaries. The
materials had reacted in wildly different fashions to the russet
stain applied during the tanning process.

He nudged Hansen and whispered, "I think those roofbeams
up there are *stone*."

Hansen glanced upward at the coffered dome over the audience hall. The lower band of decoration, ten meters above
the inlaid floor, was mosaic. The portraits and vine tendrils
running higher to the lens of clear glass at the peak of the
vault were painters' work which tried to mimic the stiffness
of the mosaics.

"Concrete, I'd guess, under the stucco," Hansen murmured

back. "But very impressive, I agree."

"The Web shapes the course of events," explained the trader at the front of the hall. "There is any number of ways that— dice can fall, let us say."

Grey's left hand came from beneath his cloak with a pair of six-sided dice between his thumb and bony forefinger. "This device thrusts possibilities to one side or the other of the event curve. The Web doesn't make things happen, your majesty, but it encourages the occurrence of possible events that *you* choose."

Grey dropped the dice. They clicked and chittered repeatedly on the stone floor before coming to rest, five pips and one, in front of the throne.

"Can you see?" whispered Hansen's neighbor. He craned his neck, pointlessly given that there were several rows of restive petitioners standing ahead of him.

"No," Hansen said.

Not quite a lie. He couldn't *see,* but he felt the Matrix warping to a particular result.

A five-meter semicircle was marked on the floor with white tesserae which stood out brilliantly from the mottled-gray marble of the remainder of the room. The white band was a deadline, literally. Except for the highest members of Venkatna's court— with permission—and Queen Esme herself, anyone who stepped across the boundary would be killed by the guard.

"I'm Salles of Peace Rock," the stranger said, offering his arm to shake. "Are you here to get your district's tribute reduced too?"

"Now, your majesty," the trader said. "Throw the dice yourself while your chamberlain here sits within the Web and controls the fall to come up six each time."

"I'll throw them, my dear," said Queen Esme. She rose from the top step of the throne where she regularly sat, leaning against the leg of her husband.

Though the seat was one of highest honor, it cannot have been particularly comfortable. Esme moved stiffly in her garments of silk brocade. The wimple which framed her face also concealed the gray of her hair, but the queen looked very old. She was her husband's senior by a dozen years;

a casual observer might have thought her Venkatna's mother rather than his wife.

"No," said Hansen. "My name's Hansen and I'm from far away. Just visiting the court I've heard so much about."

He locked his grip with that of Salles. A warrior's salute, forearm to forearm; either man's hand grasping the other near the elbow. The calluses on Salles' joints had been rubbed by years of exercise wearing a battlesuit.

Hansen remembered: *locked together with a better-armed warrior named Zieborn. Sweat in Hansen's eyes, his muscles straining, and his skin rubbed raw by the inner surface of his shoddy battlesuit. Zieborn's blazing, blue-white arc edging inexorably toward Hansen's face. . . .*

"N-n-n . . . ," Hansen whispered inaudibly.

Zieborn's face afterward. Tongue protruding. Hair and moustache out straight with the ends still smoldering from Hansen's fatal bolt.

"What's that?" Salles asked in puzzlement. He released Hansen's arm and stepped back.

"I wish you luck," Hansen said.

"Hope your namesake hears you," Salles muttered. "The god Hansen is a warrior's friend. We'll have need of him at Peace Rock if something isn't done about these new demands. My neighbors and I, we've about run out of patience with these slave-bailiffs the king's sending around."

The chamberlain wore cloth-of-gold and a scarlet sash of office, but he was a slave himself. Slaves made suitable instruments for the will of a powerful monarch like Venkatna. Slaves knew that their wealth and influence depended solely on their master—and that if the king were overthrown, they would not long survive him.

A minor noble like Salles had a tendency to think that he was every bit as good as the next man, even a king. Particularly when he'd locked down the chest plate of his battlesuit and a live arc quivered from his gauntlet. . . .

The chamberlain gingerly took the position to which Grey directed him in the center of the Web. The device was a framework of thin wires with wide gaps between them. It was not so much a structure as the silvery sketch of a structure.

Within the tracery were two couches of bare wood. The chamberlain lay down on one of them.

"It's *cold*," he objected in surprise and pique.

"Concentrate on the dice," the trader ordered. His voice was suddenly as harsh as an ice fall. "That they should fall as a six."

Queen Esme knelt and threw the dice before her. "Three and . . . three!" she called.

The chamberlain screamed. He sat bolt upright on the bench. His complexion had gone pale and his cheeks had drawn in.

"It's *cold*!" he cried. He squeezed his temples. "It's like frozen rock in my, in my . . ."

"Boardman," said Venkatna in a thin voice, "if you no longer choose to carry out the duties I give my chamberlain, I will find another place for you."

The chamberlain lay back down. His whole body trembled.

"Throw the dice again, my dear," the king said. "Six is not a fall to be remarked."

The chamberlain moaned as the dice clicked, first against each other, then onto the floor. "Four and two," Esme said. Her voice was a melodious contralto.

"And again, I think," Venkatna remarked judiciously. "Though I don't see that a toy which turns dice in the air will make my reign—"

"Six!" called Esme. "And—"

The front rank of petitioners gave out a collective gasp. Whispered comments rose and rebounded from the vaulting like distant surf.

"The second die fell on top of the first," Esme said in a controlled tone that was loud enough to be heard over the babble of lesser folk. "It is also a six."

Boardman lay on the bench breathing hoarsely. His face was ashen except for the trickle of blood from his bitten lip.

"With the right operators, your majesty," said Grey. "Two operators, that would be—this device can impose peace over the whole of your domains. *Your* peace, so that you never need to worry about internal dissent when you face enemies across your borders."

Queen Esme gave the dice to her husband and seated herself

again beneath him. Venkatna stared at the dice in his palm. His free hand stroked the back of Esme's neck.

"How will I find the operators?" the king said as if to the ivory cubes which clicked softly as they rolled against his callused palm.

"By searching," said the trader. "You are a great king, your majesty. Somewhere you will find the right two slaves to make you the greatest king who will ever live on Northworld."

Venkatna looked up. "Eh?" he said.

"An old name for the Earth, your majesty," the trader explained. Grey was turning slowly. "We use it occasionally where I came from."

The crowd of petitioners shuffled. The ranks between Hansen and the front parted as though Grey had drawn a weapon.

Hansen met the trader's gaze. Grey had only one eye. It glittered, pale and as threatening as the arc ripping from a battlesuit.

He smiled, and Hansen smiled . . . and the trader faced back to the king.

"Is the Web to your satisfaction, your majesty?" Grey asked from behind the screen of petitioners who had crowded back as soon as the trader's cold eye had been shifted in another direction.

"My, my . . . ," Salles muttered. "I don't mind telling you, Hansen, I'd watch my back around that boy. Besides, one-eyed men remind me of North the War God. He's nobody even a warrior wants to think on much."

King Venkatna nodded curtly. "Boardman," he ordered. "See to it that Master Grey here is paid his price." He paused, then repeated, "Boardman?"

Two lesser functionaries were lifting the chamberlain's recumbent body from the bench, being careful not to touch the tracery of wires. A line of drool and blood trailed from Boardman's chin.

"I'll see, to it, y-your majesty," volunteered one of the servants between gasps caused by nervousness and the chamberlain's weight.

"You've got that right, Lord Salles," Hansen muttered. "North can be a bad man to know. . . ."

≡ 2 ≡

FROM HIS ICE palace on a high peak, Fortin watched North in the guise of a trader offer a device to King Venkatna in the Open Lands. Fortin hated his father, North, almost as much as Fortin hated himself; but then, Fortin hated all things.

The view through the faceted discontinuity around which Fortin had built his palace was flawed, like that through windows frosted and glittering with reflected light. Nonetheless, the images were real, not electronic constructs. If Fortin wished, he could step through the field and enter the plane of the Matrix which he viewed.

There were eight worlds in the Matrix, and the Matrix was a world. Those who could walk between the planes unaided, shaping the event waves, were gods; but there were discontinuities where planes rubbed close to one another and beings unaided could step between them.

Fortin was a god, but the existence of this natural discontinuity was the reason he had chosen the site for his palace. The multiple images—eight simultaneous impingements, unique within the universe of the Matrix—permitted him to watch and move without leaving a ripple among folk whose lives appeared to have purpose and happiness. . . .

In the audience hall in the Open Lands, North spoke to a king as a plump underling suffered on a bench between them. Fortin couldn't tell the purpose of his father's activities; and

even North's son by an android female thought twice before
interfering with North's plans.

Several of Fortin's servants watched their master furtively.
They were afraid to be seen looking directly at him, but
terrified to be late in obeying if Fortin suddenly turned and
snapped out an order. Fortin was not usually a bad master . . .
but occasionally he was a very bad master indeed.

Fortin stepped slowly around the discontinuity to the next
facet, which looked onto a geodesic dome built in a swamp.
Mist rose from black water, draping the serpentine trees into
the semblance of monsters.

In the far distance was a range of sharp-edged hills. The
rocks bore scarcely enough vegetation to mark their ruddy
surfaces, much less break the force of the rains which cascaded
across them and glutted the lowlands.

The woman in the dwelling's doorway was too perfectly
beautiful to be human. Plane Three had been settled by survivors of a fleet crewed by androids, sent by the Consensus
to investigate when Northworld vanished from the universe
around it. Some of the androids were misshapen creatures
whose body plans departed far from the human norm, but
that was by no means universal: the same batch could give
forth monsters and visages as fine and delicate as that of the
woman in the dome.

Her complexion was white as chalk; as white as Fortin's
own skin, the genetic gift of his android mother.

Fortin moved to the next facet. He stared with a fascination
just short of sexual release. Stretching from an interminable
horizon was a plain, broken by a single hill and peopled by
stumpy columns like stalagmites of ice. There was no evident
source of light, but the stark terrain was blotched by shadows
nevertheless.

If Fortin looked with particular care, it seemed to him that
the columns bore the faces of humans in the icy agony of Hell,
and the hill looming above them had a face as well.

After a long pause, Fortin walked on.

Plane Five had been settled by a Consensus fleet also, one
of three sent to determine how Northworld had disappeared.
Gone with the planet were a colony, an exploration unit, and

the team of troubleshooters headed by Captain North, who had named the world after himself when he cleared it for colonization. . . .

Trembling with memory and expectation, Fortin stepped to the fifth facet. The sun in its final days hung—huge, red, and immobile—over a landscape of rock and desolation. There was intelligent life of a sort here, the crystalline machines which had crewed the last of the Consensus fleets. None of those glittering forms were at present visible through the discontinuity.

The only remaining life native to the plane was the patch of lichen on the face of a corniche above a shingle beach. For long ages, the lichen had been dying. Its minute roots had exhausted the nutriments they could reach in the rock, and the utter airless cold prevented the lichen from expanding outward to gain further sustenance.

To the extent that a creature so crude had feeling, the lichen was in pain. A smile touched Fortin's lips again; then his thought and his expression changed together.

The fourth time the Lords of the Consensus tried to investigate Northworld, they sent not a fleet but a man. His name was Nils Hansen. Hansen now had the powers of a god, but Fortin knew he would kill even a fellow god; though he knew the fabric of the Matrix would tear and all that was Northworld would collapse into a singularity, a black hole in spacetime.

Hansen, if he chose, would kill Fortin with the same cold certainty as Samson brought the temple down on himself and his tormenters.

Fortin's smile was a tight rictus. He walked on.

In a forest of giant conifers, six Lomeri prepared to make a slaving raid into the Open Lands. The Lomeri were lizard-featured bipeds with jaws full of cruel teeth, but the weapons and personal force-screens with which they were armed were smoothly efficient in design and execution.

The lizardmen rode ceratosaurs, bipedal carnivores with blunt nose horns and spiky brows that suggested horns as well. The beasts would eat during the raid, snatching a fifty-kilo gobbet from the flank of a human's draft animal or bolting whole a screaming child, whichever came first to hand. Half the potential slaves would probably be killed by the lizardmen's mounts; a form of inefficiency which bothered the Lomeri as little as it did Fortin.

Dimly visible, as though a mirrored mirror, the Lomeri's target shimmered across a separate discontinuity. Despite the dark blurring of the image, Fortin recognized the thatched hall and houses of Peace Rock, perched on a low plateau.

Commissioner Hansen had a long association with Peace Rock. The disaster would distress him. Fortin smiled as he moved on.

Saburo, a member of the exploration unit that first discovered the planet, had built his palace on a basalt spire that pointed like a black finger from the surface of the sea. Surf crashed on all sides, kicking froth upward to be torn by the winds into smoky streamers.

On the roof of the palace, three gas-cratered lumps of volcanic rock rested on a sand table. The surface awaited the contemplation of the palace's master, but he was not present now.

The eighth face of the discontinuity was an image of Fortin's own central hall. He wondered what would happen if he reached through frost-webbed surface and throttled the figure who sneered back at him with perfect android features. . . .

Moving with decision, Fortin walked back to the window onto Plane Five. In the distance rose Keep Starnes, the massive city/building of one of the lords descended from the humans of the first fleet the Consensus had sent to investigate Northworld's disappearance.

Outside, primitive mammals prowled a landscape of palms and cypresses, but few of the keep's teeming inhabitants had either the need or desire to leave the armored fastness. For all the ages since the settlement, the populace of Keep Starnes labored to equip armored squadrons which skirmished, pointlessly and interminably, with the forces of its neighbors. The soldiers ruled the keep, and the count ruled the soldiers.

In one particular only did Keep Starnes differ from similar keeps on Plane Five: the core of the installation was APEX, the Fleet Battle Director which had controlled all the Consensus ships. In the past, that had not mattered. Now there was a mind in Keep Starnes willing and able to use the capabilities of APEX against other keeps.

War in the neighborhood of Keep Starnes had ceased to be a gentleman's sport fought without direct involvement by the civilian establishment which supported the armies. As the walls and forcefields of other keeps crumbled, the territory under the sway of Count Starnes' self-sufficient city-state expanded proportionately.

Fortin smiled coldly as he unfurled his cloak. Its gossamer fabric bent radiation, so that a would-be observer looked *around* the wearer but thought he saw *through* a patch of empty air.

When Fortin donned the garment, he vanished from the sight of his servants. They trembled, even more fearful now than they had been before.

Within the cloak's protection, Fortin put on a pair of goggles. A hair-fine filament extended from either lens. The filaments extended through the cloak and served as the god's periscopes to the outer world.

In the center of Fortin's back and chest, supported by crossbelts, were active jammers. They could explode in dazzling radiance across the whole electro-optical spectrum. If Fortin activated the paired units, no scanner could operate in the signal flooding from them.

The half android's most important tool of defense was not a piece of equipment: it was his ability to flee through the Matrix at need, leaving Plane Five and whatever was arrayed there against him. There would be no need for that, though. Fortin had visited Keep Starnes frequently. He liked to watch in person as the count's armies ground through the defenses of keep after keep.

Starnes enslaved specialists among the population before turning the remainder out into the wild. Invariably the refugees starved, because they were unable to recognize any food except that which had been grown in hydroponic tanks before being formed into flavored bricks.

If anyone could have seen him beneath his cloak, Fortin would have looked like an angel with a beatific smile. He vanished into the Matrix, unseen and unseeable—

And Karring, Chief Engineer of Keep Starnes, watched a telltale on APEX's console begin to blink.

"Sir!" called Karring to his master. "He's slipped in again!"

≡ 3 ≡

"I DIDN'T KNOW YOU'D be here, North," Hansen said to the man who walked up behind him on the stone-railed loggia of the palace, overlooking Frekka's expanding suburbs.

North chuckled. "I'm selling my wares, Commissioner Hansen. Why are you here?"

"The only thing you have to sell," Hansen said as he turned to face the taller man, "is ways to die. What are you *doing* here?"

The breeze held a crackling undertone of warriors at battle practice in the near distance, cutting at one another with arcs on reduced settings. Occasionally, suits clashed together like anvils in collision.

Closer at hand, workmen hammered and shouted to one another during the construction of a long two-story building. Snow overlaying the job site had been trampled into muddy slush. The surface swallowed fallen tools and made the footing treacherous for folk carrying heavy loads, but the work continued.

The building would provide another barracks for the royal army. Every time King Venkatna advanced the borders of the West Kingdom, he gained an additional number of paid soldiers—for whom he would assuredly have need during the next campaigning season.

"I'm admiring your handiwork, Kommissar," North said

coolly. "I may have encouraged warriors to battle, but *you've* taught the rulers here to conquer and crush their neighbors with an iron fist. My way, it was mostly warriors who died."

He laughed again. "You must be proud of the way you've improved things," he added.

Neither man was heavily built, but North was both taller and older than Nils Hansen. Where North's lanky build was obvious even under the cloak which he now wore in the guise of a trader, Hansen was close-coupled. Planes of muscle stretched over prominent bones framed the younger man's face, while North's visage was all crags and a hooked nose.

No one would have seen a similarity between the two men—unless he looked at their eyes. The certainty that glared from beneath North's deep brow was no colder than that which flashed back in Hansen's fierce gaze.

One eye and two; but both men killers, and both of them very sure in their actions, come what might.

"*I* didn't—" Hansen said.

The denial died on his lips. He turned and faced out over the city again. He knew what he'd done. . . .

Tooley comes at Hansen over the bodies of the slain. The hostile warrior's battlesuit is striped white and red as blood. No single warrior can stop him, but when Hansen grapples with Tooley, the sidemen strike as Hansen has taught them. Tooley's spluttering armor topples, streaming the black smoke of burning flesh.

It was a cold afternoon. No one came out to share the loggia with the two men, a trader and a warrior traveling from somewhere distant called Annunciation, perhaps in the far south. Clouds lowered from the middle heights of the sky, but the snow had not yet begun for the day.

Down on the practice field, soldiers were trained in the team tactics which were Hansen's gift to Northworld. An army of professionals who fought in groups of three was unanswerably superior to feudal levies whose honor baulked at the subordination needed for the new style of war.

"I wanted them to have peace," Hansen said softly. Construction work was pretty much the same everywhere. That wasn't true about every sort of job, though.

Sometimes when Hansen closed his eyes, he could remember the former life in which he was merely Commissioner of Special Units—the armed fist of the planetary security forces on Annunciation. Then the rules were simple and straightforward: the Commissioner didn't make policy, he only enforced it; and he enforced it with a harsh certainty that left no one in any doubt as to what had been decided.

Now. . . .

"There had to be a central government to keep every lord and fifty-hectare kinglet from fighting his neighbor six days out of seven," Hansen said, speaking to North and to himself at the same time. "But it could have been a just government. It *was* a just government for years, North."

He glared at the other man. "You know that!"

North shrugged. "I know what I see, Commissioner," he said. He spread a hand idly in the direction of the slave gang unfastening a forty-meter centerpole from the draft mammoth which had dragged it to the site.

"They were from the Thrasey community, I believe," North went on. "The community fell behind with its tribute. A battalion of the royal army swept them all up to work off the debt over the next three years—those who survive."

His eye swept critically over the slave gang. A woman slipped in the slush, but she managed to slide clear before the heavy beam crushed down.

"They didn't have a prayer of resisting, of course," North said. "Not against the army *you* trained."

The Thrasey warrior has the better armor. Hansen has bitten his tongue and his muscles burn with fatigue poisons, but his arc holds his opponent for the moment it takes.

Hansen's sideman strikes. The already-extended Thrasey battlesuit fails with a bang and a shower of sparks. An arm decorated with black and white checks flies to the side. The paint is seared at the shoulder end, and the limb is no longer attached to the warrior's torso. A stump of bone protrudes as the arm spins away.

"Are you laughing at me, North?" Hansen whispered to the air.

"Yes, Commissioner," North said. "I am laughing at you.

How *do* you like the changes you've made here?"

The woman who had slipped fell again. An overseer uncoiled
his whip. The guard watched the proceedings with mild interest.
The battlesuit he wore was of poor quality, but it would do
against a coffle of unarmed slaves if they chose to object to
discipline.

Hansen gripped the railing before him. He squeezed as if he
were trying to grind the brown-mottled stone into sand with
his bare hands.

"Nobody cares but you and me, Hansen," North said. "You
know that, don't you? The others are too wrapped up in their
own affairs to notice what goes on among men."

"*Those* people care!" Hansen snapped, indicating the slave
gang with a jerk of his chin.

"The other gods," North said. "As you well know. . . . And
if you care so much about the folk here in the West Kingdom,
Hansen—perhaps you should undo what you've created?"

Hansen looked at him. North stared off into the distance.
The clouds over the practice field occasionally flickered with
the light of the arc weapons spluttering beneath.

"The fellow you were talking to in the audience hall," North
asked, careful not to catch Hansen's eye. "Salles. . . . Do you
suppose he'll get the tax burden for Peace Rock reduced?"

"He won't get his petition heard," Hansen said flatly.

North hadn't picked up Salles' name and seat during the
hubbub within the hall. He'd checked on Salles, as surely
as he'd known the answer to the question he'd just asked
Hansen.

"A moment . . . ," North murmured.

The tall man stepped to the door into the interior of the
palace and snapped his fingers to bring a footman to him. The
two held a brief, low-voiced conversation. At the end of
it, coins clinked from North's purse and the palace servant
scurried off on an errand.

Hansen's mind remained wrapped around the question,
though he knew North had asked it only to goad him.
"They'll fight, though, Salles and his neighbors," he said in
a tone of cold analysis. His job on Annunciation had been
a reactive one. He wasn't a strategist, but he was very good

at predicting what somebody else would do next—so that he could smash them down with overwhelming force.

"They've seen what happened to Thrasey, so they won't be taken by surprise." Hansen took his hands from the railing and dusted the palms softly together. He was clearing them of the grit that might cause a slip if he needed suddenly to draw a pistol.

Not here, not now; but when Hansen's conscious mind moved on these paths, his reflexes ran down their checklist of actions that had kept him alive in former days and places.

"It won't help," his hard, emotionless voice continued. "Venkatna knows they'll be waiting, so he'll send sufficient force to deal with anything a bunch of yokels can raise. But they'll fight anyway, long odds on that."

Their three opponents wear suits as good as any on Northworld. Hansen's armor glows with the charges that are about to overload its circuits. His lungs burn and his right arm swells as though he had thrust it into an oven.

Arnor, Hansen's sideman, cuts home. An enemy falls. Another of the hostile warriors swipes sideways, slashing through the neck of Arnor's tan-and-gray battlesuit.

"If you really cared . . . ," came North's voice from somewhere in the world outside of memory, " . . . you could change it all back, Kommissar. You do know that, don't you?"

"I can't unteach team tactics!" Hansen snapped. "Or do you want me to collapse the whole continent in an earthquake, North? Swallow up everybody who knows anything or even *might* know anything? Is that what you'd do?"

"I wouldn't have caused the problem in the first place, Kommissar," the taller man said. All the play, all the mockery, had left his voice. His tones were as gray and certain as the promise of snow in the clouds above. "*I* was satisfied when my Searchers gleaned only the souls of warriors killed in skirmishes which hurt no one but those involved."

"You—" Hansen began.

North overrode his protest. "It's not a joke, Hansen. I've seen it! When the Day comes, we'll need all the warriors we can get—and even *that* won't be enough to stop the hordes that come from other planes when the walls of the Matrix grow too thin to prevent them."

North swallowed, forcing his mouth to close against its own dryness. He stared in Hansen's direction, but he was looking at something much farther away.

Captain North had led the foremost team of troubleshooters in the Exploration Service of the Consensus of Worlds. The expression that Hansen saw flash across the other man's face was fear or bleak despair. Either emotion was as out of place as love in the grin of a leopard.

There were rumors among the gods about what it was North had seen in the Matrix that cost him his left eye.

The wind skirled through the stone railing, reaching under Hansen's short dress cape and tugging the fastenings of North's heavier traveling garment. The taller man grinned, fully himself again in his smirking assumption of what *he* knew that others didn't.

"If you're asking me for advice, though, Kommissar . . . ," North resumed. "As a friend and fellow, that is . . . the way men fight isn't the—cause of this."

He pointed deliberately toward the job site. The woman who had fallen was managing to stay upright only by clinging to a naked doorpost. She was obviously either sick or malnourished.

"It's the state you created to impose peace," North said. "There's where the trouble is. Bring down the West Kingdom and you'll end the worst of *that.*"

At the job site, the overseer who had lashed the woman to her feet was about to administer another whipping.

"Go back to constant wars, each lord against his neighbor, you mean?" Hansen asked harshly.

Unexpected movement caught the corner of Hansen's eye; he looked back at the construction site. A man in the ruffled livery of Venkatna's footmen was talking earnestly with the overseer and the battlesuited guard.

"They'll still be human beings, Hansen," North said softly. "They just won't be ground into the dirt by a single tyrant. . . . But *I* don't care."

"What's going on down there?" Hansen demanded.

The footman left with the sick woman in tow. Gold winked in the overseer's palm and the armored gauntlet of the guard.

North shrugged. "A little bribe," he said. "Enough that she'll be reported dead—not so very unlikely an outcome, is it, given her condition. The servant will send her on to Peace Rock, where she'll be safe for a time. She has relatives there."

He laughed. North's smile was like the crags of a cliff face, and his laughter was the surf hitting those rocks.

"You imposed this on the Open Lands against *my* will," North said. "Now we'll see if you're man enough to do something about it."

Snow began to fall onto the roofs of Venkatna's palace, but it was no colder than the ice in Hansen's glare.

≡ 4 ≡

IN AN OBJECT which could have been a small bronze handmirror, Sparrow the Smith considered the device in the audience hall of Venkatna's palace. His left hand stroked his dog's neck, where a darker ruff marked the generally tan fur. The dog sighed comfortably. She twisted to lick her master's palm.

None of the other servants came near the open door of Sparrow's suite—cell, it might have been called, deep in the rock-cut sub-basements of Saburo's dwelling. Early on, a pair of delicate, silk-clad favorites had tittered pointedly behind raised fingers at the hulking newcomer who still wore bearskin in a place of such sophistication.

They hadn't realized how long Sparrow's arms were, or that the smith would act with no more hesitation than a white bear making its kill on the ice.

Not that he killed them. Sparrow held his victims out over the sea crashing hundreds of meters below, one wrist of either gripped in his huge left hand. Sparrow plucked off their garments, seven layers each and color-coordinated according to rules so complex that they required years to understand. The bits of silk lifted in updrafts, then disappeared into the spume trailing downwind from the spire of rock.

The smith's dog was terrified by heights and the surf roaring below. She ran back and forth, yammering her concern for her master. The braces of living metal which permitted the beast to walk on her withered hind legs clicked against the limestone surface of the terrace.

Similar braces replaced Sparrow's severed hamstrings. The hard metal sharpened the shock of his heels through the rawhide boots.

When the servants were naked except for the paint on their finger- and toenails, Sparrow set them back on the terrace. One of them gripped the stones, screaming uncontrollably. The other hurled himself into the sea with a blank look in his eyes. The act might have been either suicide or a convulsion as meaningless as the kicking legs of a pithed frog.

Saburo pretended he knew nothing of what the smith had done.

No one troubled Sparrow after that. The other servants learned quickly that the smith saw things and heard things; and they already knew that he was willing to act with ruthless certainty.

Sparrow acted as if he were a god rather than a god's servant.

Tonight the smith's dog perked up suddenly in awareness of a change so subtle that it had escaped even Sparrow's senses. The bitch whined, hoping for direction; willing to fight or flee, willing to do almost anything but leave her master.

Sparrow touched the side of the object in his hand. It became no more than it had seemed at a glance before, a bronze mirror in a frame chased with delicately-fashioned serpents, each swallowing the tail of the snake before it in the frieze.

He got to his feet. He wore a long-bladed knife in a belt sheath, but the idea of a weapon was lost against the image of Sparrow's massive, careless strength.

The walls of Sparrow's suite shook as they always did with the shock and counter-shock of waves hitting the rock and shivering up the spire in dazzling harmonies. The vibrations made dust hang in the air above bins of ore and metals, stockpiles waiting for the moment that the smith needed some particular property to shape and smelt through the Matrix into—

Anything at all. There were great smiths in the Open Lands, but there was only one Sparrow.

There was an additional component to the quivering. Something was occurring, not on *this* plane of the Matrix but through the Matrix itself.

Sparrow stood, facing the apparent source and flexing his hands. The bitch crept between her master's outspread legs and bared her teeth in a silent growl.

The walls fell into a series of geometric shards.

Man and dog stood in a wormhole of octagonal sheets. Sparrow had no sense of motion, but the faceted walls/ceiling/floor rotated about him as though he were in the tailings of a spiral-cut drill, being lifted inexorably to—

They were in a glade of bamboo. In the bower before them, a young woman lounged. She had oriental features and a look of godlike hauteur.

Her name was Miyoko. She was Saburo's sister, and her mere whim would scatter the atoms of the smith's being across the eight worlds of the Matrix. Sparrow watched her without expression.

For a moment, neither of the humans spoke. Sparrow's dog, released from the trembling terror of moments before, began to take an active interest in her surroundings. Birds hopped among the tops of the tall, jointed grass, flaunting their brilliant plumage. Sparrow knelt to knead his fingers into the dog's ruff, his eyes still on those of the woman.

"I have a task for you, Sparrow," Miyoko said a heartbeat after she realized that the big smith did not intend to speak first. Pretending she had not studied the man carefully, she added, "That is your name, isn't it?"

"I've willingly performed every task my master set me, lady," Sparrow said. He spoke in a low rumble with a catch in it, as though his voice had known little use of late.

If Miyoko had been stupid, she would not have been navigating officer for a Consensus exploration unit. Her nostrils flared at what she correctly understood was not refusal—but a threat, as surely as the hideous doom that Sparrow had inflicted on those who once had forced him to

their will when he lived in the Open Lands. The dog stiffened
at the dangerous atmosphere.

But Miyoko was not stupid . . . and she had summoned this
skin-clad *animal* because she was afraid no one else could
accomplish what she required.

"Yes," she said coolly. "It's because of Saburo that I need
you. My brother is acting oddly, and I want to know why."

"Have you asked *him* why?" Sparrow said. His fingers
continued to play with the dog, controlling the beast and
providing an outlet for the smith's own nervousness. He didn't
want to die, that one, despite his demeanor. . . .

"Of course I asked him!" Miyoko snapped. "He denies that
there's anything wrong. I'm sure that he would tell the same
foolish lie to any of the rest of us who asked him."

*Not that any of the other gods would have come so far
from their own self-willed purposes as to interest themselves
in someone else . . . except perhaps for Hansen, and Hansen
would refuse to intrude into another human's personal life.*

"Anyway," Miyoko continued more calmly, "I want you to
talk with him. I know Saburo *does* talk to you sometimes."

Though I can't imagine why, she thought; and as the thought
formed, she *did* know why. This hulking brute would listen to
Saburo, as another god would not; and he would still speak flat
blunt truths to his master, as if he were unaware that a god's
mere fingersnap could doom a mortal like Sparrow to death
or eternal torture.

A smith spent much of his time in the Matrix. The Matrix
took and gave according to immutable laws, and there was
something of the same attitude in Sparrow himself.

"My brother is . . . ," Miyoko said with a gentleness which
had been missing from her tone previously. "Moody. Angry.
Withdrawn. I don't like to see him so unhappy, and he won't
let me help him."

"Stay, girl," Sparrow murmured as he stood up.

The smith's motions were deliberate. Miyoko's eyes nar-
rowed as she realized that the big man was not slow, only
perfectly controlled. If he wanted to, he could lunge across the
space between the two of them almost before the woman could
form the thought that would blast Sparrow into non-existence.

Almost. . . .

A weaver bird with a black head and brilliantly-yellow body fluttered onto Sparrow's right shoulder. It tugged at a lock of his hair. "He might not thank *me* for interfering either, lady," the smith said as if oblivious to the bird's strong, curved beak.

"If you're afraid—" Miyoko said.

Sparrow shook his head. The bird squawked and flung itself back into the air. "No, lady," he said. "I'm not afraid to do my duty. Aiding Saburo is a duty I've undertaken."

He smiled, gently enough, but his eyes were focused inward. "He's not a bad man, Saburo," Sparrow said softly. "I don't think he understands me, but we get along well enough."

The dog began edging to the side, pretending not to be disobeying her master's orders to stay. Sparrow stretched out a leg as solid as a treetrunk. He rubbed the beast's belly with his toe. When the smith's leg was extended, the leg brace glittered in the green-lit ambiance of the bower.

"I . . . ," said Miyoko. "You will not find me ungrateful. I've—noticed—that you appear to lack regular female companionship. If you would—"

"No, lady," Sparrow said. He was still smiling, but it was a very different expression now. "My master sees to it that my needs are taken care of whenever I require it." His visage softened. "That isn't a matter of great concern to me anyway. I have the Matrix and my work."

"But there was a women when you lived in the Open Lands . . . ?" Miyoko said, intrigued despite herself.

"There was a woman," Sparrow agreed. His voice was without emotion and his eyes stared at a memory in the infinite distance. "Her name was Krita, and she left me. But that's no concern of yours, lady."

The dog began to whine. She sat up and pawed at the smith's thigh to break the mood that suddenly reeked in his sweat.

Sparrow smiled and bent to scratch the back of the dog's head. "Krita is a Searcher," he said without looking up at the god who had summoned him. "You would not force Krita to your will any more than you would force . . ."

He straightened; the smile slight but real enough, the rest of the sentence left unsaid.

"But I'll talk to your brother," Sparrow went on. "If he needs help—"

The smith locked his hands behind his neck and stretched, causing his biceps to swell mountainously. "—then I'll help him to the limits of my strength."

His tone was as flat and certain as the approach of death.

≡ 5 ≡

FIVE WARRIORS CLOSED in while a sixth waited for his death, standing on a knoll with his back to an ice-slicked outcrop. The lone warrior wore armor with silver limbs and a plastron of royal blue. Servants drove his caravan of clopping pack-ponies along the muddy trail in the direction of Peace Rock and safety.

Twenty or so of the mounted freemen who accompanied the five warriors paced the caravan from a safe distance, but they did not dare close in. Two Peace Rock warriors stumbled along beside the ponies. Their armor was of low quality and wouldn't have lasted a heartbeat in close-quarters action against the group of five, but freemen without battlesuits were no more than cheese for their slicing arcs.

Salles of Peace Rock stood on the knoll in a battlesuit nearly of royal quality. His armor was better than that of any of the band sent to fetch him back to Frekka, in chains or in pieces—it was all one to King Venkatna; but they were five and he was alone, and North had sent a pair of Searchers to gather Salles' soul when the arcs seared it out.

Race and Julia held their dragonflies in one of the interstices between planes of the Matrix, watching the battle shape on the knoll beneath them. If any of the warriors chanced to look up, he would see no more than the quiver of refraction, as though a mirage had been disturbed by the rustle of black wings.

But the warriors had more pressing business than the question of what waited in the sky.

The five advanced in a shallow vee. The apex pointed away from Salles while the wings moved to envelope him. The slope was steep enough to make the footing awkward, but it was no real protection to the trapped man.

"Why don't they get it over with?" Race muttered angrily. She twisted a vernier control on her saddle, bringing the tracery of slim booms which she rode through the Matrix closer temporally to the Open Lands.

Race hung in a curtain of colored light. Dimly visible across the pastel shimmer was her companion in a separate bubble of reality, bounded by the tips of wands stretching from her dragonfly's saddle. Below, through a screen of slight asynchrony, warriors and the bleak landscape appeared in shades of gray.

Venkatna's men were in no hurry. The caravan would get away, which was a pity; but Peace Rock would be no refuge in the long run, and Salles was too dangerous an opponent to take lightly.

Salles lighted the arc from his right gauntlet, burning harsh highlights from the icy rocks behind him. His opponents paused, less than three meters away. Salles feinted to his right, watching Venkatna's warriors bunch reflexively.

Julia snorted in derision. She and Race wore battlesuits of better quality than those of the men below. The Searchers had seen more war than any warrior, and they had only scorn for the folk the king had sent to do his bidding.

Salles, on the other hand . . .

Salles lunged, not to his side but for the man in the center. Salles' legs moved stiffly. He had concentrated into his cutting arc the power that would normally have been driving the servos in his limbs.

The slope aided him. Salles' target got his own weapon up, but none of his sidemen were in time to strike with him and drain the attack's power into the defenses of Salles' battlesuit.

No single opponent could meet Salles' rush and live.

Light blazed as the arcs crossed, burning air to a plasma. The Frekka warrior's overloaded weapon failed. Salles cut home.

For a fraction of a second, his opponent's suit was shrouded in a corona that boiled snow to steam and cracked the rock underneath with transmitted heat.

The suit's defenses overloaded. Salles' arc tore a deep wedge into his opponent's shoulder. Metal sheathing burned and peeled back. The short-circuited victim collapsed, a dead man in dead armor.

In the saddle of Race's dragonfly, a delicate electronic package clucked. It was recording every nuance of the warrior's mind at the moment of his death. On the Searchers' return, their master North would turn that data to his own purposes. . . .

A Frekka warrior wheeled in time to cut as the Lord of Peace Rock crashed through the line. His extended weapon lighted the carapace of Salles' armor. The arc was too diffuse to kill, but it made Salles' servos stutter as power fed the defenses.

Salles doubled over in a somersault and rolled free. He came to his feet, facing Venkatna's men as they hesitated on the slope above him. He switched his arc off, planted his arms akimbo, and laughed.

"Race!" Julia called across the blur of nothingness. There was grim joy in her voice. "My armor to your hairband that North isn't going to get the Lord of Peace Rock *this* day!"

She brought her dragonfly closer to the plane they were observing. The Searchers were shadowy outlines to the men on the ground, while the warriors' arcs burned blue-white and vivid to the women above.

One of the Frekka warriors lunged forward as though Salles' laughter had goaded him into movement. He took two gravity-lengthened strides before his companions realized what was happening.

Salles lighted the arc in his left hand. He slashed through his opponent's ankles so swiftly that the crippling shock was his victim's first warning. The depowered battlesuit skidded downslope on its plastron, spluttering and steaming. The warrior inside screamed.

Race began to laugh. "North sent us for the wrong man," she cried to her companion. "He won't be pleased!"

Salles took a step toward his three remaining opponents.

Arcs sprang like corpse candles from Salles' right gauntlet, then his left.

The Frekka warriors moved as well, this time as a trained unit—

Until the man in the center, concentrating on his opponent, missed his footing. He shrieked as he skidded downslope on his back. His legs were splayed outward.

Salles stabbed through the man's groin. He stepped back from the smoking corpse before the other two warriors could interfere.

Venkatna's surviving men eased away also. They put their backs against the outcrop at which Salles had awaited them only minutes before. Turf smoldered on the face of the knoll where there was organic material for the arcs to ignite.

Five fresh warriors trotted down the trail. The men had decorated their battlesuits with their personal colors, but each helmet bore the crimson-in-gold rosette of Venkatna's royal army. They spread out as they closed on the Lord of Peace Rock from behind.

"It's not fair!" Julia cried.

"Since when was North fair?" Race replied bitterly. "He wants the souls of warriors, and he'll have his way no matter what."

Julia twisted a control. "Not Salles," she said simply. "Not this time."

The Searcher and her dragonfly sprang into perfect focus with the landscape beneath them. Julia slid forward the joystick on her pommel, sending the vehicle downward at a sharp slant. Its four jointed legs flexed as the feet touched down. The booms folded and telescoped as the dragonfly came to rest. Julia sprang from the saddle.

Race landed beside her companion. The dragonflies trailed tendrils of ozone as their electronics meshed with the new temporal ambiance. That ionized harshness was lost in the effluvium of the arc weapons of the oncoming warriors.

The fresh squad of Venkatna's men hesitated at the Searcher's sudden appearance. Race and Julia gave them no time to consider their course of action.

Race, wearing a battlesuit colored orange with bronze

highlights, stepped forward—struck with her right hand—
and switched the power instantly to her left gauntlet. Her arc
doubled Julia's stroke at the leading warrior's sideman.

The Searchers' armor was of the highest quality attainable,
the ideal within the Matrix which smiths in the Open Lands
attempted to replicate. The chest of the man struck by the
paired blow exploded in a yellow blast like that of raw sodium
dropped into water. His helmet and both arms separated as the
mangled suit toppled backward.

Race strode forward and cut into the hip of the warrior at
whom she had feinted initially. Julia, clad in a scale-patterned
suit of scarlet, silver, and mauve, ran down the man who fled
screaming that the gods fought against them.

Not the gods. . . .

Julia's powerful arc licked out and caught her opponent
three meters away. His suit concentrated all its energies on
defense; the warrior fell over because the servos in his leg
armor froze while he was in an unstable position. Julia stepped
forward, a pace and then a second. The defensive screen
overloaded and the victim's carapace burst into a fountain
of burning steel and shorted electronics.

Salles looked over his shoulder; but only for an instant,
because the survivors of the group he'd fought started the
rush they'd intended to coordinate with the newcomers' attack.
Salles parried one slash with his right hand, then pivoted as
he tried to keep the second warrior at a distance with a
dangerously-weak arc from the other gauntlet.

Race and Julia attacked their remaining opponents. Venkatna's men stood, but they made only the feeblest of attempts
to defend themselves. The sudden turn of events had left them
with no more volition than calves in the slaughter chute.

Behind the Searchers, the Lord of Peace Rock swiveled to
put both royal warriors in line before him. He struck high at the
nearer with the full power of his arc, then leaped the headless
battlesuit to meet the sole survivor before the man could decide
whether to lunge or backpedal.

The two warriors grappled. The long shadows cast by the
sun through the pines danced with discharges from the straining
battlesuits.

Salles got his left arm into the position he wanted. He directed a full-power arc from that gauntlet into his opponent's throat. Circuits blew out with a bang.

Venkatna's man fell backward. For a moment, currents played across the blackened surface of his armor in fluctuating patterns. One of the dragonflies chuckled as it drank another soul.

The Lord of Peace Rock swayed. Paint had blistered from his plastron and right forearm, but all his opponents were down.

Freemen rode east along the trail. They carried word to King Venkatna, who had tried to forestall a rebellion by assassinating its leader. Venkatna would try again, but for now the fighting was over.

"Who are you?" Salles called to the figures, faceless in their battlesuits. "Why did you—"

The figure in orange and bronze raised its arm. It might have been about to speak. Before it could do so, the shadow of a great hand blurred across the landscape and gathered Salles' rescuers into the Matrix.

≡ 6 ≡

FORTIN SLIPPED THROUGH the Matrix like a silverfish crawling between the pages of a book. His soft, cling-soled footgear stepped without a tremor onto the floor of a corridor within Count Starnes' fortress.

Fortin was on one of the lower levels of Keep Starnes, beneath many layers of shielding. Except for one of the cleaning personnel in an orange uniform, sucking grit from the thin carpet with a static broom, the men and women in the corridor wore blue serge outfits. They belonged to units which directly supported the army.

Fortin in his light-bending cape was completely invisible to them.

A colonel in magenta and gold strode down the hall like a battleship under way, looking neither to his right nor his left. He had a train of six subordinates—all of them in blue. Even the lowliest of the elite who crewed Count Starnes' war vehicles was too grand a personage to perform in a servile capacity within the keep.

Civilians stood at attention against the sides of the corridor. The cleaner knelt and pressed his forehead to the dull green carpet. His broom whined unattended. The cleaner's hand patted the floor in tiny arcs, hoping to find the off switch. He was afraid to open his eyes to guide his movements.

Fortin fell into line at the end of the colonel's entourage.

They came to a rotunda. Armored doors hung ready to seal any or all the corridors which starred off from this center. The civilians present were in the retinues of the score or more soldiers striding along on their business. This deep within Keep Starnes, each corridor was a community from which civilian staff members moved only upon direct orders of the military.

There were six sets of paired elevators in the center of the rotunda. The colonel stepped into one cage; his servants got into the other half of the pair.

Fortin, grinning with the spice of near danger, hopped into the cage behind the colonel.

This side of the elevator had a full set of controls, but the colonel did not deign to touch them. The cages dropped together, under the direction of one of the servants.

The elevator stopped four levels down, just above the Citadel. The atmosphere pulsed with the life of the keep itself: relays which clicked like beetles mating; the soft susurrus of the ventilation system; the hollow echo of water which had seeped through the rock walls of the enormous structure, being pumped up to the surface for disposal with the sewage.

The tremble of the Fleet Battle Director operating in the Citadel beneath was omnipresent.

The colonel got off and strode down an empty corridor. He didn't bother to look to see that his entourage had fallen into place behind him.

Fortin tapped the control for Citadel level as the elevator door began to close. The cameras which peered from all four corners of the cage ceiling could not see his smile of superiority.

The elevator resumed its descent. Fortin prepared to slip out quickly when the cage stopped.

Fortin knew he was the cleverest of all those who lived in Northworld. There was no situation from which his cunning would not extricate him; and anyway, he could always escape through the Matrix.

But there was no point in taking risks. . . .

"He's entered Elevator Four with Colonel Markesan," said Karring. "He's coming here, as we expected."

The Citadel was the lowest inhabited level of Keep Starnes.
Its rotunda had a forty-meter ceiling, but a far greater mass
of metal and crystalline armor separated the Citadel from the
nearest portion of the keep above it.

The single corridor that led off from the rotunda held the
nodular immensity of APEX, a computer capable of controlling
the largest battle fleets of the Consensus of Worlds. It was now
the domain of Karring, Count Starnes' chief engineer.

"Why doesn't Markesan see him?" Count Starnes asked.
He was stocky and very broad; a physically-powerful man
whose uniform was tailored to conceal the extra weight of
middle age.

Starnes' build ran true to the dominant genotype on Plane
Five—on Earth, Starnes would have said, though there were
still folk who used the name Northworld. Northworld was
a term from the distant past, associated with the myth that
humans had come from a wholly different planet to settle
here. . . .

Lena, Starnes' elder daughter, operated from one of the
four remote consoles in the rotunda. She reclined like a huge
spider at the heart of a web formed by all the systems of
Keep Starnes which fed into her semi-circular workstation.
"Markesan couldn't find his ass with both hands," she said.
"Or," she added with a giggle, "his prick."

The pair of lovers standing behind Lena's contoured chair
chuckled with practiced appreciation. Both wore leather briefs;
one of them had added a studded leather cross-belt and balanced
pistol holsters as ornamentation. The men were as thick-set as
their mistress, but their bodies were densely muscular while
Lena was fat. A sheen of oil glistened on their skins.

"The intruder is shielding himself from all normal observation," Karring explained. At his mental direction, APEX
projected a holographic image of the elevator's interior in
the air above Count Starnes. "We can't see him either."

Colonel Markesan stood in a formal at-ease posture, even
though he must have believed himself to be unobserved. There
was nothing near him but the walls of the descending elevator.

"It might not be *him*," said Lisa, Starnes' other daughter. "It
might be *her*."

Lena guffawed. The count turned away to conceal a smile.

Lisa was a sport, a throwback to a body type which had become increasingly rare in Plane Five's limited gene pool. She was as tall as her father, but she weighed less than a third of his 160 kilograms. Where her elder sister wore a net bra and crotchless briefs, Lisa affected the uniform of a private soldier.

"We'll know soon enough," Karring said mildly. "I'm going to Bay 20 to prepare for our visitor."

"Well, it *might* be," Lisa muttered.

She lifted the bulky helmet fabricated to Karring's specifications. The face of the helmet was solid and featureless. A ten-centimeter tube stuck out to either side, like the periscopic lenses of a range-finder hood. She put the helmet on.

Air began to sigh in the single elevator shaft which penetrated the Citadel's cap.

"And I'll get ready too," said Count Starnes with a tone of satisfaction. At last he would face a new kind of enemy; an enemy who *might* provide the challenge which he no longer found in grinding to dust the neighboring keeps on Earth.

The squat master of Keep Starnes opened the hatch in the rear face of his personal war vehicle, a miniaturized tank three meters long and almost equally broad. The tank's frontal armor was collapsed uranium sloped at a 70° angle. It was thick enough to resist even a slug of the same material fired from a railgun like the tank's own weapon.

The interior of the vehicle fitted Count Starnes like a glove. All the available space was filled by the operator, the railgun, or the fusion powerplant on which the tank's weapon and repulsion drive depended. Additional internal volume would require additional armor to protect it. The present defensive load was at the limits of what a magnetic flux could raise a workable distance above the surface.

The hatch clanged shut. The vehicle quivered as Starnes brought its systems to life.

In the huge curving screen in front of Lena, a three-dimensional schematic of Keep Starnes spread with the complexity of a taproot's microstructure. Passages were color-coded as to purpose and level. There were almost a

hundred shades in the pattern, and Lena recognized every one
of them.

The display changed as APEX responded to the huge
woman's mental directions. Her lovers preened and posed
behind her couch, waiting patiently for the next demand on
their particular skills. They knew from experience that their
mistress' requirements would not be long in coming.

The Fleet Battle Director extended over twenty bays, offset
from one another so that the corridor between them jogged
like a series of square waves. Though Karring walked quickly,
it took him over a minute to reach his destination.

A tracery of wires hung in the air above the entrance to
Bay 20 without physical connection to any other solid object.
Karring looked at it in grim satisfaction. The object's existence
was only partly within the dimension in which it had been built.
APEX converted into a map display the changes in potential
which the device recognized.

If ordered, APEX could modulate the device that looked like
no more than a wire cage; and through the device, the fabric
of spacetime. . . .

≡7≡

SPARROW SETTLED HIS mount at the edge of a plain so flat that an optical illusion made it seem to rise in the far distance. The setting sun cast long shadows.

For as far as the eye could see, the ground was covered with warriors battling.

Duration meant nothing to immortals like Miyoko and her brother. They might choose to walk or might slip through the Matrix to their destination in a nerve-freezing flash; it was all the same to the gods.

Sparrow was a man. He rode to North's battleplain to find Saburo.

The vehicle was one the smith had built himself. It was a dragonfly in general form, capable of travel between the planes of the Matrix as well as flying at speeds high enough that its forcefield glowed with the collisions with air molecules. Sparrow had modified the vehicle so that the pressure of his knees and bootheels controlled speed and direction in-plane, as he would control a pony.

Sparrow could use dials and rocker switches, just as he was comfortable with either a crossbow or a battlesuit. He had chosen a unique design for *his* dragonfly because he was the greatest smith in the eight planes of Northworld.

To the gods, creation was a thought or a fingersnap; but they did not understand the process by which they controlled event waves. Sparrow entered the Matrix in a trance; found the pattern of his desire; and re-formed piles of ore and rubble into smooth crystalline machines in which atoms were spaced and arranged just as they were in the ideal he dreamed.

Other smiths built battlesuits. Sparrow built anything he chose. He was the master of all patterns within the Matrix, and the Matrix was the pattern of all existence on Northworld.

Saburo stood alone, a silent figure in layers of peach-colored silk. Before him, battle clashed into the observable distance.

The combatants could be identified by the colors and flashings which each warrior had worn when he died. Now, however, their battlesuits were uniformly of the highest quality: armor that only Sparrow or a handful of other smiths could have duplicated, and that with great effort. The air between the two opposing lines glowed as arc weapons shorted against one another.

Sparrow watched with critical interest for a moment. Though the battlesuits were all ideal, there were variations among the warriors. Neither side had been able to advance since combat began at dawn, but suits lay dead and blackened all along the line of conflict.

Turtle-backed machines slid across the plain, gathering limbs and helmets to the torsos from which they had been sheared. When the machines moved on, the armor they left behind was perfect again, though it lacked the sheen that indicated its systems were alive.

"Good evening, lord," Sparrow said.

Saburo spun around. At once a bubble of silence surrounded the two men, isolating them from the arcs' continuous snarl and an occasional crash as a forcefield was loaded to the point of failure.

"Ah," said Saburo. "Master Sparrow. I—didn't expect to see you here."

His tone might have been one of disapproval, if Sparrow had chosen to take it that way.

Sparrow smiled. Saburo could blast him into atoms—but he could not control *this* servant by subtleties of intonation. "One wouldn't expect to find you here, either, milord," he said bluntly. "It's Lord North's domain, one would say."

He glanced past his master toward the continuing battle. "Or Lord Hansen's, perhaps."

"Commissioner Hansen never visits the battleplain," Saburo remarked. He turned to view the fighting again himself.

Saburo was a slight man with delicate features, though Sparrow had never made the mistake of thinking that his master was soft. They were very different in personality; but Sparrow would never have taken service with someone he did not respect.

"They're quite splendid in their way, aren't they?" Saburo said. "There's a poetry of sorts in their motion. It's all a matter of understanding the idiom."

Sparrow snorted, though he could see that his master's observation had a certain validity—

For someone who had never worn a battlesuit. Who hadn't chafed his limbs in long hours of practice, straining against the delay before the suit's servos translated the wearer's motion into the swing of an armored leg. Who hadn't felt the heat build up during battle, until the interior of the suit was an oven which burned the wearer's lungs and boiled the juices from his cramping limbs.

Who hadn't seen his vision displays break up into multicolored snow which meant the battlesuit was about to explode in coruscating flames, carbonizing all portions of the wearer near the point of failure.

The warriors still on their feet at evening on the battleplain were the best of the best. Their movements of attack and defense were so skillful that they might have been dancers.

But every one of them had died in battle in the Open Lands, or they would not be fighting again here.

"No one could stand against them, don't you think?" Saburo said. Despite his phrasing, the slight man was speaking to himself rather than his servant. "One could lead a group of them on a raid into another of the planes and—whisk off a slave very easily. If one wished."

"*And* tear a hole in the fabric of the Matrix," Sparrow said. "*And* start the Final Day, when the armies of the other planes come through the hole you've torn."

Saburo turned. "It might not do that," he said sharply. "If

perhaps only a few of the—of the warriors crossed. There needn't be a serious disruption of the Matrix."

"Which plane?" said Sparrow.

"This is purely an intellectual problem of the sort your crude—"

"*Which* plane, milord?" Sparrow repeated. He did not bother to raise his voice, but no one who knew the smith could doubt that he would continue pressing until he had an answer—or Saburo gave him his death for asking.

"Say—as an intellectual exercise," Saburo said. "Say Plane Three. The androids would be easily surprised. In and out. And no repercussions. There very likely wouldn't be any repercussions."

"The androids," the smith said, "aren't defenseless, milord . . . but that wouldn't really matter. Seeings that the holds on Plane Three are all within the swamps, the androids wouldn't need to defend themselves. That lot—"

Sparrow jerked his bushy, cinnamon beard to indicate the warriors struggling in the last moments of full daylight.

"—would sink out of sight on the first piece of soft ground, which they'd find the first step they took out of the Matrix."

He fixed Saburo with eyes as frosty as metal burned in the casting crucible. "What is it that you really want, milord?" Sparrow asked.

Saburo tented his hands. "You can't help me," he said to his fingertips.

"I can't help you until you tell me what you want," the smith replied.

The sun dipped below the horizon, though refracted light continued to brighten the sky: lemon yellow in the west, a rich and saturated blue on the opposite horizon. The warriors still on their feet froze in position. Their arc weapons vanished like the visual aftershocks of a myriad lightning bolts, and the luster of the battlesuits dulled.

"All right," said Saburo with a calm that belied the struggle before he permitted himself to speak. "I'll show you, Master Sparrow."

He waved a hand. Master and servant vanished together from the battleplain as though they had never been.

The turtle-backed repair vehicles continued to crawl among the casualties as yet unrepaired.

The severed limbs were hollow. The battlesuits fought without anyone inside them.

≡ 8 ≡

THE RISING SUN cast North's shadow across the island toward Race and Julia. Though the sea was calm, waves slid far up the slimy surface which could not be more than a hundred meters in diameter at this stage of the tide.

Gulls wheeled a half kilometer upwind, calling shrilly and occasionally diving into the pale green water. Scales flashed in their beaks as the birds climbed back to altitude, and the odors of salt and fish mingled in the air.

"So . . . ," said North in a voice as bitter and reptilian as the shrieks of the gulls. "My will is nothing to you?"

Race fell to her knees; Julia was trembling despite herself.

There was nothing in North's physical appearance to demand respect: he was merely a tall, craggy man past middle age, wearing Exploration Service coveralls. An expert might have noted that the butt of North's holstered pistol was worn and that he wore his rank badges on the underside of his collar where they would not target him for a distant marksman—

But Race and Julia dealt almost exclusively with men of war, and they had themselves faced death many times. The power of all Northworld emanated from the space where this man stood, as though he were a window for its majesty.

Julia covered her face with her hands. "F-father . . . ," she whispered. "Father, forgive me."

The Searchers' armor had vanished along with their dragonflies. The two women stood in the garments which they had worn under their battlesuits, a linen shift for Julia and Race in a singlet of thin suede, sweat-stained and rumpled. They were both big, both of them strawberry blondes, and—though they were not related—similar enough in appearance to have been sisters.

The gulls and the chuckling sea were the only speakers for moments that stretched toward a lifetime.

"Why should I forgive you . . . ," said North at last, " . . . ladies?" He spoke mildly. The whip-sting was in the epithet rather than in the tone with which he delivered it.

"You took my service of your own free will," he continued. "And you laughed when you played me false. My will and your oath were *nothing* to you."

The horizon was without shore in any direction. In a broad arc to the west, a gray slant of rain joined the darker gray of clouds to the sea. The breeze picked up. Thunder became an undertone without noticeable peaks.

"He was so brave, m-majesty," Race whispered. She didn't fear death, but the power that wore North like a garment was greater than life and death.

"It was my sin, master," Julia said. She lowered her hands slowly. "He was strong and brave, and I didn't want to see him murdered like a dog."

She swallowed. Tears were streaming down her broad cheeks. "Forgive me, master. I . . ."

"Oh," said North in bitter derision. "I won't punish you, ladies. You're beneath my contempt, aren't you? Oathbreakers? I'll simply set you down in the Open Lands and be shut of you."

A sheet of lightning leaped across peaks of the oncoming storm. The flash glinted from North's strong teeth and deep-set right eye.

"Your kin are long dead, but I couldn't do anything about that even if I chose," North said. "The sense of honor you displayed to me fits you admirably to live as whores."

Thunder from the storm front rolled across the island. Julia knelt as though an unbearable weight had crushed her down.

Her eyes were closed, and her mouth drooped open.

"Slay us, master," Race said. "Or give us leave to kill ourselves. . . ."

The Searcher wrung her hands together, rasping callus against callus where her body rubbed in her battlesuit. She tried to recall the feeling of bravado with which she had plunged into the skirmish in the Open Lands. Her only fear *then* had been of arc weapons, of the skill and numbers of Venkatna's troops; and that was less fear than a thrill of excitement. The will of North the War God was the farthest thing from her mind—

Then.

"Are you truly contrite?" North asked. His voice seemed softer, though it was hard to say just what the change in timbre had been. His words were audible through the now-constant thunder. "Do you truly wish to redeem yourselves? Though I warn you, the task I will set you, *if* you choose, will be a hard one."

"Anything, master," Julia whispered. She opened her eyes.

"Anything . . . ," Race said. She spoke so softly that the word was in the form of her lips and tongue rather than sound.

"Good Searchers," the god in gray coveralls mused, "are too valuable to waste. So . . ."

Water sluicing over the ridged surface of the island licked unnoticed at the Searchers' toes. The ground began to rock with the rhythm of the thunder.

"It is my *will*," continued North, "that you serve the human I choose for as long as he lives and requires you. That you carry out his orders with abject obedience. And if you do so—"

The lightning flash was so bright that it dimmed the risen sun for the instant of the discharge. The thunder was nearly simultaneous, and it echoed from the dome of the sky.

"—then it may be that you will become Searchers again," North continued through the pulsing roar, his tone audible and awful. "But I promise you nothing except the chance to live as the slaves of the man to whom I give you!"

"As you will," Race murmured.

She linked her right hand with Julia's left. They rose to their feet. A sullen wave broke over them from behind. The water was warm.

"As you will, your majesty!" the Searchers cried in unison to the figure of North, which swelled from the sea's surface to the heavens without losing solidity.

The rays of the sun streamed from the clear eastern horizon. The light, polarized between the sea and the overhanging cloudbank, tinged the women green. The storm broke over them in a blast of huge cold drops.

"Do you think it will be Salles we serve?" Race shouted into the ear of her companion.

The figure of the god disappeared. His laughter boomed across Race and Julia, louder than the thunder and more terrible than the scintillant ropes of lightning above them.

The island humped upward, ridge after green-black ridge, tumorous with barnacles and streaming ropes of seaweed. Almost a kilometer away, great flukes rose to hide the sun.

The beast dived. The storm-lashed sea swept over the place the Searchers had stood, but Race and Julia were no longer on this plane of the Matrix.

≡ 9 ≡

THE CAGE OF Fortin's elevator opened into the armored heart of APEX.

With the right will and mind controlling it, a Fleet Battle Director could design weapons and draft tactics superior by an order of magnitude to those of any other keep on the planet. Count Starnes' was the will, Karring's the subtle mind. Together they could succeed within their generation in reducing all hostile keeps—all civilization on Plane Five outside Keep Starnes itself—to smoking ruin.

Fortin had observed the beginning of their destruction with a pleasure greater than any he achieved during brief moments of sexual climax. He grinned as he stepped once more into the Citadel, concealed in his wrapper of bent light. The keep's technicians would spend days tracing the fault in the elevator system which had caused a pair of cages to descend to Citadel level, but they would find nothing. . . .

A high-pitched alarm signal began to warble. The sound was not loud, but it cut through the vibration which funneled from the corridor containing APEX.

Fortin frowned. The alarm was new, and so were other aspects of the Citadel. . . .

Four remote consoles were spaced around the periphery of the rotunda. In the center of the circular room was the bank of elevators. The figure walking toward the elevators—toward

Fortin—must be Lisa, because there was virtually no one else in Keep Starnes so thin.

A bulbous helmet with horns and shoulder braces covered her head. It was apparently opaque, because she moved with the care of a blind man in an unfamiliar room. Lisa swiveled her torso, back and forth like a scythe stroke, every time she placed her foot.

Her sister, Lena, lay as usual in the center of a huge console. She concentrated on a display which, to Fortin's cursory glance and lack of interest, appeared to be a palette of blurred pastels. Her body gleamed with a thin film of sweat.

The huge woman's current pair of lovers stood—or posed—behind her couch. They flexed muscles and plucked nervously at their harness as they watched Lisa's deliberate progress across the rotunda. The lovers had no part in present events, but they obviously felt they were at risk.

Karring wasn't in the rotunda, but that was no surprise. The chief engineer's normal lair was Bay 20, at the far end of the APEX corridor. Others were not barred from entering that sanctum—Starnes and his daughters would have flayed alive anyone, even Karring, who presumed to dictate where they could or could not go in their own keep. Nonetheless, Karring was important enough to be allowed his privacy, so long as it didn't become a point of honor. Keep Starnes was a huge place, and its rulers had no desire to visit every cranny of their domain.

Count Starnes was not visible either, but the tank across the rotunda from Lena's console was alive and ready for action. The elevator shafts had been cleared so that the massive vehicle could be lowered into the Citadel. It was always parked here, where it provided Starnes' last refuge against an enemy who had penetrated the myriad lines of defense above.

Fortin had never before seen the tank with its systems up.

The railgun's fat barrel was pointed only generally in the intruder's direction. A slug from *that* weapon could penetrate a hundred meters into living rock. A human as close to the muzzle as Fortin was would splash if the meteor-swift projectile struck him. Even a human with the powers of a god. . . .

Fortin smiled and shivered. He pretended to himself that he was unaware of the danger, but the danger itself was what brought him to this place of war.

"Try to your right," Lena called. She could pivot her couch to watch her sister, but she didn't choose to do so.

Lisa obediently turned and took another step—toward Fortin. She was still about ten meters away.

Real concern blanked the frown from the half android's face. He walked across the rotunda with the quick, stiff steps of a dog in a modest hurry.

Fortin understood the operation of Lisa's helmet now. The short booms to either side projected coherent light. The interference pattern the beams should form where they crossed five meters from the source was calibrated to within angstroms. The slightest variation in the path of one of the beams would disrupt the pattern—

And locate the intruder, despite the near perfection of his light-bending suit, with precision.

"He's heading for APEX!" Lena shouted. She leaned forward in the heat of excitement; her couch rolled up to follow her, continuing to cradle the woman's head and shoulders.

Fortin did *not* understand where Lena's console got its input. It seemed to be only an approximation, but not even that should have been possible to Starnes' daughter. They were using the Fleet Battle Director to track him. Fortin needed to learn how.

His heart was beating fast, though there was no real risk. The elevators were too dangerous for Fortin to attempt again, but he could escape directly into the Matrix.

Not, however, before he learned how Karring had detected his presence. It had to be Karring.

Lisa followed Fortin down the corridor at a quicker shuffle. The two of them were playing a game of blind-man's bluff, but the quarry could move. There was no risk, even though Lisa wore the pistol holster that was a badge of rank on Plane Five.

The corridor was five meters broad, but it jogged repeatedly where the banks of equipment projected farthest into it. APEX lowered over its surroundings like a giant carnivore bearing down on prey.

The Fleet Battle Director was constructed in twenty linked nodes. The designers' intention was both to minimize battle damage from a single hit and to provide shielding between segments so that sets of operations would not interfere fratricidally with one another. The armored bays contained individual input and output hardware. Input was via the operator's mental command, if so desired, or through a number of physical options. Primary output came in the form of holographic images which glowed in the air above each terminal.

Meter-thick conduits cross-connected the nodes and snaked through the walls of the Citadel, putting APEX in uninterruptible touch with every aspect of Keep Starnes. High overhead, the corridor ceiling crowded with a maze of lesser lines and the girders which supported them.

So close to APEX, the air was alive with a chittering like that of myriad goats, gnawing at the fabric of the universe.

Fortin walked on. His smile was becoming fixed. There was only a dim glow in the unoccupied bays he passed. Lisa's grotesquely distorted silhouette followed, backlit by the faint ambiance reflecting in from the rotunda.

The terminal at the far end of APEX was lighted. Rapidly-changing holographic displays modulated the pool of radiance which spilled from the bay into the corridor.

Karring was responsible. . . .

"He's still ahead of you," Lena directed her sister. Her throaty contralto rang from the speakers in the ceiling of each alcove. Their varying distance from Fortin blurred the words into reptilian menace.

Fortin reached Bay 20. Behind him, Lisa began to jog forward.

Karring sat upright at a terminal not dissimilar from the outstation at which Lena performed in the rotunda. Between the bald, aging engineer and the display hung a one-meter globe. Only careful study showed that it was constructed of matter rather than light. It glittered as it spun unsupported.

On the display—

Fortin squinted as his eyes tried to focus on holographic lines that seemed to be not quite in the same plane of existence.

It was a pattern of translucent octahedrons with mass and depth that went beyond the three spacial dimensions; they were distorted, and as APEX twisted the globe in response to a silent order from Karring—

"I see—" Lisa cried from the mouth of the bay.

Fortin's jamming pods fired a blast of radiance matched to the helmet's input frequency. He ran back down the corridor, past Lisa.

Six of Count Starnes' soldiers poised in the shadows above Bay 18. In preparation for this moment, the cables had been removed from the conduit feeding that node and two others. The armored tubes now provided secret paths into the Citadel. Special troops crawled into position while Lisa drew the intruder's attention.

A mesh as fine as spidersilk drifted down onto Fortin from the maze of pipes and wires in the corridor ceiling. The strands were monomolecular. Any one of them was strong enough to serve as the tow-rope of a truck.

The pattern on Karring's display slipped over itself, torquing and rotating until one of the octohedrons was crushed almost to non-existence. The chief engineer turned. He smiled.

The net tightened.

Fortin's brain was ice cold. He shifted himself into the Matrix, conscious only of his need to escape.

He couldn't move in the Matrix, either. Fortin's right hand clutched and wriggled in the free ambiance that was all eight planes and the paths between them—but only his hand. The vent that should have sucked the god in as the surface of a pool does a diver did not form.

Karring's globe spun faster as it distorted. The grip of the Matrix on Fortin's wrist was fiercer yet. He began to scream.

Glowing with the nimbus created by induced magnetic fields, moving at a walking pace, Count Starnes' tank slid down the corridor.

The bore of its railgun was centered on Fortin's chest.

≡ 10 ≡

THE ROOM'S EIGHT windows were so clear, and the scenes they displayed were so diverse, that Sparrow doubted for a moment that he was inside a building after all. He reached out toward the image of courtiers and petitioners gathered in King Venkatna's audience hall to see if he could—

Saburo's nostrils pinched. Seven of the windows, including that displaying the Open Lands, went a gray as solid as stone and featureless as vacuum.

In the remaining window, a black geodesic dome squatted on a mud island in a swamp. Around the stagnant lake, tree-ferns reached through the mists to spread the feathery fronds which sprouted from the sides of their trunks.

"Who made this place, milord?" Sparrow asked. He looked around with undisguised interest.

The windows met, edge to edge, in a complete circuit, but the room had no door. It was only accessible in the fashion by which Saburo had brought his servant here: through the Matrix.

"Why do you say 'made'?" Saburo asked. There was a touch of asperity in his voice. "Discontinuities between planes exist throughout the eight worlds. North as our leader could of course choose to place his dwelling around the best of those natural sports."

Saburo knew that his own palace—perfectly sited and balanced with its surroundings though it was—had not impressed Sparrow. The opinion of an artisan, scarcely better than a savage, was of course of no importance; but still. . . .

Sparrow snorted. "I've seen nature," he said. "Don't tell me I can't recognize craftsmanship."

He ran his index and middle fingers down the edge of the unclouded window, where the frame would be if it had a physical frame. The material was without temperature, neither hot nor cold. The only property it imparted to Sparrow's touch was the feeling of adamantine solidity.

"North built this himself, did he?" the smith said in marvel.

"I believe that is the case, yes," his guide and master replied. Saburo's voice was as colorless as the seven windows he had closed.

"I give him best, then," Sparrow said softly. His hand worked slowly up and down the gray, as though polishing a surface already smoother than matter could be. "*I* couldn't have built this, and I never thought I'd say that of a thing I could see."

"Master Sparrow—"

"I wonder what it cost him," the smith said. He wasn't interrupting Saburo; he was simply oblivious to everything except wonder at the construct in which he stood. "I know what it costs to turn the Matrix on itself, and to do it on this scale—"

"*Master* Sparrow," Saburo hissed in a towering fury.

The smith blinked, then immediately knelt—in contrition rather than fear. "Milord," he said, "Lord Saburo—I was inattentive when my duty was to you. It will not happen again."

"I—" Saburo said. He was startled to receive a sincere apology from this man. The smith's stiff-necked honor and controlled violence were as much a part of him as his cinnamon beard and hair. "I should have realized that this room would be of interest to someone of your—talents. But rise, please rise."

Sparrow stood and turned again to the window. This time he examined the scene rather than the structure which displayed it.

The water which surrounded the dome looked silver where sunlight glanced from it, deep black with dissolved tannin outside the angle of reflection. Meter-tall horsetails grew at the margins of the pool, wearing their branches like successive crowns sprouting at each joint of their stems.

Trees rose from the humps and ridges of higher ground nearby. The soil even of the hillocks was almost liquid, so that roots had to spread broadly across the surface in order to support modest thirty-meter trunks.

"Not battlesuits," Sparrow muttered, smug to see his off-hand assessment borne out by further evidence. "Not unless they're on stilts. Which I suppose I could . . ."

Saburo brought the image in the window nearer without giving an audible command. A wall of the same black plastic as the dome encircled the small island. The vertical corrugations every few meters looked at first to be structural stiffeners, but closer observation showed that each rib had a narrow shutter. The posts supporting the wall's single gate were thicker than the remaining ribs.

Because of the swamp's flat terrain, the ports the shutters masked could sweep for almost a kilometer in every direction. That judgment assumed the wall's defensive weapons were sufficiently powerful, of course; but the smith had a high opinion of the products of the androids' craft.

"The place *could* be captured . . . ," Sparrow murmured; considering ways and means, considering the tools he would build for the task.

He turned to his master again. "I don't know how long it could be held, though," he added.

"It wouldn't have to be held," said Saburo. "However . . ."

The image closed nearer yet and slid through the faceted dome of the structure. In the center of an open room knelt a woman—

An android, this was Plane Three—

A *girl* with perfect features. Her hair was in a tight bun, and she had painted her face chalk white over the naturally pallid android complexion. Black make-up emphasized her eyes, and her lips and spots high on either cheek were brilliant carmine.

She was arranging a spray of ferns and seed pods on the low table before her.

"She is . . . ," Saburo whispered.

Sparrow expected his master to continue with *'perfect,'* because that was the word which glowed from Saburo's eyes as he spoke.

Instead, Saburo said, " . . . Mala. She is the daughter of King Nainfari. She is—"

Saburo's voice strengthened as he spoke, until it crashed out with godlike force, "—the woman whom I have wanted for my wife ever since I amused myself here in North's vantage point."

His face tightened. The image drew back with the suddenness of a crossbow releasing. Mud, black plastic, and dozing armaments filled the window.

"Amused myself like a fool," Saburo continued harshly. "And saw her by chance, whom I could never have. Because for me to enter Plane Three with the necessary force would mean . . ."

The slim god's eyes stared at a day, a Day, that he had been unable to prevent himself from seeing. The Final Day, seen once in the Matrix and forever after in memory.

Sparrow smiled coldly. "You swim in the Matrix, my lord," he said mildly, "and you still believe in Chance?"

The smith had memories too. . . .

Sparrow shook himself like a bear dragging itself onto an ice floe. "So . . . ," he said, rotating the dome and its defenses in his mind. "You want the girl."

He focused again on his master. "All right," he said. "I'll bring her to you."

For a moment, Saburo's face looked beatific. Then he frowned and said colorlessly, "Master Sparrow, I have the greatest respect for your abilities, as an artisan and as a . . ."

His voice trailed off. Perhaps he would have said 'man,' had he continued in that vein. Instead, Saburo resumed with, "The terrain is swamp, and the temperatures there are very high. Not the sort of climate to which you are accustomed. Also—"

Saburo's voice returned by imperceptible stages to that of the technical expert he had been in an exploration unit. "—the defenses are strong, extremely strong. I've examined them at length. I don't believe one man, however equipped . . ."

He broke off when he realized that the smith was smiling at him. The expression had humor in it, but the underlying emotion was quite different.

"Lord Saburo," Sparrow said to the smaller man, "we both know that I serve you—"

"Serve me very well," Saburo broke in, afraid of what the smith might say next.

"—on my own terms," Sparrow continued without deigning to notice the interruption. "Which is all right, so long as neither of us makes a point of it . . . very often."

He paused.

"Go on," Saburo said. His voice was like the blue heart of a glacier.

"My terms are, milord . . ." Sparrow continued softly, " . . . that I will serve your need to the best of my ability, and that you will permit me to do so. I *will* do this thing for you, Lord Saburo."

"Then do so," Saburo said. His eyes were focused on the memory of the slim figure to whom his heart belonged. "And if you succeed . . . your will shall be my will, Master Smith."

≡ 11 ≡

MARKETDAY CROWDS SWEPT by the entrance, but a hush filled the interior of the shop of the merchant prince.

It was even cool—by the standards of southern sweatboxes like the port of Simplain. Brett, the underchamberlain, lowered the dampened linen kerchief with which he had been patting his face since an hour before sunrise.

D'Auber, the warrior who was both Brett's escort and his fellow envoy, continued to flap the throat of his tunic. The warrior insisted on wearing wool, no matter what the temperature was. Brett suspected that D'Auber would report the underchamberlain's switch to local materials as treason against Venkatna.

"Well, where's the guy with the slaves?" D'Auber demanded. "Where's Guest?"

The guards at the door were a pair of dark men wearing baggy white shirts and pantaloons. They carried broad-bladed halberds for show. Warriors in battlesuits stood in alcoves nearby where potted ferns discreetly camouflaged them.

Guest's entrance hall was a circular room whose high alabaster ceiling imitated the sag and folding of a tent roof. The clerestory level was a screen of filigreed stone. It and the vaguely-translucent ceiling provided adequate illumination, once the envoy's eyes had readapted from the dazzling blaze outside.

Water trickled down the steps of an artificial rill at the rear of the hall. It smoothed the raucous street cries from outside and contributed significantly to the room's coolness.

"Where's *Guest?*" D'Auber repeated, since everyone within hearing had ignored him the first time. "And what's the matter with the damned water? Does the place leak?"

Another white-suited servant entered the hall. This fellow was nearly two meters tall. "Lord Guest will join you now," the servant declaimed in a loud voice without looking at either of the envoys.

He stepped aside. A whole line of additional servants bustled in with an ivory stool, peacock-feather fans, and—incongruous within a masonry building—a parasol of either cloth-of-gold or gold foil on a thin backing.

Two servants ceremonially unfolded the stool. The man who sat on it seemed to appear from nowhere.

He was tall, almost as tall as his annunciator, but the gray silk he wore had been concealed behind his servants' shimmering garments. Fans waved, the parasol extended above his head, and the white-clad entourage made a formal bow to their master.

"So . . . ," said Guest. His voice was deep and powerful, that of a younger man than Brett had expected from the merchant prince's gray beard. "You are the couriers from the West Kingdom, responding to my offer."

"*I'm* a warrior," D'Auber rejoined harshly. "Not some messenger. And we've come from the Empire of Venkatna the First to escort back his slaves."

A train of heavy beasts passed in the street outside. They hooted at the city crowds and clanked the chains which some of them dragged to permit their mahouts to snub them up if they failed to respond to direction. The elephants of the region of Simplain had straight tusks and bare gray hides, unlike the black-wooled mammoths familiar to the northern envoys. The beasts, like the dark-skinned humans, were just close enough to familiar models that their *wrongness* was all the more disturbing.

Guest's complexion appeared to be as pale as Brett's own. It was hard to be certain as the fans moved in the dim light.

The merchant prince chuckled. "Ah, styles change faster than I can keep up with them. So long as your master's gold assays to the required purity, he has my leave to call himself whatever he pleases."

"The gold is of course being checked by your clerks, ah, Lord Guest," Brett said. "But there'll be no difficulty with its purity."

The underchamberlain had jumped in quickly because he was concerned about where D'Auber's temper was going to lead the conversation. It was all well and good to say in the privacy to your tent that Guest was nothing but a mere trader, of less account than a royal—than an imperial—slave.

In Simplain, though, Guest was a person of obvious importance. The battlesuits in which his guards watched from the edge of the hall were as good as the one which D'Auber had left perforce in the envoy's quarters. And Frekka was very far away . . .

"Even down in this hellhole," D'Auber said, mopping his face with the end of his sash, "you ought to be careful about what you say about the emperor. North the War God stands behind him, you know."

Perhaps the warrior was concerned about the risk also, because his neutral tone robbed his words of the threatening implications which they might otherwise have held.

"Ah, well," said Guest without obvious offense. "We in Simplain have many gods, and I fear that your North isn't widely worshipped here. Still, I wish Emperor Venkatna well, as I hope to do much business with him in the future."

"When may we hope to see the present merchandise?" Brett said brightly, another desperate attempt to turn the discussion into safer fields.

Guest clapped his left fingertips into his right palm. "At once, good sirs, at once," he said.

The curtains behind the merchant prince billowed again. Male servants entered, guiding a pair of women. To Brett's surprise, the females were not from the Simplain region at all. Both of them were pale and blonde. They weren't fat, but they were larger than the local women—and indeed, larger than most of the local men.

"Step forward, girls," Guest said. "Give the gentlemen a good look at you."

He smiled as he added to the envoys, "They will meet your master's requirements perfectly, good sirs. In the lands where they come from, the use of such devices is well known and they are experts in it."

"They'd better be," D'Auber growled. "At what the emperor is paying for them."

"Half now," said Guest easily. "Half when they have proved their abilities. What could be more fair?"

Brett stepped closer to the new slaves. Something about them was—not right, though the underchamberlain couldn't put his finger on precisely what it was.

The expression with which they met his eyes was not so much cowed as resigned. Certainly there was no indication of rebelliousness or danger.

"It's only . . . ," D'Auber went on angrily, " . . . that some folk, I don't mean you, Gues—*Lord* Guest. Some folk down here to Simplain, that is—"

Brett turned. "D'Auber, stop it *now*," he hissed with as much authority as he could assert without making the situation worse than it already was.

"What's a palace flunky think he's doing," D'Auber snarled, "tryin' to give orders to a front-rank warrior, anyhow?"

Guest laughed with unexpected relish. "That's telling him, Lord D'Auber!" he said.

D'Auber, not in the least mollified by the support, snapped his attention back to the merchant prince. "Like I was saying," he said, "folk down here might think they could cheat us and not worry about it. Well, you can laugh at North if you like, but he's the chief of gods in Simplain as well—and before he's done, he'll have brought the whole world under the Peace of King Venkatna!"

Brett saw his chance. "*Emperor* Venkatna!" he said. "Now shut up, D'Auber, before you blurt *more* treason."

The warrior backed a step in shock. He opened his mouth like a gaffed fish. D'Auber had drunk enough of the local wine this morning to stain his tongue and palate dark.

"I envy your friend his certainty," Guest said to the

underchamberlain in a conversational tone. "Few of us here in the southern lands are so sure of the gods' will."

Brett stepped to the side to put his body between D'Auber and the merchant prince. "The emperor looks forward to paying the remainder of the purchase price," he said. "If these are the experts you say, milord, there might well be a bonus."

Flummery, soap to lubricate the path of commerce—though it was by no means impossible that Venkatna would add a bonus. If the Web performed to its claimed capacity, the emperor could well afford to do so.

The underchamberlain frowned. He suddenly realized what was unusual about these slaves. They had calluses on all their visible joints, just as if they were warriors who practiced regularly in their battlesuits.

"I assure you," said Guest, "that this pair will be your master's most dutiful slaves. They will carry out his orders as though they were the injunctions of a god."

He laughed again.

Brett shivered despite himself. The particular sort of humor that suffused the sound was more disquieting than another man's rage.

"Do they have names?" he asked to break the spell.

"Race," said Guest, pointing, "and Julia."

Guest rose abruptly. Though the action was sudden, servants whisked the fans and parasol clear. He was scarcely upright before other servants were refolding the ivory stool.

"They will bring your master the fortune he deserves," Guest added before he vanished again through the curtains.

Until Guest stood up again, Brett had not noticed that the merchant prince had only one eye.

≡ 12 ≡

THE MAN HANGING in the center of the white bottle babbled. Count Starnes watched the image of Lena's console with a smile of accomplishment.

" . . . *anything you want* . . . ," the prisoner's voice whispered through a console speaker. His haggard face, the only non-white object in the containment facility, filled the huge curved screen. " . . . *only let me go . . . power . . . wealth . . . anything, I swear by the Matrix, only let me go . . .* "

"About ready, I would say, Karring," Starnes said complacently.

Lena split the screen to add a full-length view of the prisoner. She giggled like heavy soup bubbling. "He's so skinny," she said. "Just right for you, hey, Lisa?"

Her sister colored and turned away from the screen.

One of Lena's lovers smirked. When he saw Lisa's expression, his face blanked. He shifted so that his partner stood between him and the count's younger daughter. Lena could not protect her lovers from fury like *that* if it were unleashed.

Not, in all likelihood, that Lena would care. The men who serviced her were fungible goods.

" . . . *all the power in the world . . . only . . .* "

"As you say, milord," Karring agreed coolly. "Though had you permitted me to try, I'm confident that APEX could have sucked from him all the information that you could wish."

Starnes shook his head. "No, Karring," he said. "The old ways are best. For old problems, at least."

The bottle which held the prisoner sat in Bay 20, at the focus of the device by which Karring closed the escape route through dimensions. The chief engineer was more at home in the heart of APEX than anywhere else; but the others, even Count Starnes, found the inner recesses of the Fleet Battle Director to be as disquieting as a crocodile's den. They observed the bottle's internal pick-ups at Lena's outstation in the rotunda rather than on Bay 20's integral displays.

The internal security squad which captured the prisoner had stripped him through the meshes and inserted intravenous drips into his arms. Then they hung the intruder, still trussed, within the containment bottle.

In the three months since the capture, the prisoner had been without sensory input. The inner walls of the bottle maintained an even white glow. Even the water that flushed his wastes was held at precisely blood temperature.

After a time, the prisoner began to talk . . .

"In a way," Starnes said, "I'm sorry we've captured him. For a time, there, when we knew he was entering the keep . . . there was a new challenge, a *real* challenge again."

"There are the other keeps to conquer, father," Lisa said. She was still dressed—she was invariably dressed—as a common soldier. She spoke without emotion, but her eyes feasted on the pale, slender body of the man on the screen.

"Pft!" Count Starnes said. "That's gotten to be like kicking over anthills now. Oh, I'll go through with it, eliminate the rest of them, because I've started. But there's none of them that'll give me a fight . . . and when I'm done, what *then?*"

" . . . *a god . . . power beyond your dreams, just . . .*"

"There will be others where he came from, milord," Karring said. His voice held the same wistfulness as his master's had a moment earlier. "Dangerous opponents, perhaps, though we will defeat them. You and I and APEX . . ."

Lena blanked the screens. She reached down the front of her briefs and began to masturbate herself idly. Without looking back at the others around the console, she said, "All right, you've broken him. Are you going to go on from here? Because if you're not, father dear, I have better things to do with my time than watch a thin stick like him drool."

Count Starnes looked down at his daughter without expression. "Yes," he said after a moment. "All right, I'll speak with him."

The images blinked back onto the screen. "Prisoner!" the count ordered sharply. "What is your name?"

"*. . . gold and jewels and slaves for torture for any pleasure . . .*"

"Prisoner!"

The prisoner's eyes were open. They snapped shut, and he said in a cracked whisper with no hint of inflection, "My name is Fortin and I am a god and I will make you—"

"Prisoner!" Starnes repeated, slapping off the chain of syllables. "Fortin. Who sent you here?"

"No one sent me, your majesty," Fortin replied. His eyes reopened. A chilling intelligence had returned to their amber depths. Karring, perhaps the only one of the observers to notice, frowned. "I came as a visitor, meaning no harm and harming nothing of your wonderful power."

The close-up image smiled vastly. "I can make you still more powerful, if you only release me."

Karring shrugged. "He has nothing we need, milord," the chief engineer said.

Starnes pursed his lips. "The fabric that concealed him was interesting," he said.

"It took time to analyze," Karring agreed. "But it only conceals someone who isn't using any active sensors himself, much less weapons. Frippery, and anyway, we can duplicate it now ourselves."

"He's not even a soldier," Lisa said abruptly. "Give him to me, father. I might have use for a servant."

Lena chuckled. She was now toying with both her lovers as they stood to either side of her couch. Her eyes were on the holographic display.

"I could bring you an expert in war," Fortin said with an ingratiating smile. "Someone who could teach you to fight even better, who—"

"We don't need to be *taught* war," snapped the count. "We need an opponent worthy of our mettle."

He sniffed and added, "As *you* certainly were not."

"Though for a time, milord," Karring said, "it looked as if . . ."

"I can bring you an opponent, Count Starnes," the prisoner said. His face twisted into a look of horrible anticipation. "I can bring you a . . . soldier of my own people, to challenge you, if you like."

"No," said Karring abruptly. "I don't think that would be safe."

"Safe?" the count said. He looked at his chief engineer. "I don't see the danger."

"He may be a scout, milord," Karring explained. "He could return with an army of—I can only guess. We don't *know* the size of the keeps and their armies where he comes from."

"I'll bring him alone, your majesty," Fortin said, reverting to inflated address. "I'll send him, and he'll come without weapons, just as I did. No army, only one man, and you can run him like a rat in your maze. I swear by the Matrix!"

He licked his lips to keep from drooling again.

"His word's worth nothing, of course," Count Starnes said. His eyes were narrow with calculation.

"The Matrix . . ." repeated the chief engineer. "Prisoner: this Matrix is the medium through which you entered Keep Starnes?"

"Yes, yes," Fortin said. "And the oath has power, power to bind even me, even a god, milord."

He bobbed his head as he hung, still wrapped in unbreakable meshes. Fortin didn't know what Karring intended by the question, but he knew that anything was better than an eternity of white silence. . . .

"Is it alive, the Matrix?" Starnes asked his chief engineer.

"No," said Fortin.

"Y—" Karring began. He looked curiously at Fortin's expanded image.

"From what APEX tells me, milord," Karring continued when he saw that the prisoner had nothing to add, "I rather think that this Matrix may be alive in some fashion. But I don't see that it matters to us at present."

"You don't have anything to gain from me, your majesty," Fortin said quickly. "But I can bring you an opponent, a *safe* challenge. A game worthy of your skill and powers."

"We've caught him," Lisa said. "There's no reason to let him go. I'll take him for—for a time."

Lena chortled. "Just because you're skinny, you don't have to make do with *that*," she said.

She roused herself in the couch. It obediently shaped to continue supporting her as she twisted to look directly at her younger sister. "Here, take one of the boys. Take them both, child, it'll do you a *world* of good."

"Shut up," said Lisa distinctly, "or I'll—"

"Daughters!" snapped Count Starnes.

The women ostentatiously turned away, from one another and from their father as well.

"*I* say," Lena murmured, "let's send him back, and see if the next one is full grown."

"There's a risk, Count Starnes," the chief engineer said simply. "Even to us."

For a moment, Starnes pursed his lips. Then he shrugged and said, "If they can send one scout, they can send another. Keeping this one or killing him, that won't change anything."

Count Starnes reached past Lena and touched a mechanical switch for certainty. "The prisoner can't hear us now," the count said. "Karring, can you take our forces through this Matrix?"

"N—" the chief engineer began. He pursed his lips, then continued, "Not as yet, milord. Every time this one comes or goes, APEX gathers more data. Very shortly, I—we—might be able to do that."

Count Starnes smiled, a look very like that of the prisoner when he started to drool with anticipation. He opened the audio channel to the exclusion bottle again. "If this one can send us a single soldier . . . then that might be an interesting game, don't you think, Karring?"

"I'll send him, your majesty," Fortin's voice pleaded from the console. "One man, a soldier."

"Unarmed!" said the chief engineer. "Swear by your Matrix

that he will come without any weapon."

"I swear by the Matrix . . . ," Fortin whispered. "His name will be Hansen."

Starnes looked at Karring. "All right," Starnes ordered.

The globe in Bay 20 ceased abruptly to spin. As it did so, the net within the containment bottle fell limp as the prisoner vanished into the Matrix.

APEX murmured to itself, waiting as it had waited through the eons since the settlement of Plane Five.

≡ 13 ≡

SOME OF THE chaotic crowd eyed Hansen, but that was normal interest rather than doubt about his presence here in Heimrtal.

Kings Lukanov, Wenceslas, and Young had come as envoys of the Mirala District to treat with Emperor Venkatna. None of the three knew every member of the other entourages, and there were hundreds of warriors from the imperial army besides.

No one thought that Hansen was out of place. The short wolfskin cape which he wore over gray velvet emphasized the breadth of his shoulders and compact strength. His thick wrists bore the calluses of long practice in a battlesuit, and he moved with the stiff-legged arrogance of a warrior.

A warrior, or a mammoth-killing sabertooth.

No, he wasn't out of place. Heimr Town was a scene of blood and destruction; precisely where Nils Hansen belonged . . . especially since Hansen was the root cause of the desolation himself.

An imperial servant blew notice on his twisted brass horn. Warriors in the crowd moved closer to the court Venkatna had set up in the marketplace on Water Street, where merchants bartered with the citizenry of Heimrtal in former days.

No more. Though the houses surrounding the marketplace had burned, the heavy timbers of the ground floors still remained. Imperial troops had nailed Heimrtal's warriors there, bodies dragged from the battlefield dead as well as men who had surrendered when the Heimrtal line collapsed.

Some of the latter were still alive. Night would take care of
that, when the air dropped below freezing. The only warmth
the victims had was that of the posts smoldering at their
backs.

"Lord Nettley, step forward!" called a strong-lunged usher,
one of the bureaucratic entourage which accompanied Venkatna
even on campaign.

Not bureaucrats alone, however. The only warriors in armor
in Heimr Town now were imperial troops, and there were
enough of them to handle any trouble the Mirala delegation
might want to start.

Venkatna wore red silk brocade and a puff-sleeved jacket
rich with gold embroidery. Six champions in battlesuits stood
beside and behind the emperor where they could protect him
from sudden attack. More warriors were stationed along the
rear of the marketplace and at the edge of the circle cleared
in front of Venkatna.

The imperial troops had reverted to painting their battlesuits
with personal colors. A generation before, the professionals
of the West Kingdom buffed their armor to bare metal and
went to battle in the white, with only the rank badges flashed
on their helmets to differentiate the units of their disciplined
mass. . . .

*Marshal Maharg's helmet is marked with seven chevrons,
alternating black and yellow. His gauntlets glow dull red with
the weight of current flowing through them as he withstands
the attack of two Solfygg champions.*

*The servos in the joints of Maharg's armor have been
robbed of power to feed the defenses. He steps backward
anyway, fighting the whole mass of his battlesuit. He is a
true champion; worthy of his father, worthy of Nils Hansen,
his father's greatest friend.*

"*Maharg, I'm—*" Hansen shouts. *Breath flays Hansen's
lungs with knives of ozone. The skin of his right arm feels
as though it has melted into the charred suede lining of his
battlesuit. His legs stride forward in slow motion.*

*Maharg moves like a cat killing. He shunts full power into a
thrust that blows one opponent's circuitry in a dazzling fireball.*

The remaining Solfygg warrior carves through Maharg's backplate.

"—coming!" shouts Hansen as he strikes, too late for anything but revenge.

A man jostled Hansen's left elbow.

When the horn sounded, the delegation from the Mirala District came out of the shock to which Heimr Town had reduced it. Warriors pushed to the front of the crowd. Hansen sat on an overturned wagon from which one could see over the armored bulk of the imperial guards. King Wenceslas and his entourage determined to take the wagon as a vantage point.

Hansen was still in a waking trance as he turned toward the warrior who pushed him. Whatever was on Hansen's face was enough to throw the other man back like a hammerblow. Wenceslas and his warriors settled around Hansen like snow drifting across a waiting lynx.

"Lord Nettley," Venkatna said. "You have proved yourself our faithful servant many times in the past."

The emperor's voice lacked the deep-chested fullness that his usher had shown a moment before, but it snapped with stone-hard authority. He sat on a stool. Though the piece was light and could be folded for travel, Hansen noticed that it had five short steps below the seat.

"Nettley? *That* little booger?" grumbled the warrior who'd bumped Hansen. "Bloody traitor, that's what *he* is."

"Left his rightful lord two summers back," agreed another of Wenceslas' attendant warriors. "Then led Venkatna back t' his home here to gut it, he did."

Nettley was a solid-looking man in his thirties. He moved well. If Hansen had been putting together an army, he would have hired Nettley without concern . . . so far as competence went. Nettley was very much the sort that a wise leader kept an eye on.

Venkatna was smart enough to know the risk of treachery. The ruins of Heimr Town proved the emperor was ruthless enough to obviate the risk as well.

"Kneel, Lord Nettley," Venkatna ordered. "In the name of the powers which the gods have vested in me as their vicar on Earth—"

The immediate crowd hushed so thoroughly that the cries of women in the background soughed through the marketplace. Over a hundred of them—freeborn, not slaves until disaster engulfed the Heimrtal levy the previous afternoon—were being marched off toward Frekka in chains.

"—and before the assembly of the people, I name you Duke of Heimrtal and Mayor of Heimr Town, with the rights of high and low justice without reference to custom or the authority of the elders—"

The crowd gasped. The man beside Hansen blurted to Wenceslas, "*You* don't have that authority, Vince, and you're a king!"

"I don't have a thousand warriors to call from Frekka when the freeholders get up in arms against me, either, Blood," King Wenceslas replied bluntly.

"—and the right to administer all land within the district as imperial land, beneath my authority," Venkatna concluded. "Rise, Duke Nettley."

Imperial troops cheered. Battlesuit speakers amplified the voices of armored warriors into terrifying threats. No one else in the crowd made a sound. When the shouts died away, the keening of the women could be heard again.

A warrior near Hansen mumbled a curse.

Hansen absorbed the scene as if none of it touched him emotionally. He was gathering data. The way his hands flexed as if toward a gun butt when the women cried meant nothing to the men around him.

"Isn't a bloody lot left t' be duke *of*," the warrior called Blood whispered.

Most of the district's freemen were unharmed; even some of the warriors would have fled to the woods and escaped instead of trying to face Venkatna's professionals. Nettley would have no difficulty finding willing tools to promote into the seats of the fallen lords, just as the emperor had found Nettley to replace the late King of Heimrtal. . . .

The new-made duke stepped out of the circle. His face was smug and gleaming with sweat.

"I have here," the emperor continued, waving a document from whose wax seal fluttered ribbons of blue and crimson, "a petition from the Mirala District, in the names of Lukanov, Wenceslas, and Young—"

"Bloody well about time!" said a warrior under his breath.

"—requesting, I should almost say *demanding,* a meeting with me," Venkatna said. "Regarding what they term 'the traditionally free relations of their district with the West Kingdom.' "

King Lukanov, an old man and so fat that he seemed to balance his weight on a briar-root walking stick, tried to enter the cleared circle. An imperial warrior stretched out his arm to block the aged monarch.

Lukanov squawked. Wenceslas cursed under his breath, but *he'd* had the judgment not to move before he was invited to do so.

Venkatna tossed the document behind him. An aide caught it in the air, but the meaning was clear.

"Their petition is denied," the emperor said flatly. "The gods have appointed me vicar of *all* the Earth."

He stood up and continued in a sharp, carrying voice, "My friends from Mirala can see around them how I deal with those who oppose the gods' will. They can talk to Duke Nettley to learn how I treat those who support me in North's great enterprise, the bringing of peace to all corners of the Earth. Next spring, my armies and I will meet them in Mirala, and we will see whether they have learned the lesson from others, or whether I will have to teach them myself."

Venkatna clapped his hands.

"This council is dismissed!" the usher cried. Horns blew a raucous discord.

Wenceslas turned and stalked off through the dispersing crowd, his face white with rage.

"That stuck-up sonuvabitch!" growled one of the warriors tagging along in the petty king's wake. "Who does he think he is!"

Hansen's face was as still as a cocked gunlock. That *question was an easy one to answer. Where you might get an argument was over whether the sonuvabitch was right.*

He wasn't right if Nils Hansen had anything to do with it.

Venkatna spoke briefly with his aides. A courier handed him a document tied with the crimson ribbon of the chamberlain's office, and a pair of body servants folded the portable throne. The emperor's bodyguards spaced themselves in a circle around him; more alert, not less, in the clamor of the thinning crowd.

Queen—it would be Empress now—Esme, flanked by a pair of armored warriors, walked past the overturned wagon on her way to her husband. Behind her followed a mixed group of male slaves and well-dressed young women. A hitch in Esme's step reminded Hansen of King Lukanov a few minutes earlier.

Venkatna broke off his discussion and strode over to his wife. "Darling!" he said as he gripped Esme's arms. He kissed her on the forehead, just beneath her wimple. "You shouldn't be walking around like this. You should have waited in the tent."

Esme indeed looked slight and cold, despite the bright sunshine and the cloak of white bearskin which she wore. She smiled toward her husband with genuine happiness and said, "No, no, dearest. It does me good to get out. And—"

She half-turned and gestured toward the women whom the slaves were herding into a line abreast, facing the emperor.

"—I wanted you to see the selection of girls I've made while it's still daylight," Esme continued. "Only the six on the left are virgins, but I thought the other four were too interesting not to include. Lamps and torches do so blur the finer points, don't you think?"

One of the women was sobbing. The others stood silent. Their faces reflected a range of expressions from interest to wide-eyed shock like that which Hansen had seen on a man he'd gut-shot.

"Well, they're all very nice, Esme," Venkatna said with a cursory glance toward the women. "Very nice, I do appreciate it. But actually, I think I'll start back immediately with the vanguard. You see—"

"You won't be riding all night, dearest," the empress said sharply. "You'll sleep somewhere, won't you?"

Venkatna flashed a perfunctory smile. "Yes, quite right, my darling."

He looked past Esme's shoulder again. "The two in the middle, shall we say? They'll do nicely."

He stepped back from his wife and waved the document from his chancellor. "What I wanted to tell you, though," he said, "is that Saxtorph says he's succeeded in finding slaves who can work the Web as it should be worked! He's waiting for my return before he gives them a serious test, though."

Esme turned her head. She looked at the envoys from Mirala, already striking their tents and loading impedimenta onto draft mammoths. "As you think right, dear," she said. "But those fellows over there mean you no good, and you know it."

Venkatna laughed in loud triumph. "I *want* them to get home, dearest. Fear defeats more enemies for me than I've had to face in open battle. And it saves me potential subjects, recruits for—"

He looked at the bodies nailed to ruined walls, stiffening and still moaning.

"—my armies."

"As you say, dear," Esme said. "But I don't think the Mirala District will come without a fight."

The empress glanced around the marketplace. Her eyes met those of Nils Hansen, sitting alone now on the wrecked wagon. He smiled at her.

A smart woman. Hansen didn't think Mirala would give up without a fight either.

If he could arrange it, that would be a fight the imperial forces lost. . . .

≡ 14 ≡

SPARROW'S DOG THRUST her nose under the smith's hand and joggled him, because he'd been concentrating too hard to pet her willingly. He muttered a curse, but his fingers were gently firm as they flexed to scratch the animal's ruff.

Sparrow had said—Sparrow had boasted—that he would bring Saburo his bride; and so he would.

But precisely how was another matter.

Sparrow's handmirror held a tiny image of Plane Three; raw swamp, not Mala's dome kilometers to the west of where the smith now focused. He would enter the plane through a discontinuity rather than by forcing a hole in the Matrix. To do otherwise would be to alert the entire android defense structure, and Sparrow was under no illusions as to his ability to battle through *that*.

He had nothing against kidnapping the princess against her will. Saburo had directed him to bring the girl; if Saburo felt there should be limitations on the methods his servant chose to use, then he should have said so from the start. But Sparrow had no intention of getting into a biting match with a sabertooth, either.

So . . . Sparrow would have to enter Plane Three at some distance from his objective and travel through the swamp to Mala's outlying bower. The terrain was unpleasant; and, while the wildlife didn't include sabertooths, there were some hazards of a similar line.

The beast which Sparrow studied through his window on other realities was a dimetrodon several meters long. It would weigh several hundred kilos after a good meal. It lay on a rock, sideways to the dawn. The sail arching high on the dimetrodon's back would warm its blood more quickly to splay-foot after its prey. Such beasts wouldn't be the real danger of the journey, but they weren't negligible either.

The dog peered at the dimetrodon's reduced image. She growled from the back of her throat, uncertain of what she saw but disquieted by it. Sparrow stroked his pet.

The smith adjusted the handmirror, returning—for he had stared at this during three hours of the past four—to a scene in the Open Lands. In the palace of the Emperor Venkatna, a tracery of metal and silk-fine semi-conductor crystals waited for operators who could drive it to capacity.

Sparrow shifted his viewpoint down into the Web's microstructure. He did not understand the mechanism by which the construct channeled event waves, but he could *use* one. . . .

There were, of course, risks.

The big man stood up in sudden decision. He switched off the viewing mirror which he had built according to shadows in the Matrix that no one but he could have seen.

What Sparrow built now would be a still greater triumph of his craft.

The bitch rubbed against her master's legs. The braces of living metal which Sparrow had made for both of them clicked together. She could sense his excitement, and she felt it was too long since they had hunted together. . . .

It took the smith over an hour to gather the raw materials which he needed, then to array them precisely to the side of the split-log bench. Any surface would do when he entered the Matrix, but the old symbols were best.

The dog waited, alert but patient. The smith lay down on the bench and closed his eyes. After a moment, the pile of raw materials began to shift. Stones grew webs of gossamer crystals, doped with traces of other elements at the necessary points in the silicon lattice.

Chance *could* have brought the molecules together in this

fashion. Somewhere in the infinite universes, chance had done so.

The will of Sparrow the Smith picked atoms from the pile he had prepared and shifted them in accordance with the pattern only *he* could have discerned in the Matrix. From the ores and scraps of metal grew a delicate object—small, but in every other respect a duplicate of the probability generator in Venkatna's audience hall.

≡ 15 ≡

HANSEN TURNED WHEN he heard a mechanical sound over the snorts and murmurs of the Y-horned titanotheres browsing around him on the plateau.

A high-powered unicycle was headed his way. Its hub-mounted motor howled every time the wheel bounced into the air from a pothole. The rider sat easily erect, dressed in black leathers. His mirror-polished visor was a reflective ball. On it a medial horizon separated the rich azure sky from a distorted panorama of the rough terrain.

On *that* vehicle, the visitor could only be Fortin; and in Hansen's book, there was never a good time to see Fortin.

The unicycle slowed as it neared the titanotheres. The multi-tonne beasts were loosely spread over the landscape; calves, generally in pairs, close to their mothers, and a huge male stationed downwind of the herd he dominated.

Fortin picked the last thousand meters of his way carefully, trying to reach Hansen at the center of the herd without approaching any of the titanotheres. The ball of his helmet spun from side to side as he tried to look in all directions at once.

A young male titanothere bellowed and did a sudden curvette, snapping at its haunches. Apparently the beast had mistaken the sound of the unicycle for that of a horsefly about to light. Fortin wobbled and almost fell: though the dim-sighted browser was unaware of the vehicle's presence, the titanothere's circular rush nearly trampled unicycle and rider accidentally.

Fortin pulled up beside Hansen and switched off his engine. He stepped to the ground. The sidestand bit into the friable soil, and the unicycle fell over beside its rider.

The drive motor was hydraulic. The smell of hot oil made Hansen's nose wrinkle.

Fortin touched his helmet. The front half snicked back and merged with the rear. His white android features were no paler than usual in the near dusk. "What a bloody place!" he snarled. "Can't you find somewhere decent to be, Commissioner?"

"I suppose if I felt like human company just now," Hansen said, "I'd be back in the Open Lands with Lord Salles."

Hansen smiled. It was not a particularly-pleasant expression, but there was enough humor in it to raise a question of how pointed he meant the insult to be when he added, "Human company or yours, Fortin."

The android laughed. "And here I came to do you a favor, Hansen," he said.

The two men—the man and the android—were close to the same height, but Hansen's build was much solider without being heavy. Despite that, Fortin had a wiry strength—as a weasel does, and it was coupled with a weasel's mad urge to slaughter.

Well, Hansen hadn't always needed much of a reason to kill either; though sometimes he dreamed about it afterward, nightmares in which all the faces became one face with glazing eyes. . . .

"You never did anybody a favor, Fortin," Hansen said without overt emotion. He stepped over to the unicycle and raised it, since its rider wasn't about to.

The little vehicle was extremely dense. Hansen grunted, letting his knees do the work to save his back. His toe teased closer a broad, fibrous chip of titanothere dung, years and perhaps decades old. He slid it under the stand. The chip spread the weight enough to keep the unicycle from toppling when he let go of the handlebars.

Fortin's face hardened as it had not at the verbal insult.

"Perhaps," he said to Hansen's back, "you'd rather that I just go away and not bother you with what I've learned?"

"Don't play games, Fortin," Hansen said. He turned and met his visitor's eyes. "I know, duration doesn't matter to us any more . . . but I don't have much taste for silly games."

A titanothere forty meters away drew Hansen's attention when it flopped down. Its ribs boomed a drumbeat against the ground.

The beast rolled on the light soil, kicking its four-toed forefeet in the air and gouging the dirt with its nose horn. Small birds hopped in and out of the dust cloud, snapping at insects the titanothere roused.

Fortin watched, frowning as he tried to divine what it was that Hansen saw in the spectacle to hold his rapt attention. If Hansen had hunted the huge beasts—

—had blasted the animals to gobbets of flesh which lost life and then even the semblance of life—

—the android could have understood; but instead Hansen merely observed. He was so gentle with beasts that Fortin could almost forget the lethal violence gleaming at the back of the ex-policeman's green eyes.

"All right . . . ," Fortin said aloud. "It's simple enough, really. You came here to learn how Captain North made this world vanish from the outside universe, did you not?"

"That's why the Consensus sent me to Northworld, yes," Hansen said. He looked over his shoulder at Fortin. "Do you know the answer?" he added without emotion.

Fortin quirked an ingratiating smile. "I know who does," he said. "Or more accurately, I know where the information is. But I don't suppose you consider that you have a duty to the Consensus of Worlds any longer, now that you've become a god . . . ?"

"I'll worry about my duty, friend," Hansen said softly. "Why don't you tell me what you think you know?"

"The folk on Plane Five are descended from the human crews of the fleet the Consensus sent first to search for Northworld," Fortin said. "When Captain North made us vanish. They're settled in keeps, and they fight each other."

Hansen nodded. "Fight each other within limitations," he

corrected. "Armies fight each other, but they pretty much leave each other's homes alone so they don't spoil the game for the future."

He grinned harshly and added, "God forbid that anybody decides to live in peace anywhere on Northworld."

"It used to be that way on Plane Five," Fortin said. "All the millennia since the settlement. But the current Count Starnes is destroying all his neighbors, one by one. So I went to see how."

The dust-bathing titanothere rolled to its feet and woofed like a huge dog. It ambled toward another young male, then charged. The beasts thudded together in a mock courtship battle.

"You *would* like that, wouldn't you, Fortin?" Hansen said. His eyes were on the great herbivores and his voice was controlled, but the android noticed Hansen's fingers twitched as though reaching for a pistol. "People killed, people left to starve; people chained in labor gangs, all for no reason. . . ."

"I'm *trying* to do you a favor, Commissioner," Fortin said sharply.

Hansen turned. He was dressed in Open Lands style, a leather jerkin over his wool blouse and breeches. He wore no weapon, but the threat of murder was in his eyes.

"Then do it, Fortin, and get out," Hansen said. He spoke with difficulty, as though his throat were choked with dust. "I decided a long time ago that I shouldn't kill people just because they were evil little bastards . . . but I've been known to make exceptions."

"If you kill me, Hansen . . . ," the android whispered. "If you kill any of us gods, the whole Matrix collapses and there's *nothing* left."

"Yep," said Hansen. "I've been told that."

Fortin's mind turned inward to a vision of nothingness so icy and perfect that his body shivered in rapture. The very motion drew him back to where he stood, on a plateau on Plane Eight, where titanotheres gamboled in the dusk.

"Yes," the android said to clear his throat and mind.

"All the keeps on Plane Five have powerful computers," he resumed in a voice as light as the breeze. "That of Keep

Starnes is the original Fleet Battle Director, an APEX system, that came with the settlement. It outclasses the other systems as the sun does a candle. That's how Count Starnes is able to overwhelm his neighbors."

"Go on," Hansen said. His voice had lost its edge. He didn't see Fortin's point as yet, but he was now sure there was a point.

"Don't you see, Commissioner?" the android crowed. "APEX is powerful enough to determine how North took us beyond the outside universe. But in all the time the unit has sat on Plane Five, nobody bothered to ask it the question!"

The titanotheres began to move off in the direction of the setting sun. The odor of their bodies and the alkaline bite of the dust they stirred filled the muttering gloom. A big female passed within a few meters of the humans, unaware or unconcerned.

Fortin could no longer make out Hansen's features. "I'm telling you this because I thought you'd want to know," the android went on. "But I advise you not to attempt to access the data. It's too dangerous."

He tried to conceal his anxiety that Hansen wasn't going to react; that the ex-Commissioner would ignore the duty that had sent him to Northworld in the first place.

But—when the Matrix gave humans power that made them gods, it also accentuated the primary traits of each human's underlying personality. Duty must have been important to Commissioner Nils Hansen long before the Consensus sent him to Northworld.

Whereas Fortin's personality—

"Count Starnes says he'll let you use APEX," Fortin said, "but it's not really safe to visit Plane Five, is it? Since we can draw power from the Matrix only here and in the Open Lands."

Hansen did not appear to be listening. His eyes followed the titanotheres, black humps against a crimson sky. The fingers of his left hand played across the seat of Fortin's unicycle.

"Besides," the android added, desperate in his fear and his evil, "Starnes says he'll see you only if you come to him unarmed. He's not to be trusted. I'm afraid that if he has you in the center of his keep, he'll strike you down."

Hansen stretched his arms out to the sides, then twisted them behind him and craned his neck back as well. "Will he just?" he murmured. "Quite a boy that Starnes, hey?"

"Look," said Fortin. "I've told you what I surmise and I've given you my recommendation: stay away, it's too dangerous for you. I have nothing more to do with it."

His voice rose without his being aware of it. A titanothere straggling behind the rest of the herd broke into a snorting trot in the direction of the sound.

Fortin's left hand splayed out. A ball of orange sparks devoured a section of the landscape, expanding until it struck a vertical plane separating it from the titanothere. The ball winked out with the hollow *whoomp* of an implosion.

The titanothere skidded, then galloped off in the opposite direction.

Hansen lowered his own left hand. "He wasn't going to do any harm," he said to the android. "Usually they don't charge home; and anyway, they're too clumsy to chase you down if you dodge."

"I have better things to do than play games with mindless beef!" Fortin snarled. He threw his leg over the saddle of the unicycle and locked his face shield down.

"I'd feel naked, going into a place like Keep Starnes without a pistol," Hansen said conversationally. "T' tell the truth, I feel naked even out here without a pistol. Maybe that's why I come, d'ye think?"

"I think nothing!" the android snapped. "What you do is your own affair, Commissioner Hansen."

He touched a switch on the left handgrip. White radiance fanned across the landscape from the unicycle's headlamp. The wheel spun in the light soil, tilting the saddle forward despite the stabilized suspension. The little vehicle tore off into the night in the direction the titanotheres had gone.

Hansen dusted his palms absently over his thighs, brushing away grit that the unicycle had thrown onto him. He could return to the Open Lands at the moment of his departure, so that he would seem never to have been gone.

He could as easily travel through the Matrix to the dwelling he kept here on Plane Eight, a dozen kilometers in less than an eyeblink.

But duration no longer mattered to him, and he needed to think. He started to walk through the gathering dark, an easy pace that would get him where he was going in the short term . . .

And perhaps by then he would know what he intended to do in the larger sense.

≡ 16 ≡

THE LEGS OF Sparrow's dragonfly clicked delicately as he set the vehicle down on the shingle beach. Jade-green waters swelled in the sunlight, bubbling over the pebbles. Similar white ruffs in the distance marked other islets.

Above the surf lapping toward the dragonfly hung the image of a swamp, glimpsed as though through a frosty mirror: a discontinuity into Plane Three.

Sparrow's dog leaped from the cradle of his arm. She darted forward and yapped at the waves, then ran back with a curve of foam pursuing her. The omnipresent rustle of water against air and stone thinned the barking to chirps indistinguishable from those of distant gulls.

Sparrow opened his vehicle's side compartments. Ordinary dragonflies were fitted with the electronics necessary for them to carry out the tasks North set his Searchers. Sparrow used the space to haul limited amounts of cargo.

Birds circling the island dropped lower. Their wings were jointed crescents against the clear sky. The metal braces which gleamed like fishscales as the smith and his dog moved drew their interest.

The dog hopped up on her hind legs, snapping at the gulls as opponents she could understand. The big birds shrieked disdainfully, then flared their wings to rise again.

Sparrow laid a ground sheet over the shingle. He took out

the first parcel and unwrapped the soft leather covering of a bell-muzzled energy weapon, a mob gun. It had a sling and a short stock, but it could be fired as easily with one hand.

When Sparrow asked Hansen for advice about weapons which were not in use in the Open Lands, the god had suggested this one. Hansen's careful neutrality cloaked obvious doubts about anybody who chose to enter a dangerous situation carrying arms which—however effective in themselves—were not natural to him.

Sparrow set the mob gun on the ground sheet. The second parcel contained a pair of gauntlets. He tried them on. They were massive, heavier even than they would have been if the smith had fashioned them entirely from steel. The wrist flares covered half the length of his forearms.

The gauntlets' thumb and finger joints slid like miniature waterfalls when Sparrow clenched his fists and opened them. He could pick an egg out of a nest and not break its shell.

Sparrow clashed the gauntlets together and laughed. His dog sprinted toward him from where she had been chasing waves. Her feet spurned pebbles as she barked in concern.

Hansen was right. Sparrow had practiced with the mob gun. He'd been impressed by the way its discharge converted cubic meters of landscape into a fireball . . . but the mob gun would stay here, and Sparrow would wear the gauntlets into Plane Three.

The smith wore a sleeveless shirt and short breeches of undyed wool. His sandals were laced halfway up his calves. They had heavy soles with hobnails, though he didn't suppose the studs would help his footing in the soup to which he was headed.

He'd been in swamps before. He'd killed a bogged mammoth once, moving cautiously because he was as much at risk as the beast which screamed and tried to twist enough to wrap the tiny human in its trunk. The water had been cool, even though it was midsummer when the sun set for less than an hour. Gnats had covered Sparrow like a black skin as he eased forward with his spear poised. . . .

The dog jumped up, barking worriedly as she clawed Sparrow through his thin breeches.

"North gut you!" the smith swore by habit and reached down; but the mass of the gauntlet slowed and reminded him. He rubbed the base of the animal's ears with his armored fingertip, then patted its flank in reassurance before he stepped to the compartment on the other side of the dragonfly.

There was only one object in this compartment. Because of its delicacy, Sparrow had fastened it with dozens of flexible restraints instead of trusting a padded wrapper. Now he undid the clips one by one until finally he removed the ovoid construct of metals and semi-metals grown as monocrystals rather than being pulled through a drawplate.

The wire egg was about twenty centimeters through the long axis and some fifteen across the center of the swell. It flexed slightly and began to glow in the violet-magenta range as the smith held it by the ends.

A pattern of water droplets shimmered above the breaking waves. As Sparrow concentrated, Brownian motion drew a corridor through the mist. Merely a pocket in the fabric of random chance. . . .

Sparrow sighed and hung the probability generator from the pair of hooks he had worked through his supple bearskin belt. The device was as sturdy as he could make it and still retain its powers. If that wasn't sufficient for field use, then Sparrow would succeed without it.

He grimaced. When he used the device, it felt as though a cat drew icy claws across the surface of his mind.

Through the discontinuity, heat bent horizontal waves across horsetails growing from the mud of the swamp. Sparrow flexed his gauntlets. It was tempting to consider letting the dragonfly carry him across the muggy wasteland to his destination—

But the dragonfly would trip alarms all over Plane Three's single continental land mass. They would come for him, the androids, with force he could not withstand.

The discomfort of the trek would be only an incident. Sparrow's face and arms had swollen to twice their normal size from gnat bites after he slew the mammoth in the bog, but he hadn't noticed the insects until after his spear thrust home. . . .

Sparrow stepped into the surf. It foamed suddenly to knee

height, then dropped back. The dog ran back and forth along the tide line, yapping frantically.

Sparrow turned. "Come on, then!" he shouted. "Or stay, I don't care. I'll be back for you."

The dog tested the salt water with a paw. A wave licked forward. The animal tumbled over herself scrambling backward. She sat on her haunches and yowled piteously.

"You damned fool," the big smith said. To an outsider, he appeared to be talking to his dog.

He waded back onto the shingle and scooped the animal up in his left arm, cradling her carefully so that she didn't kick the wire egg on his belt. The bitch raised her muzzle and began to lick Sparrow's ear. Her canines were white and powerful.

Sparrow splashed into the surf, carrying the thirty-kilo animal as though she weighed no more than the sunlight on his cinnamon-gold hair. As he neared the discontinuity, frost thickened across its surface. The scene beyond was lost in diffracted light.

Sparrow lurched forward. The waves advanced to meet him, but when they drew back, the man and his dog were gone.

≡ 17 ≡

THE POINT OF black light in front of Hansen lost itself for a moment, then twitched inside out like an origami sculpture. The light became the figure of a black-haired woman on a dragonfly, landing in the courtyard of the Searcher Barracks.

A whiff of ozone dissipated quickly in the fresh breeze; the substrate of heated resins and polymers, the spoor of electronics seeing hard use, remained somewhat longer.

"A manual touch-down, Krita?" Hansen said in amusement. "As smooth as the automatic systems could have managed, I'll grant."

"Hello, Nils!" the Searcher said brightly as she swung off the saddle of her dragonfly. The dimensional vehicle's four legs were jointed into V-struts like the hind limbs of jumping insects. They bobbed when the rider's weight came off them.

Krita was a small woman, coming to a little above the shoulder of Hansen, who was of only average height for a man. Like Hansen, she was densely muscled and callused from battle practice; but she was a woman beyond doubt.

She wore soft boots and a white linen shift which had embroidered borders at the hem, armholes, and deeply-scooped neckline. Her breasts were wide-set on a broad chest, much more prominent when she was nude than through even a thin garment. The shift was cut to mid-thigh so that she could wear it comfortably in a battlesuit; her legs as she dismounted were smooth and tanned all the way to the black pubic wedge.

Krita put her arms around Hansen and kissed him. She smelled faintly of female sweat, modified by the fruit-oil soap with which she had recently washed her hair.

The barracks were apartments on three sides of a courtyard whose fourth face was closed by the towering majesty of North's palace. Dragonflies waited before many of the twenty-seven units. Another Searcher opened the door beside Krita's, noticed the couple embracing—

Recognized Hansen and jumped back so quickly that the panel of carved light shivered in its frame as it slammed.

Krita chuckled. "Come on in," she said, tugging at the edge of Hansen's marten-fur cape. "Seeing the gods here—"

She laughed again.

"—disturbs some of the girls."

"I've offered you a place of your own," Hansen said somberly as he stepped into Krita's suite.

If one looked carefully at the walls, one could see they were created of points of light disappearing into the infinite distance, like a clear winter sky compressed into a few centimeters. The design was North's business and that of those who chose to live in the War God's outbuildings. It reminded Hansen of Plane Four, where souls existed in ice and torture. . . .

Maybe that was what it reminded North of also.

Krita lifted on tiptoe to kiss Hansen again. She paused and said, "You know I won't do that."

"Sure," he agreed, looking around him. The walls were hung with tapestries, finely-wrought drinking horns, and the bows and spears of the chase. Very like a lord's hall in the Open Lands, but without the soot and bustle and *life* of that other plane. "No strings, though."

"I said *no,*" Krita snapped. "You heard me the first time, and all the times since."

Hansen sucked his lips in. "Yeah, sorry," he said. "It's just I—"

He sat on a bench covered with a bearskin. As if changing the subject, he said, "There's something I'm thinking of doing."

Hansen gestured. In the air appeared a simulacrum of Keep Starnes, a dome a meter across glowing with the pale blue aura of a magnetic screen.

"On Plane Five?" the Searcher asked. Her anger was gone. The tone of her voice was cautious. Her mind had run ahead of what her lover was saying to what she knew he *was:* the most accomplished man of violence that she or Northworld had ever seen.

Krita sat down on the bench, an arm's length from the man.

"Right," Hansen said. "Count Starnes' keep. Fortin says there's a Fleet Battle Director there, a computer from the settlement."

As Hansen spoke, layers stripped one by one from the image. First the glow faded, exposing the underlying surface of collapsed metal and crystals grown in seamless, refractory sheets.

"A unit like that," Hansen continued in a tone half playful, half appraising, "might have the data I was sent to Northworld to find. Fortin says Count Starnes claims he'd let me access it."

The uppermost layers of the keep were given over to huge plasma weapons and missile batteries, artillery that could scar the face of the moon—but which could be used only if ports were opened in the defenses. For all their seeming power, an attempt to use the banks of weapons would be next to suicidal.

"That's nonsense!" Krita snapped. "You can't possibly trust him."

Hansen raised an eyebrow. "You know Count Starnes?" he asked.

"*You* know Fortin," she retorted. "Everybody knows Fortin! Whatever he says is a lie."

"Yeah," Hansen agreed/said. "There's that."

The living spaces and the workshops of Keep Starnes appeared as the plane of vision sliced deeper. The warrens of the lower classes near the top; deeper in, technicians' apartments, scarcely more spacious.

The overwhelming majority of the production lines that

opened, layer by layer, were given over to armaments.

"Whoever sent you here has no authority now," Krita said. "You're a *god,* Lord Hansen. Nobody can force you to do anything!"

Hansen's face hardened from its neutral set. "Nobody *ever* had to order me to do my job," he said, more harshly than perhaps he had intended.

Krita's lips parted to let her breath hiss in.

The Searcher's eyes focused on the image of Keep Starnes. The lower levels, where Count Starnes' soldiers and their dependents lived, were laid out on a more spacious floorplan than those of civilians. Even so, the suites were harsh concretions of straight lines and right angles.

After a moment Krita said, "Yes, I see. I've . . . always wanted to see the Fifth Plane. Maybe I can arrange for Etienne—"

Hansen shook his head.

"—and Sula to take over my—"

"*No,* Krita," he said softly. He took her by the shoulders and deliberately met her eyes squarely.

"Why not?" she demanded. She shook herself violently, so that Hansen jerked his hands away. "Tell me why you can go but I can't?"

"Because," he said, his voice low, his words as precise as the clicking of a weapon coming to battery, "because if I go, there'll be problems enough—"

"Danger, damn you!" the woman shouted. "Say the word, *danger.*"

"There'll be *danger* enough," Hansen said. "Without me having to nursemaid somebody raised in the Open Lands without a clue about how to conduct herself in a technological environment."

He got to his feet.

Krita closed her eyes. She said, "You could be killed, Nils. You c-could very possibly be killed."

"*If* I go. And I told you . . . ," Hansen added with intended tenderness as he stepped to the woman's side, "I'd like to make you a place of your own before I leave."

The woman jumped up and slapped his hand away as though

it were a snake. "D'ye think I'm a whore?" she shouted. "Is that what you think?"

Hansen swallowed, massaging the red mark on the back of his right hand with the lean, strong fingers of his left. "I think," he said quietly, "that every time I try to do something with people, I fuck up."

He turned to the door muttering, almost under his breath, "Except when I've got a gun in my hand."

"Wait," Krita said.

Hansen looked back over his shoulder. Krita was rummaging among a pile of furs in an alcove, rich skins marked like red fox but the size of oxhides. Her short garment rode up over the curve of her buttocks.

"I have someth . . . here it is."

She straightened and turned, holding in her hands a low helmet of black plastic. There was a frosty jewel the size of Hansen's thumbnail in the center of the forehead.

"Here," Krita said. "Take it."

Hansen obeyed. The plastic was colder than the air around it. "Where did you get this, then?" he asked, his intonations faintly sing-song.

"North gave it to me when he brought me here," the Searcher said flatly. "Before you were a god. But he said—"

Hansen lowered the helmet carefully over his head. He continued to hold the rim as though he expected the material to burn his scalp.

"—that I should give it to you when the time came," Krita continued. "That I would know—"

"To *me*?" Hansen said in amazement.

"*My name is Third,*" said/thought the artificial intelligence in the helmet.

"Bloody hell!" Hansen snarled as he snatched the helmet off.

"What's the matter?" Krita asked, concern breaking through the cold visage of a moment before. "Did it . . . ?"

She didn't know how to complete the sentence. The helmet had shaped itself to her skull when she once had tried it on; but it was otherwise cold and dead to her, a construct of dense black plastic.

"Nothing's wrong," said Hansen. "I've used . . . one of these before. It's a command helmet."

His thumb rubbed the bezel which clamped the jewel. "Yeah," he added, "it might come in handy."

Krita tossed her head. Her hair hung down to the middle of her back. When she shook it, it rolled like a black waterfall.

"I may not be here when you get back," she said in a distant voice. Her eyes were focused on a patch of wall slightly above Hansen's left shoulder. "I'm going to arrange with some of the others to handle my duties for a time. I need a break—"

She turned her back.

"And I have business. Of my own."

"Right," said Hansen. "Ah, sure. We'll get together again soon."

He started to don the helmet, then thought the better of it. With the object in his left hand, he took a step toward the door.

"Is that all?" Krita demanded on a rising note. When Hansen looked around, she was facing a sidewall of black light.

"Aren't we going to make love, Nils?" she went on stumblingly. "For old times' sake at least?"

"Oh, love," Hansen said.

He tossed the helmet onto the pile of furs and put his arms around the woman. She was crying silently, but her hands uncinched the hooks of her waistbelt when Hansen fumbled them.

They made rough, passionate love on the bearskin Hansen slid from the bench beside them. The jewel in the command helmet gleamed down on them like a cold gray star.

≡ 18 ≡

BRETT, THE SEARCHERS' escort, stepped into the audience hall between Race and Julia. He came to a dead halt when he realized that the throne was empty. No one was present except guards in battlesuits at the room's three sets of doors.

"I was told . . . ," the underchamberlain said to the warrior in black-and-silver armor at the door giving onto the imperial apartments. "Ah, that the emperor wished to see me at once?"

The volume of the large domed room turned Brett's voice into a pattern of cicada raspings. Without the usual crowd to give it life, the audience hall was a tomb.

"Don't get your bowels in 'n uproar, pretty-boy," the guard boomed harshly through his suit speaker. "Himself'll be here when he chooses t' be, don't you worry."

Julia grinned at Brett. "Little toad," she said distinctly. The Searchers were sworn to obey Venkatna in all things . . . but the underchamberlain had attempted to turn imperial authority into personal favors from the new slaves on the road back from Simplain.

Race held Brett while Julia singed the hairs off Brett's scrotum with a candleflame. It had taken the underchamberlain some time and a serious blister to realize that he would be much better off if he held absolutely still. . . .

"I wouldn't mind a piece of that, though," Race said, nodding toward the black-and-silver guard.

Julia laughed. Their uninhibited voices rang clearly from the ceiling vaults. "You don't know what there is inside," she said. "Might be like an oyster, all gray and shriveled up."

"I know," said Race, as though the object of their discussion were on another planet instead of listening in amazement from a few meters away, "that if he's got armor that good—"

The black-and-silver suit was at least third-class, maybe second.

"—then he's worth my time to see how he handles himself shucked."

The warrior at the staff entrance, through which Brett had brought the Searchers, rumbled a peal of amplified laughter.

Julia walked over to the Web and ran her hand through the air, just above one of the crystalline struts. "This must be what they want us for," she said.

"For North's sake!" the underchamberlain blurted. "Don't *touch* that."

"Says who, sonny?" Race snapped. She giggled. "Baldie, I mean."

"Like a maze," Julia said, leaning with her hands on her thighs to peer toward the benches within the apparatus. The rearward thrust of her hips to balance drew the eyes of the four men in the room. "You know what it looks like . . . ?"

"Something Sparrow might have done," Race agreed, suddenly sober. "I hear he's—"

She shrugged. "Up there, now, you know? Serving Saburo."

Brett and the nearest guard stiffened to hear a god's name in this context. Though children were named for gods, and the slaves might have meant—

"Saburo's a brave man, then," Julia said without irony. The men overhearing her relaxed.

The tall Searcher knelt. Someone her size would have to hunch forward like a gnome to reach the benches.

"Yeah," agreed Race. "Giving orders to Sparrow would be like giving orders to Lord Hansen: they better be the right orders. Those two have got tempers as cold as North's heart."

The warrior and underchamberlain looked at one another. They stood very still.

Servants pulled open the door behind the black-and-silver guard, then hopped aside. Emperor Venkatna stepped through with his right arm around Esme and a worried look on his face. "Really, my dear," he said. "There's no need for you to be up at all."

His wife patted his hand. Her face beneath the heavy make-up had a grayish pallor. "Nonsense," she said. "Nonsense. A little touch of indigestion isn't going to keep me down."

Esme straightened with an effort, but her voice gained strength as she did so. "These are the slaves, then? I hadn't realized they'd be so attractive. Do you suppose . . . ?"

"No, no," Venkatna said with a touch of peevishness. "They're far too valuable to waste warming my bed."

He frowned. "If they have the skills they're supposed to, that is."

"I only want you happy, dearest," Esme said.

Race looked at Julia. Julia rocked her left hand in the air, palm down. Venkatna wasn't a badly set-up man. A bit on the soft side, but athletic ability on the battlefield didn't necessarily translate to skill on a good, firm mattress.

Anyway, the Searchers would perform whatever tasks their master required, for as long as he lived. . . .

Venkatna tried to support Esme up the low steps of the throne, but she now resisted the coddling. "Go on," she said crisply, gesturing to the seat. "I'll not sit down before you, you know that."

The emperor made a moue that flexed the tips of his moustache, then settled himself on the throne. His wife lowered herself primly to the top step. She put her hand affectionately on Venkatna's knee.

Venkatna patted Esme's hand. "All right," he said, looking from one Searcher to the other. "I understand you are skilled in the use of the Web?"

"Yes, that's right, your majesty," Brett interjected. Old Saxtorph, who had replaced the brain-dead Boardman as chamberlain, couldn't last long. Brett's risk in calling himself to the emperor's attention was—possibly, very possibly—worth the chance of being remembered when it came time to appoint another chamberlain.

"Be silent, fool," Esme said without bothering to look at him.

Race pursed her lips. "Ah . . . ," she said. "What is it that your majesty wishes us to do, exactly?"

"Get into the Web and use it," Venkatna said with a flash of anger. "The merchant who sold it to me said that it could affect my whole domains. I want you to do that. I want you to bring peace to my entire Empire!"

Julia glanced at her companion, then back to the emperor. "Peace, your majesty? When you say peace, do you mean . . . ?"

Venkatna lunged up from his throne. "I mean peace!" he shouted. "I mean that no one in the Empire takes up arms against my orders. Peace!"

Race looked at the Web. The benches were to lie on, that was clear enough. For the rest, the device was an amalgam of nodes and shimmers almost too delicate to be material. It was as incomprehensible as North's purpose in sending her here to Venkatna.

But North *had* a purpose, of that she and Julia could be sure.

"Your orders are our fate, your majesty," the tall Searcher said. She bent and crawled within the Web through a gap—not an entrance, there was no proper entrance. Julia found another opening across the Web's humped form.

The bench felt cool to Race's back. The glimmering pattern of which the Web was woven did not so much illuminate the Searchers inside as it distorted the humans and architecture when Race tried to look beyond it. She closed her eyes because she could think of nothing else to do—

There was a globe of infinite vastness, and she had no being. It was colder than thought, and her not-self trembled.

Peace . . . boomed a voice/memory.

She concentrated. Tiny figures skittered across a landscape dwarfed by the hugeness of the frame on which it appeared. Arc weapons flashed, spikes in the limitless dark.

Race *pushed* as she would move the controls of her dragonfly. The cold gnawed at her heart and marrow. In the distance she heard moaning; Julia, or it might have been Race's own voice.

The arcs vanished . . . sprang up elsewhere in emptiness and winked out . . . elsewhere. . . . Nothing was constant but the cold that sucked away life and juices.

Your orders are our fate.

She thought she heard North's titanic laughter trail across the black sky.

≡ 19 ≡

"THIS ONE SAYS he come t' fight the tax men with us, Lord Salles," called the guard stumbling down the trail behind Hansen. "But *I* don't know."

The response lag of servos in the guard's battlesuit was so long that the fellow was lucky not to fall on his face. If he'd survived even a single battle in armor so shoddy, he was either lucky or improbably skillful.

"He knows," said Hansen as he dismounted in the center of the neat bivouac, "that I'm carrying the best battlesuit he's ever seen in his life. And he hasn't figured out that a man who owns armor like mine might just be more use to rebels like yourselves than his hardware is."

"This man's a friend of mine, Bosey," Salles said, exaggerating a brief meeting in Venkatna's audience hall. He clasped the newcomer, forearm to forearm. "Glad to have you with us, Lord Hansen. We'll need all the help we can get to defend our ancestral rights."

You'll need more than that, with an imperial battalion on its way. You'll need a bloody miracle. . . .

Wood smoke drifted through the roofs of the stick-built hutments and hung in a vaguely-sickening layer above the cold ground. A dozen warriors were at battle practice behind the circle of dwellings. About a hundred other folk could be seen in the small camp; some of them probably warriors, but the bulk freemen and slaves.

Salles released Hansen's arm and stepped to the side to view the trio of ponies which were the newcomer's only companions. "Where are your servants?" he asked in surprise.

Hansen smiled wryly. "Just me," he said. "I never much cared for folks poking around me when I'm trying to get dressed, and I figured I could dip my own stew out of the dinner pot if I had to."

"He could still be a spy," Bosey objected. His battlesuit was a black-and-green plaid. The paint was fresh but it had been applied by an amateur, probably Bosey himself. Even an expert would have been hard put to conceal the ragged welds which joined the portions of Bosey's battlesuit into a wretched whole.

"Bosey, get back to your position," Salles ordered sharply. To Hansen he added apologetically, "From high ground, suit sensors—even Bosey's suit sensors—can give us three kilometers' warning of any force approaching from the east. Assuming they move with at least a few guards suited up in live armor, that is."

"I'll give you more warning than that," Hansen said coldly as he surveyed the encampment. "Venkatna's troops are about two days out. Less if they push, but they won't bother to."

Salles swallowed, then nodded crisply. "How many?" he asked in a nonchalant tone.

Hansen stretched his head backward and kneaded his buttocks with his fingertips. Not a lot of fat there, which was as it should be; but not a lot of padding for a pony's saddle, either.

"A battalion," he said, looking toward the tops of the pine trees. The latest snowfall had slipped from the upper branches. There were collars of half ice, half crusted snow, on the shadowed needles partway down the trunk.

Before the next snow fell, most of the people in this camp would be dead.

"About a hundred battlesuits," Hansen continued to the sky. "The co-commanders are named Ashley and D'Auber, I'm told."

"D'Auber's a butcher," Bosey said. The cracking of his voice was accentuated by the bad reproduction in his battlesuit amplifiers. "He'll kill every damned thing down t' the rats in the garbage, he will."

Hansen turned like a hawk stooping. "If you're not back to your post in two minutes," he shouted at Bosey, "I'll stuff your head up your worthless asshole and save D'Auber the trouble! *Move,* you scut!"

Bosey stumbled back a step, turned, and made off toward his vantage point at the best speed his battlesuit could manage. Warriors playing chess in front of the nearest hut jumped to their feet. The freemen leading away Hansen's ponies stopped; one of them dropped the reins in his hand. A woman, very possibly a noble from the quality of her fur-trimmed cloak, watched Hansen with particular intensity.

Hansen knelt, rubbing his forehead with his fingertips and kneading his cheeks hard with his thumbs. From a great distance he heard Salles say gently, "He's loyal, you know. He didn't leave my service when he realized we were going to fight the tyrant in Frekka."

Hansen's arc cuts off the warrior's head and the man's outstretched left forearm. The legs and brown-mottled torso of the battlesuit fall front down, away from the surprise attack.

The men at the back of the enemy line do not expect close-quarters battle. They cannot survive more than a few seconds when battle finds them. Warriors in red and green and an ill-painted pattern of silver stars try to turn. Their battlesuits, like that of the first victim, are scarred by frequent repairs. Each sequence of damage and repair further degrades the armor's capabilities.

Hansen slices through both men at chest level. He doesn't have time to pick weak points for his arc, nor is there any need to do so with this caliber of opponent. The sectioned battlesuits topple into the mud, sparking modestly. The victims' armor does not carry enough power to create an impressive display, even when it is vented in a dead short. . . .

"All they're good for is to die," Hansen muttered. The pressure of his hands on his cheeks slurred his voice. "T' say that they're warriors, 'n' t' die the first time they happen t' get in the way of somebody with a real suit."

"Bosey can keep watch for us," Salles said. "Him and Aldo and a couple of the others. And they can keep Venkatna's freemen out of our camp while, while the battle's still going on."

His voice was thinner than before and had an artificial lilt. Salles had been badly shaken by Hansen's news.

What the hell had he *expected* was going to happen? That Venkatna would ignore a rebellion just because the rebel warriors had moved out of their keeps?

Hansen got to his feet. His back was to Salles. He didn't turn. A warrior in a black battlesuit had left the practice field and was walking toward Salles and the newcomer.

"Got any more troops than these?" Hansen asked mildly.

"About this many more, three kilometers west with Lord Richtig," Salles replied. "Thirty-one all told. Thirty-two with— if you join us."

"I've joined," Hansen said. "I'm fucking here, aren't I?"

On bivouac Salles wore rough garments, homespun wool without embroidered designs. They suited him much better than court clothes. He moved well, too. Hansen didn't doubt that he'd be a tough opponent with anything like parity of equipment.

"I rather thought . . . ," Salles said. "That perhaps they'd send a smaller force initially, and we could overwhelm it. Of course, there'd be a battalion the next time. . . ."

Hansen turned. "What are you going to do now?" he demanded harshly. "Surrender?"

Salles met his glare. "If we surrendered," said the Lord of Peace Rock, "they'd execute us anyway. It won't make any difference to the civilians back at the keeps, since they'll be enslaved in either event."

"As they would have been in any case when the district was unable to meet its autumn tribute," said the woman in the fur-trimmed cloak. She had walked up behind Hansen. "As I well know."

"Lucille is my cousin," Salles said without looking at the woman. "She was married to the Lord of Thrasey . . . who failed to pay his tribute last year. I thought she'd been killed when the keep was sacked, until she escaped to me last month."

"What are you going to *do*?" Hansen repeated.

"Fight," Salles said flatly. "Die in battle if that's the will of North . . . but battles have been won against the odds before."

Hansen snorted.

"Why are you here, then, Lord Hansen?" Salles said sharply. "This isn't your fight, and you've obviously formed an opinion about our chances of establishing our rights against Frekka."

"What do *you* think your chances are, b-b—milord?" Hansen retorted.

He grimaced. Before the Lord of Peace Rock could snap out the dismissal that the barely-swallowed '*boyo*' demanded, Hansen knelt and said, "Sorry, Lord Salles. The injustice of the situation bothers me, and I, I'm taking it out on the victims."

"For the gods' sweet sake," said Lucille calmly, "get out of that mud, milord. We have better use for you than that you should catch your death of cold."

She touched Salles' forearm. "This is the man who bought me out of the labor gang, cousin. The usher who carried the bribe said the money came from a warrior named Hansen, a stranger."

Which explained Lucille's pallor. Quite an attractive woman, if you liked them thin and with hair colored something between brown and blond.

It didn't explain the game North was playing; but you could never be sure about that. . . .

"Gods, I'm sorry!" blurted Salles, clasping Hansen's arm again. "I didn't realize! I—"

"You thought I was some prick come to laugh at you when you were about to die," Hansen said wryly. "Reasonable guess, the way I was acting."

His face sobered. "I knew some folk from this district a long time since," he added. *About a hundred years ago, as time runs in the Open Lands.* "Nobody you'd know, but—I figure they wouldn't want me to walk away from this fight if they were still around."

Aubray wears armor decorated with black-and-cream rosettes. Hansen doesn't remember the sideman's features. The Colimore arc shears off the front of Aubray's helmet, igniting

*Aubray's hair and beard in an orange frame for the warrior's
screaming face.*

The blow was meant for Hansen. . . .

"Hansen?" Lucille said from very close by. "Milord?"

Hansen shook himself. "I'm all right," he said before his
eyes had focused again. Lucille stood beside him, ready to
grab him if he started to fall.

"Maybe the gods will slay Venkatna," muttered the Lord of
Peace Rock. "His exactions are an affront to them, surely."

"The gods don't interfere that way," said the warrior in black
armor who had finally reached them from the practice ground.
"Events have a balance. Trying to bend them by brute force
means that they'll snap back in a way you won't much like."

"Let me introduce you to our other new recruit," Salles said.
"Like you, he says he used to have friends in this area. Lord
Hansen, this is—"

The warrior gripped the latch of the battlesuit and pulled
open the frontal plate.

"—Lord Kriton."

*Even though her hair is cropped short and she wears a
quilted jacket, how could they think Krita was a man? But
they saw only the hard eyes, and skill with a battlesuit that
not even Salles himself could overmatch.*

"I've met Kriton before, Lord Salles," Hansen said. "With
warriors of his quality and yours—and mine . . . I think maybe
we can survive the present problem. Then we can reach the
Mirala District in time to do some real good."

Hansen offered his arm for Krita to grip as she got out of her
battlesuit. She swayed against him. *Breasts as firm as apples,
with dark nipples extending as he kissed them. . . .*

"I'm glad to see you here also, Lord Hansen," the Searcher
said as she met her lover's eyes.

≡ 20 ≡

HANSEN SENSED A presence in North's palace of carved light, though the owner himself was not in his gleaming hall. Someone waited in the sheets and columns of material radiance. . . .

"Dowson?" called Nils Hansen. "I'd like to talk to you."

A plane of light dissolved, uncovering a wall niche. In it were a stalagmite of multi-hued ice and a tank of clear crystal—

Which held a human brain.

The outermost layer of the stalagmite scaled away like dry ice subliming. A lilac bubble, almost too pale to be called pastel, expanded from the stalagmite. When the bubble's edge intersected Hansen, he heard Dowson's voice say, "I'm always glad to help you, Commissioner Hansen."

The cold equivalent of laughter swept from the cone as a hint of yellow. "I'm always glad," Dowson added, "to interact with any of you who still have flesh."

Hansen walked closer to the tank, though there was no need to do so. The floor beneath his feet appeared to be parquetry of black and white slabs. Closer observation showed that the black was absolute void, while the white shimmered like sections from the heart of a sun.

"I may visit Plane Five," Hansen said. Gas beaded at the bottom of the tank and rose sluggishly through the fluid in which the brain was suspended. "I wanted to know about the

Fleet Battle Director that I'm told is there."

Mauve and blue-violet sprang from the ice cone. Dowson's voice was cool and dry, but that had probably been true when the speaker was a man and not a disembodied brain.

"Fortin told you that APEX is in Keep Starnes," said the voice in Hansen's mind. "Which is true. And he told you that APEX knows how North took us out of the universe, how he stole all Northworld from the Consensus. . . ."

"Is *that* true?" Hansen demanded. He couldn't help staring at the once-man when he spoke to him/it, but he kept his face rigidly blank. "Does APEX . . . have that information?"

"I don't know, Commissioner," whispered the moss-green scales which drifted past Hansen. "I would tell you if I knew, but I do not know."

If the voice were fully human, Hansen would have said there was a wistful quality to it.

He turned from the encased brain and looked across the hall. When North wished, the lines of congealed light could reach infinitely high, and there were a thousand bright gates in the walls.

When North wished.

"Commissioner," Dowson's voice said. "You came to me because I live in the Matrix—"

"Because you see it all," Hansen said with the harshness of disappointment. "Because I can look here or look there, but I'll miss the context. And the context is everything."

His voice echoed from the distant wall with a sound like that of keys turning in a tumbler lock, inhuman and inanimate. *He'd wanted a simple answer, This Is or This Is Not, so that he wouldn't have to make a decision himself. So that Commissioner Nils Hansen could just follow orders without being responsible for whatever resulted from his actions.*

"I live all that exists in the Matrix," Dowson corrected gently. "But Plane Five has its own rules, Commissioner; as you know."

Hansen spread his arms. He felt the bubble of tawny thought tingle through them on its way across the hall's expanse. He turned again and crooked a smile to the crystal tank.

"I'm afraid, you see," Hansen said quietly. He had

been twenty-nine years old when he entered Northworld; a powerfully built man who was even quicker than he was strong.

His body was still that of the man he had been, but his eyes were ageless and terrible.

"If APEX knows how North took the planet . . . ," he said. He squatted down, resting his forearms on his knees. He stared at the floor beneath the tank as he used Dowson as a mental sounding board. "Then I'll go there and get the information. But I don't trust Fortin—"

"Not even a madman would trust Fortin, Commissioner," said a dusting of blue light.

"—and Fortin himself says that Count Starnes isn't to be trusted."

"You're afraid to die?" Dowson asked, as though he were compiling emotional data to add to his complete knowledge of objects and events.

Hansen looked up, still balanced on the balls of his feet. He smiled again.

"No, Dowson," he said. The lilt in his voice was a defense mechanism, an instinctive trick to prevent listeners from believing the truth that they were about to hear. "I'm afraid that I want to die, because—"

Hansen laughed. The sound was as humorless as chains rattling.

"Because so many other people have, you see?" he went on. "Either because they tried to help when I got in over my head, or because they were in my way and I was, I was . . ."

"APEX may have been able to analyze Captain North's actions," Dowson said. His words were olive and soothing in their emotionlessness. "But no one can command you now, Nils Hansen. Not the Consensus, not North himself. You have free will."

A drift of thought so faint that it was gray by default trailed Dowson's voice across Hansen. "As those who followed you and faced you had free will."

Hansen stood up in a single smooth motion. "When *I* choose to do something," he said, "it makes things worse! Have you seen what the West Kingdom is like, Dowson?"

"I live all things in the Matrix, Commissioner," the brain responded in a shower of sublimed azure. "You see here and see there; and you miss the context, as you say. Don't—"

"I—" shouted Hansen.

A wash of orange thought swept over Hansen with the force of the surf combing a beach. "You pretend that until you have all knowledge, you are unable to act on your own decision, Nils Hansen. I tell you now: when you have all knowledge, you will be like me—unable to act at all."

Another bead of gas lifted from the bottom of the tank. It began to crawl upward, hugging the convoluted surface of Dowson's brain.

Hansen stretched and laughed cleanly. When he bent backward, he closed his eyes so that the saturated radiance of the hall's high arches wouldn't dazzle him.

"Guess I'll go talk to Count Starnes in a little while, then," he said as he straightened. "Thank'ee, my friend."

He grinned, wondering if Dowson could see the expression; whether Dowson could actually *see* anything at all. There was humor in the smile, and in Hansen's tone as he added, "Not because the Consensus ordered me to do it. I'm going because I'm curious to see what I'll learn, and—"

Although Hansen's expression did not precisely change, the planes of solid muscle drew taut over his cheekbones. They formed a visage more terrible than a grinning skull.

"—from what I hear, there are some things that ought to be fixed on Plane Five. Nobody's paying me to fix things nowadays, but if Fortin's little friend the count wants to make it my business . . ."

Hansen's words blurred off into savage laughter, echoing from the vaults and niches.

"Then you will oblige him," said Dowson in a thought of pure blood red.

"Nobody better," Hansen agreed. He flexed his supple, gunman's hands and grinned. "Nobody better at fixing *that* sort in the twelve hundred fucking worlds of the Consensus."

"Hansen . . . ?" Dowson asked as his visitor started to leave. The curtain of light was in place again, so the scales of ultramarine seemed to expand from a solid wall.

"Yeah?"

"When you say 'friend,' as you did," Dowson's voice continued, "that is a mere form of address, is it not?"

"It can be," Hansen said. "That's not how I meant it this time, though."

The trim, cat-muscled killer turned toward the portal leading out of the enormous hall. As he left, he called over his shoulder, "I'll be back to see you when I get back, friend."

≡ 21 ≡

SMOKE FROM IMPERIAL cookfires formed a haze where land met the sky. Hansen began counting the bell tents which stood in a straggling circuit of the hilltop. Each was pennoned according to the rank of the quartet of warriors to which it was assigned.

The freemen and slaves serving Venkatna's troops were now seeing to their own shelter: ground sheets, tarpaulins laid across bushes on the gentle sideslopes, or nothing at all. The day had been clear. Though the temperature tonight would probably drop to freezing, the air was dry. A blanket roll was sufficient for men hardened to campaign.

Some of them wouldn't be around long enough to worry about the pre-dawn chill.

The imperial servants weren't a problem, not even the freemen who scouted for the armored warriors when the battleline advanced; but there were going to be some of them who got in the way. Salles' rebels—*Hansen's* rebels now, in all but name—didn't have time to pick and choose. When they went in, anything imperial that moved would be a target. . . .

A single armored warrior stood at the edge of the imperial camp. He was probably bored, but that would change quickly enough when his battlesuit display indicated the presence of thirty-two rebel warriors.

At the moment, the sentinel saw nothing except a birch-shaded covert a hundred meters east of the campsite. The battlesuits of Salles and his men stood empty behind the ambush line. Until the rebels closed the frontal plates over themselves, the suits remained unpowered. Cold, the armor provided no emanations for Venkatna's sensors to receive and report.

Soon dusk would cloak the lower slopes of the hill. Warriors using the image intensifiers of their battlesuits would not be affected.

The imperial troops, relaxing over their meals, wouldn't be sure what was happening until the line of armored rebels burst into the camp with their arc weapons lighting the way.

Very soon. . . .

Lord Salles stood beside Hansen on the right flank. A courier, panting from having run the length of the rebel line, gasped a message to him. When the courier finished speaking, he darted his head back as though he feared a blow.

The man probably did. Nobles were not permitted by law and custom to kill out of hand freemen like the courier . . . but a courier who brought a haughty message from one warrior to another couldn't assume mere law would be sufficient protection.

Salles laughed harshly. The Lord of Peace Rock had been moving ever since his rebels reached their ambush site; but he was restive, not nervous, like a thoroughbred which curvettes at the starting line.

"*Tell* your master," Salles said, "that he will await our signal—as he agreed under oath. Tell him!"

"It won't be long," Hansen added in a mild tone. He wondered if *he* sounded nervous. His mouth was dry and he wanted to piss, but at the moment he didn't like the thought of having his dick bare and unprotected. . . .

The courier nodded gloomily and started back toward Lord Richtig. His boots popped and rustled through the litter. The noise wasn't audible for any distance—certainly not the fifty meters to the nearest imperial servants—but it was unnecessary. . . .

"I'm worried about Richtig," Salles muttered to Hansen.

"He's likely to suit up and attack on his own."

Servants behind the ambush line edged closer. They turned their faces away, so that they could hear the leaders without being obvious about it. It wasn't just warriors who were in this, particularly if the attack failed.

"That's all right," Hansen said. "He won't."

He looked at the sky through the tracery of bare branches. Still pale blue. After another few minutes, though. . . .

"You don't know Richtig!" Salles snapped.

"I know his type," Hansen said calmly. *Didn't he just!* "That's why I put Kri—Kriton beside him."

Bells chimed from the imperial baggage mammoths which grazed on the lush meadow west of the camp. The location of the grass had determined where Hansen's force could lie in wait. The beasts would not have been fooled by a screen of trees and the lack of electronic warning; but all they cared for now was to fill their vast rumbling bellies.

"Eh?" said Salles.

"If Richtig tries to get an early start," Hansen explained, "Kriton'll stick a knife into the seam of his battlesuit so that it won't close and show up on our friend's—" he nodded toward the imperial sentinel "—sensors."

Hansen smiled in bleak humor. "If sh—Kriton's in a good mood, he won't put the point a centimeter into Richtig's side t' remind him about orders."

Lord Salles blanked his face as he considered the statement. "You know Kriton well, then?" he asked in a neutral tone.

"You bet," Hansen said.

Black hair so short that it scarcely brushes his cheek when she bends over him on the couch. Her dark nipples on his chest, the taut muscles over her ribs and under the swell of her buttocks as he pulls her down to engulf him. . . .

The slope to the imperial camp was a rich purple-blue.

"Mount up," Hansen ordered as he turned to his own battlesuit. "But nobody close their suits till the gong sounds."

There was a freeman standing behind each warrior with orders to jam a stick into the seam of any suit whose owner tried to close up early. Venkatna's forces would certainly torture to death *everyone* they captured if the surprise assault

failed. It was just possible that some of the freemen would obey
Hansen's orders, though they knew how angry any warrior so
treated would be.

The motion of warriors getting into their battlesuits shifted
down the line like a wave. The act itself was a visual signal
to the next man over, though trees hid each rebel from all
but a few of his fellows in either direction. A gong signal
would warn the imperial forces early, and each battlesuit's
frequency-hopping radio was shut down with the rest of its
electronics until the plastron latched into the backplate.

The suede lining of Hansen's armor felt cold, but its pressure
encircling his legs and arms was a relief. The plastron, including
the front portion of the helmet, remained open. He laced his
gauntleted hands over it, ready to slam the piece closed and bring
up the suit's systems as soon as the whole force was ready.

He waited.

*His hand fumbling with Krita's sash for the first time, so
clumsy that she chuckles and slips the tie herself. . . .*

"Lord Kriton says they're ready on our end, sir!" gasped a
puffing runner.

"Sound the gong," said Hansen as he slammed shut his
frontal plate. He'd forgotten that the Lord of Peace Rock
was in titular command, but the waiting slave forgot also and
hammered the fat bronze tube.

"Suit!" Hansen shouted to switch on his armor's artificial
intelligence as he pounded uphill. "Full daylight equivalent—"
the display became a clear window before his eyes as the AI
enhanced the scene to what it would have been at noon "—
and carat friendlies white in all displays!"

"Hansen the War God!" Krita shouted as a battlecry as she
burst from the woods on the opposite end of the line.

Little minx.

A battlesuit weighed in the order of a hundred kilos. Servo
motors in the joints amplified the wearer's movements, but
the speed and strength of the response depended on the suit's
quality. Running in a suit as poor as that of Bosey or those of
several other rebel warriors was only marginally less punishing
than jogging with an anvil.

The diverse rebel force couldn't possibly hit the imperial

camp as a unit unless all the troops governed the speed of their charge to that of the men with the poorest equipment—

In which case the enemy would have most of his triply superior numbers armed and ready to meet them. Hansen had arrayed the rebels with the best battlesuits on the flanks— he and Salles on the right, Krita and Lord Richtig on the left. The rest were spaced inward in declining order of their armor's quality. That way the attack would, with luck, display a smoothly concave front to Venkatna's startled men.

"Alarm!" the imperial sentinel cried. "We're attacked! Alarm!"

He was using his radio, not the loudspeaker in his helmet. None of his unsuited fellows could hear him.

An imperial freeman tried to run from Hansen's approach. The man slipped and curled into a screaming ball. Hansen would have spared him, but a slave behind the line of rebel warriors smashed the fellow's skull with the mallet which had just rung the gong.

A slave with a club was a better man than a warrior caught halfway into his armor. This was no time to be choosy about technique.

Hansen sucked air in through his open mouth, but his lungs hadn't begun to burn yet. Ten meters before he reached the imperial camp, he glanced to his left. Salles was a pace behind him, handicapped by having lighted his arc weapon. The discharge drained some power that would otherwise have fed his servos.

Krita's black battlesuit was parallel to Hansen's and a hundred meters away, while Richtig was several strides behind her.

The rest of the force . . . was coming at its best speed, with only a few drop-outs, for a wonder. Even Bosey, though he had sprawled and was just picking himself up again. Hansen's artificial intelligence—and that of all the other rebels, if the order had passed as it should on the suit-to-suit data link— inserted a white plume above the helmet of every friendly figure glimpsed on the display.

It was time.

"Cut!" Hansen shouted with his right thumb and forefinger

spread wide. His AI obeyed by switching on his weapon for a long looping cut.

Three tents ignited at the arc's touch. The wool burned orange with sparklings from the strands of metal woven into the pennons.

"Hansen the War God!" shouted a rebel other than Krita.

There were half a dozen men in the tents, relaxing warriors or those serving them. They had only enough time to leap to their feet. Hansen's blue-white arc slashed across their unarmored bodies. Flesh exploded into steam and droplets of blazing fat.

Hansen strode into the inferno, clearing his path with quick blind slashes of his arc. The stench of burning wool was overpowering despite his battlesuit's filters. A long bandage of tent-flap swaddled Hansen's helmet when he stepped into what should have been the clear area in the camp's center. He flailed his arms to rid himself of the encumbrance.

The sentinel was the only imperial warrior wearing a battlesuit. The man rushed Hansen with a cry of fury.

Lord Salles stepped through the gap between two tents. He flicked the sentinel with an arc extended to three meters. Salles' weapon was too attenuated to cut, but it licked like a serpent's tongue over the defensive screens of the imperial battlesuit—draining so much power from the servos that the sentinel froze in mid-step.

Hansen thrust through the sentinel's plastron. The victim fell onto his back. There was a black hole in his chest and a rim of molten metal bubbling around the edges of the cut.

"Hansen the War God!" Hansen screamed, why not, as he charged a group of imperial warriors desperately trying to get into their battlesuits.

It was going to work. They'd caught Venkatna's men completely unaware. There'd be casualties, sure, at the end when they had to deal with the few imperials who managed to arm themselves, but all the rebels were engaged and half the camp was already aflame.

He felt it change.

The Matrix shrugged; that was the only word Hansen could think of to describe the sensation. He wasn't affected himself—

his arc ripped a pair of empty battlesuits and the screaming imperial warrior who changed his mind too late about getting into one—

But the other rebels switched off their weapons and began opening their battlesuits.

"Don't!" Hansen cried incredulously. *The probability generator, the Web, that North had sold Venkatna. It was now operating.* "For pity's sake, don't stop now!"

An imperial warrior slammed his plastron closed. He cut Bosey in half. Bosey's black-and-green armor was poor stuff to begin with, but the young rebel—*sixteen and he'd never see seventeen now*—had started to climb out even as the arc swept toward him.

"Take them prisoner!" ordered a steely voice on what Hansen's display noted was the imperial command channel. His AI decoded even the lock-out push of lesser battlesuits. "Don't kill them till we learn what's happened!"

Half a dozen of Venkatna's troops, wearing their armor, approached Hansen in a tight group. He backed away.

Lord Salles stepped clear of his battlesuit. He looked at Hansen in surprise. "What are you doing, Lord Hansen?" demanded the one-time rebel leader. "We shouldn't take up arms against Emperor Venkatna."

Krita got out of her armor. She was not immune to the forces twisting through the Web.

"Get him!" cried an imperial warrior as he started for the only rebel still in armor.

Hansen's arc touched the man as he started his rush from several meters away. The imperial was off-balance when his servos lost power. His shout turned to a squawk. He fell forward, tripping the pair of warriors following him most closely.

Hansen plunged into the smoky flames of the tent behind him.

Imperial warriors surrounded the tent immediately. The only things they found when the fire died down were the corpses of their fellows, killed in the rebel onrush.

≣ 22 ≣

THE AIR WHICH Sparrow drew into his lungs was as humid as the contents of a warm bath; the tang of salt was gone.

The dog yipped in startlement. The smith set her down. She ran from one plant to another, snuffling furiously at their spreading roots. There was no true ground cover; thin, russet mud splashed the dog's feet and belly, though the muck slid from her leg braces like grease from heated iron.

Sparrow shrugged to loosen his woolen blouse. A streak of sweat between his shoulderblades already glued the fabric to his back. He could see the tops of trees kilometers away; some of them spiked, others with ribbons of foliage clumped into pompons. Closer to hand grew horsetails and low cycads like scaly balls tufted with fronds. They disappeared into the mist within a hundred meters.

Sparrow didn't bother to sigh. He was a hunter, long used to the punishment of climate and terrain: bitter cold, sleet storms, or this muggy swamp—it was all the same, and all to be accepted.

Besides, he knew what Hell was. On a plain so cold that metal cracked, frozen souls oozed forward like slime molds; infinitely slowly and forever, until the Final Day ended time. This was not Hell.

When Sparrow opened his small mirror to determine his course, the face immediately beaded with condensate. He took off one gauntlet and wiped the screen with the edge of his palm; then repeated the motion. The difference in temperature across the discontinuity—and the saturated atmosphere here— had blurred the surface a second time.

Mala's fortress bower squatted on the screen. Part of the haze fogging the image was on the far side of the view. A red bead on the mirror's bronze frame gave Sparrow a vector to his destination.

"C'mon, you fool dog!" the smith called as he set off. Mud swelled over his feet at every step, but the high laces would prevent the sandals from being stripped off. Not that Sparrow couldn't go on barefoot—or naked and weaponless—but he didn't intend to do so.

The dog could find her master by scent easily enough, but Sparrow was worried about the sorts of things he knew lurked in this swamp. Not worried for himself, but the fool dog didn't have any sense at all. . . .

When there was something like firm ground running in the proper direction, they followed it. When open water crossed their path, Sparrow waded and the dog swam. The warm, sluggish waters didn't disturb the bitch the way living surf had done.

The dog barked in a high-pitched, enthusiastic tone and with the regularity of a metronome while she paddled. Sparrow glowered until there was a sudden commotion on the far bank of the stream they were crossing. The unfamiliar yapping had panicked a fat-bodied amphibian, three meters long and far too big to prey on fish. It bolted through the marsh in the opposite direction.

The dog hopped onto the bank and shook herself violently. "Fool animal . . . ," Sparrow murmured as he climbed out beside her. He scratched between her ears, his touch as delicate as a delivering midwife's despite his gauntlets.

They passed numbers of sail-backed edaphosaurs chewing vegetation with peglike teeth. For the most part, the herbivores ignored the human and his dog, though one—a male with scarlet wattles—grunted a challenge. All the edaphosaurs wore collars of black plastic: control devices, marking these beasts as members of a herd.

Nainfari's cattle; so Nainfari's hold would not be far distant.

After three hours of slogging, Sparrow paused and sat on a cycad. Fronds, squashed outward by the smith's weight, tickled the backs of his calves. Insects were lured by pink flowers growing from the cycad's scaly trunk. They buzzed around Sparrow in confusion at his mammalian odor.

The smith and his dog had just crossed from a headland between a pair of streams emptying into a pond. It had been deep wading, and for a moment Sparrow thought he too would have to swim. His equipment was waterproof, and the smith wouldn't shrink either; but it was a reasonable time to settle for a moment and wring some of the muck from his blouse and breeches.

Edaphosaurs browsed the horsetails on the margins of the pond. A swimming reptile, scarcely the length of the smith's forearm, surfaced in the center of the standing water. A fish glittered in its tiny jaws. It vanished again as suddenly into the black fluid again.

Sparrow rose to his feet. His dog, panting and mud-stained except for her nose and forehead, remained sprawled on the ground with only her head lifted. "All right, dog," the smith grumbled. "You wanted to come, so I brought—"

The dog jumped up with a snarl.

Sparrow turned, quick as a baited bear. The dimetrodon, ten meters from them and poised to rush, hunched back in surprise. Its jaws of large, ragged teeth gaped wider, but the blush darkening the big carnivore's fin indicated fear and consternation rather than anger.

The dimetrodon grunted. The dog backed between Sparrow's legs. Her growl sounded like a saw cutting rock many kilometers away.

"There's no need for trouble," Sparrow murmured. His arms were splayed at his sides. He began to edge away. The pond was to his right.

The herd of edaphosaurs shuddered into a slow-motion stampede. Those nearest to the dimetrodon waddled off, and their motion warned the next rank of the beasts. The edaphosaurs' sails wobbled with the sinuous motion of their lizardlike bodies.

"No trouble at all . . . ," the smith said.

The dimetrodon rocked forward and back on its four splayed legs. It wasn't likely to charge now; but there was limited room for reflexes in the sail-backed carnivore's small brain. You couldn't be sure which one was going to trip the beast into motion.

Spray like the base of a waterfall lifted from the far edge of the pond. A dozen figures on repulsion skimmers tore through the horsetails, heading across the surface of the black water. Edaphosaurs which had splashed midway into the pond for fear of the carnivore now swam in terrified circles.

The leader of the band on skimmers was a four-armed android, but the remainder of his party wore slave collars. The bulk of them were either humans from the Open Lands or Lomeri, the scaled, bipedal lizardmen who inhabited Plane Two. One female had the squat somatotype of Plane Five.

The newcomers were dressed in leather harnesses and rags which they wore for their brilliant hues rather than protection or modesty. Knives, handguns, and shoulder weapons on slings bounced and jangled as the party crossed the water.

The android held his skimmer's controls with one pair of hands and aimed a multibarreled weapon with the other. The gun belched a white flash and a hypersonic *c-crack-k-k* from its twenty muzzles. A volley of fléchettes spewed toward the dimetrodon.

The beast blatted in surprise. At least a half dozen of the miniature projectiles punched out scales or made bloody dimples in the thin fabric of the carnivore's sail. The animal sound was submerged by the slave gang's roaring weapons.

Bullets, laser light, a sulphurous bolt of plasma, and a sheaf of thumb-sized rockets raked the area of the dimetrodon in a deafening salvo. Most missed their intended target. A human's laser sheared through the control column of a Lomeri's skimmer, sending the latter tumbling wildly across the water.

Enough of the salvo hit to rip the carnivore to bloody rags. Explosive projectiles sawed almost through the dimetrodon's short neck, while the plasma bolt reduced the beast's sail to blackened spines from which the connecting tissue had burned.

The reptile thrashed in the mud. Individual muscles retained vitality which the entity as a whole had lost.

The hunters swept up onto the bank. They grounded their skimmers, then got off and formed a semicircle around Sparrow at the distance of two or three meters. The Fifth Plane female scooped up the lizardman from the disabled skimmer. She tossed him negligently to the mud at the edge of the pond.

The band's weapons smoked or glowed from the recent firing. They pointed in various directions, but most of them pointed at Sparrow. The dog crouched between the smith's legs, growling below the range of audibility.

"Hey, Morfari," the squat female called to her android leader. "Give him t' me, hey? He's just about the right size."

"Balls to that!" snorted the human male with the laser. He was grinning. "*I'm* not getting sloppy tenths again!"

"You can share, can't you, Lilius?" Morfari said. He broke open his volley gun, ejecting the fired casings so that he could reload with another bundle of fléchettes from a belt pouch. "You don't need the same part, after all."

"Use the Chewer," chittered a Lomeri slave, pointing his snub-nosed rocket launcher at the quivering dimetrodon.

"Naw, it's a female. That rules it out for Lilius."

Morfari's arms were muscular and well-shaped. He waggled his reloaded volley gun in a one-handed arc that lifted the weapon's point of aim over Sparrow's head and lowered it again to the other side.

"Greetings, stranger," the android said. "I'm Morfari. My father, Nainfari, is the king hereabouts, and me 'n the crew guard his cattle."

The big female chuckled. One of the Lomeri began to pick his pointed teeth theatrically with a dagger.

"Now . . . ," Morfari continued. "Just who might *you* be?"

The smith shrugged. "My name's Sparrow," he said. "I'm passing through your father's domains, but I'll do no hurt to his herds."

"You can say that again, sweetie," said a human slave whose automatic rifle was pointed at Sparrow's belly. The slave ran a finger around his collar in a habitual action. The plastic had chafed a callus on his neck.

"We saved his life," said the Fifth Plane female, more than half serious. "He owes us a little entertainment at least."

"Lady . . . ," said the smith in a voice as detached as distant lightning. "My master sent a man who could fight his own battles."

He opened his iron-shod hands. Sparrow's grip would span the trunk of the largest tree on this island. "I thank you for killing the monster, but I would have avoided it had you not arrived . . . and if the beast would not be avoided, then I would have torn its head off—"

He smiled, an expression of power and implacable determination. "—as you have done yourselves, with your weapons."

Sparrow cocked his right hip so that he could scratch his dog behind the ears with his left fingertips. The touch wouldn't calm her, but it would keep her steady . . . and it would keep the smith steady also, at a time when death could come as easily as when the rock of a sheer cliff began to flake under the weight of the climber.

Three of the lizardmen chirped to one another in their own language. A human said, "You know, he just mighta done that thing," as his thumb polished a worn place on the receiver of his grenade launcher.

"I'm a courier," Sparrow said as he straightened. "My master sent me with a message for the Princess Mala. I'll deliver it and leave."

The slave gang responded with hoots and guffaws. Their collars were control devices. A signal, from the lavaliere bouncing on Morfari's chest or from the base unit at Nainfari's hold, would inject pain or even death through the collars.

But Morfari and his hunting party were clearly united in enthusiasm for what they did—and the ways they were permitted to do it.

The android chuckled. He rubbed his chin with one hand and scratched his back with another. All the time, his remaining pair of arms kept the volley gun aimed at Sparrow's belly.

"Well, Master Sparrow," Morfari said. "I don't think that's a good idea at all. Even if you got past—and I grant you might, big fellow—the Chewers—"

He nodded toward the dimetrodon; one of the beast's hind legs still clawed the air slowly.

"—and the Gulpers, there's what my sister's put up to keep her privacy."

To the side, a joke between a pair of Lomeri turned ugly. One of the lizardmen snatched out a knife. The Fifth Plane human, apparently Morfari's adjutant, knocked the knife-wielder down with a clout across the temple.

"The outer ring," Morfari continued, seemingly oblivious to the fuss among his slaves, "that'll cut you apart while you're still a kilometer away, even if you—"

His pale, perfect face smiled.

"—slide on your belly through the mud. Inside her walls, nothing bigger than a roach can live, without dear Mala gives it special dispensation. That's pretty good defenses, don't you think?"

Sparrow shrugged. His eyes were on Morfari; his expression calm, almost bovine.

"And besides *that* . . . ," the android continued.

His tone was sharper from irritation at the smith's placidity. The slaves stopped their japes and looked to their weapons.

" . . . my father's told his cattle guards to slay all vagabonds they find in the neighborhood of Mala's bower. What do you think of that, Master Vagabond?"

Sparrow shrugged again. "My master sent me with a message," he said calmly. "I have to deliver it."

"What would you say," Morfari snarled, "if I told you that we were going to kill you right here in the mud?"

"Gloves," said Sparrow as he spread the thumbs and forefingers of his arc gauntlets. "Cut!"

≡ 23 ≡

VENKATNA'S DOZEN TOP advisors stood, each man shoulder-to-shoulder with two fellows, in the audience hall at Frekka. Torches flaring from wall sconces lighted the gathering.

Venkatna enthroned was the diamond mounted on the ring of his advisors.

"There's no question now," said old Bontempo. "The Mirala kings are getting aid from outside the district."

"Hiring mercenaries!" snorted Weast. "Everybody does it when they know war's coming."

"Heimrtal did it," another laughed.

The women in the Web behind the council circle moaned softly, but the sound had been going on for hours. No one took notice of it or of them. The bands of soft light moved so slowly across the surface of the device that the patterns appeared to be static.

"I don't mean mercenaries!" Bontempo protested. Anger made him wheeze, but he couldn't raise the volume of his voice. "They're being *joined* by others, some from as far away as the deep South—just to stop us!"

"And by rebels from within our borders . . . ," added Kleber in a tone of dry concern. Kleber viewed battlesuits with disdain. His cold competence in combat—as in all things—had gained him respect though not affection.

A quick knock and the creak of the outer door drew

Venkatna's eyes. Several of his advisors glanced around also. The armored guard at the door talked with an usher, then turned and boomed over his loudspeaker, "Your majesty? Lord D'Auber is here."

"Send him in, then!" the emperor said curtly. In a slightly warmer tone he added toward the council, "Since we're discussing rebels."

D'Auber had ridden hard and hastened to the council without bothering to dress or change. His breeches were black with the sweat of his ponies. The warrior's effluvium made the advisors in court dress blink at two meters' distance.

"Another failure with Salles, is it?" Kleber said, guessing aloud from D'Auber's haste and anger.

"Like bloody hell!" the warrior snapped. He raised his eyes to Venkatna. "Your majesty, we've captured the whole lot of them—Salles, Richtig, everydamnbody but a couple got killed. And that pussy bastard Ashley you sent with me, *he* says not to execute 'em without you say so! *He* says you gave him the right to overrule my decisions even though we're supposed t' be co-commanders!"

"Too bloody right, we did," Weast muttered.

"I want you t' give me a chit says—" D'Auber continued.

"One moment!" Venkatna said. He leaned forward on the five-step throne. "You captured the rebel warriors alive? You surprised them in bivouac, then?"

"Ah—" D'Auber said. The question shocked him back to a memory of Lord Ashley's nattering after the battle. This was obviously on the way to becoming the same discussion: *'You idiot, D'Auber! We can't kill them until we know what's going on. Don't you even wonder why this happened?'*

D'Auber *didn't* wonder about that at all. He just knew that the best time to kick an enemy was when he was down. When you had the chance to execute thirty rebels, you didn't stand around talking about it.

Other people, particularly ranking people, didn't always see the things that appeared obvious to D'Auber.

"Ah," he repeated. "Actually, it was a battle. They, ah, kind of surprised us, but then they gave up."

In sudden anger at a question which none of the advisors

had enough information to ask, D'Auber shouted, "We'd have beat 'em anyway! I was getting things organized!"

"Ashley did well," Venkatna said.

The emperor stood up slowly. Reflected torchlight made his cloth-of-gold robe gleam and turned its ermine trim into a serpent of lambent flame. "Gentlemen!" Venkatna cried. "Let us give thanks to North who rules men's fate! The Web works!"

As if the word were a signal, the women on their benches within the device moaned in unison. They shook themselves, like people awakening from nightmare. All the advisors turned. Even D'Auber was shocked enough out of his confusion to glance around.

The internal lights faded from the Web. The two slaves sat up, shivering. They grasped one another instinctively as they rose to their feet.

The women's eyes were closed or slitted, but they walked out of the maze of wire with the slow grace of a fluid flowing past barriers in a lighter medium. It was as though the location of each portion of the Web was burned into their very cells.

"Who the hell are they, then?" D'Auber asked.

"Your majesty," Race said. "We must rest."

"Food . . . ," Julia whimpered.

"We've done your task," Race continued. She managed to open her eyes. The Searchers huddled together, shuddering uncontrollably though the room was reasonably warm and sealed against drafts. "The Matrix stretches. It will hold its present shape without us f-f-forcing it."

Her eyes scrunched shut again. "For a time."

"Food. . . ."

"Saxtorph!" the emperor shouted. He sat down again. The chamberlain and all of his staff had been excluded from the chamber before the council of war began.

"You at the door," Venkatna said, amending his address to summon the guard. "Get in somebody to take care of these girls. Set up one of the antechambers for them to eat and rest."

He looked at the Searchers, still huddled together. "One of you—Bontempo, your cloak would do for a tent. Put it over them, will you?"

"They're slaves!" cried Weast, not Bontempo himself.

"They are doing my will," said Venkatna in a thin voice. "See to it that you do the same, Count Weast. . . ."

Bontempo draped his garment of foxfur and red velvet over the women. For a moment, they appeared unaware of what was happening. Then Julia raised a trembling hand to grip the garment and hold it in place.

"But the prisoners?" D'Auber said. He hadn't understood what was going on, and it wouldn't have interested him if someone had bothered to explain. "Ashley says—"

"We don't have to kill them now," mused young Trigane; blond, handsome, and as ambitious as he was unprincipled.

"They're still rebels!" snapped Weast. He was angry at his rebuke and determined to take it out on a relatively-safe target.

"They *were* rebels," the emperor said mildly.

Weast winced and formed his mouth into a tight line, his back to the throne.

"Now they're . . . I wonder just how loyal they are?" Venkatna said/asked.

Race replied with her eyes closed, "Perfectly loyal, your majesty. All those subject to you within your empire will do your will."

Brett and four slaves bustled into the chamber with food and bedclothes. The underchamberlain watched Venkatna out of the corner of his eye. He was afraid to cross the emperor, but the message which the guard had shouted down the hall could have been misconstrued a dozen different—potentially fatal—ways.

"They're warriors, your majesty," Trigane said. "*Use* them as warriors."

"Yes, use them as the front line against Mirala," the emperor agreed. With growing enthusiasm he went on, "Yes, and against all the other enemies of the peace North chose me to impose on his world! And—"

Venkatna rose to his feet again.

"—those who survive when Earth is united, then they too shall have peace!"

"They'll mostly have found peace before that, your majesty,"

Kleber said with a tight smile. "The peace of North's battleplain."

The emperor began to laugh. The others joined in, both from inclination and a desire not to stand out; all but D'Auber, who still didn't understand.

The door to the royal apartments opened, so slowly that for a moment no one noticed it. Esme stepped into the large hall, walking carefully.

Venkatna jumped directly to the stone floor and strode to her. "Darling!" he said. "You shouldn't be up when you don't feel well."

"I'm fine, dearest," said Esme, but she took his offered hand with more than conventional ardor. The empress looked as gray and drawn as the two Searchers. "Just a touch of indigestion. And I do like to be with you, you know."

Venkatna's advisors formed small groups, each man with his face turned determinedly away from the imperial couple. D'Auber started to interrupt, but Kleber and Trigane took the warrior firmly aside and spoke to him urgently.

"The Web has done just what . . . ," Venkatna said as he walked his wife toward the throne, his left arm around her and both of her cold hands in his.

He looked at Esme more carefully and his voice softened. "Darling," Venkatna said, "you really *don't* look well."

"If I can just sit down for a moment, I'll be fine," the empress insisted with forced good cheer.

Venkatna set her on the top step, lifting the slight woman despite her protests that she wasn't a cripple. "Dearest?" he asked. "Would you like me to share your bed tonight? It's been far too long, what with—"

Esme looked beatified. "Oh, darling," she said. "When you're under such strain, you should have someone young and pretty to relax you. I don't need—"

"Nonsense!" said the emperor. The conversations beyond the throne buzzed pointedly louder. "You know you're the only woman I could ever love."

"Oh, darling," Esme murmured as she nestled her face against Venkatna's broad, gold-clad shoulder.

≡ 24 ≡

THE RED-BEARDED WARRIOR to Hansen's right in the broad, sunlit bowl of Mirala's Assembly Valley turned and stared.

"Got a problem, friend?" Hansen asked in a voice as emotionless as stone. He was uneasily aware that the fellow was a member of King Wenceslas' household, with a dozen battle comrades within spitting distance . . . while Hansen was alone.

As usual, and more or less as he chose, he guessed.

"Naw, no problem," said the other warrior. He was a little taller than Hansen and a little bulkier, though he carried no more flesh than was necessary to clothe his heavy bones. "Only I saw you before. At Heimr Town."

"I was there," Hansen agreed. *The guy who'd shouldered him on the cart, then backed off.*

Redbeard wasn't looking for a fight, but he too knew that he had a lot of friends around him. He was going to get answers. The best way for Hansen to respond was openly, as a friendly stranger who didn't notice the threat implied by the situation itself.

A petty chieftain on the Speaker's Rock droned about the traditional freedoms of Mirala. There were over a thousand men in the valley. The whole male population of the district, slave and free, was summoned to a war assembly. Only a few

hundred of the crowd were warriors, though, on whose skill
and arc weapons the speaker's 'traditional freedoms' would
depend when Venkatna came.

There would be more slaves than warriors present if the
Mirala District marched to meet the Empire. Feeding and
dressing the warriors; setting up shelters and polishing
battlesuits.

Not infrequently rushing into the battleline if their master
fell, trying to succor him in a whirl of carnage where the
accidental touch of an arc weapon would be instantly fatal
to a rag-clad slave. Hansen could never figure out why they
did it, why anybody followed anybody.

Least of all why anybody followed Commissioner Nils
Hansen; though they did, and though they'd died in windrows
following him. . . .

"Right, I thought so," Redbeard said. His tone lost a trifle
of the cautious veneer. "Only I thought you was with King
Young . . . and he decided he'd rather be a baron for Venkatna
than a king on his own, didn't he?"

Hansen smiled. Denying a former place in Young's entourage
would lead to other questions—and there wasn't any need for it.
Redbeard had just given Hansen a background that he didn't
even have to lie to claim.

"If Young didn't want t' fight those bastards in Frekka, then
I figure there's people who do," Hansen said. "I joined Lord
Salles and then *he* went over. So I came here."

"You came the right place," Redbeard said after a brief
pause. "I guess they'll get done jawin' sometime soon."

He thrust out his right hand. "I'm King Wenceslas' sideman,"
he said. "My name's Weatherhill, but ever'body calls me
Blood."

Hansen clasped Blood's proffered forearm. He remembered
doing the same thing with Lord Salles in the timeless present.

A different speaker was prating now, a king of fifty hectares
named Kawalec. He looked the same as the previous man; his
words were the same mush of nonsense and braggadocio; and
if there was a distinction at all, it was that Kawalec's voice
had a nasal twang which made it even more unpleasant than
was guaranteed by the pointlessness of his words.

In the north of the continent was a watercourse called the Assembly River. It meandered through sands and stagnant marshes without ever getting anywhere.

"My name's Hansen," Hansen said. At Blood's raised eyebrow, he added, "The name's been in my family a long time. It doesn't mean my parents thought I was a god."

If they thought anything at all. Nils Hansen had been raised in a State Creche, but no one in the Open Lands would understand that.

Hansen didn't really understand it himself. If you were going to create a child, you didn't throw it away like a lump of wet clay for the State to mold . . . did you?

Blood pursed his lips. "How good's your armor?" he asked.

"The best," Hansen said; knowing that Blood would discount the flat truth of the statement by one or even two levels. "It's a royal-quality piece."

Blood smiled slightly. *Every guy lies about how good his battlesuit is, and how good he is in bed.* "Right," he said. "But if you left King Young and then got out of Peace Rock in a hurry besides, I don't guess you've got much of a personal train, do you?"

"Too true," Hansen agreed. "I'm here with two ponies, my armor, and my traps. Not so much as a slave t' boil my breakfast."

Blood pursed his lips again. "No fooling?" he said, mentally knocking the quality of Hansen's battlesuit down another couple stages. "Well, when all this bumf is over, I'll take you over and interduce you t' the king. He's not a bad guy t' fight for . . . though ye mustn't worry much about what he says after a couple cups in the evening, he don't mean nothing by it."

Hansen smiled slightly at the assumption that everybody had to have a formal place in the structure. There couldn't be individual do-gooders who just wanted to help remove a tyrant. People had to be fitted into place, for their own good and for society's.

Aloud he said, "I wouldn't mind that."

Blood, having just recruited another warrior for his master's entourage, looked around him in satisfaction. The places immediately beneath the Speaker's Rock were held by warriors.

The score or so of nobles attending the assembly sat on stools on the rock itself.

"I'd take you t' see Vince right now," Blood said, "only he's waiting t' speak himself. All this talk is bullshit, but it's like putting on your best clothes on assembly day, y' see. Somethin' you gotta do."

He grinned at the ranks of warriors. "We're going t' stuff this empire bullshit right up Venkatna's ass. We'll roll right over them Frekka nancy-boys."

"I'd like to think that," Hansen said soberly. He'd seen armies of individuals like this meet trained soldiers before. . . .

Hansen faces a Syndic in gold armor and a pair of his bodyguards. Three meters separate the lines. Men to either side of Hansen shout and wave their arcs, but they do not close and the Syndics wait also, trusting in their greater numbers.

To Hansen's right flank, the shouts have given way to screams and the rip of battlesuits failing under the onslaught of multiple arcs. The shock troops which Hansen trained are rolling down the enemy line like a scythe through wheat.

The Syndic turns to run. Hansen lunges. A bodyguard in pale green stripes blocks his path. Hansen's arc shears through the bodyguard's chest. Blood and metal bubble away from the cut. . . .

"Hey?" said Blood, his voice a mix between anger and surprised fear. "What . . . ?"

Hansen forced a smile. Memory had frozen his visage. He felt as though the skin over his cheekbones should crack like icebergs calving from the face of a glacier.

"Sorry," he said. "Just thinking."

"I guess you were . . . ," Blood said in something more than agreement. "Look, you don't like our chances? *Look* at these guys. And there'll be more when we march, not less. They're comin' from all over, just like you. Ever'body who hates the West Kingdom."

Another speaker rose on the flat prow of rock overlooking Assembly Valley. He was thin and abnormally tall, wearing a cloak of gray fox skins as lustrous as the seas of the far north.

"There's good men here," Hansen said, "and a lot of them. But they'll fight as so many men, and Venkatna's troops will fight like one man. And that'll be all she wrote. . . ."

There was a commotion on the Speaker's Rock. Kawalec, the kinglet who had just spoken, was refusing to give way. "I'll not be followed by a merchant!" he shouted nasally. "And a foreigner besides!"

Two of the other nobles assisted King Lukanov to his feet. Lukanov led the district because of his age. No member of Mirala's nobility had a real edge on the others by wealth or number of retainers. Nobody was sure how far seniority alone would go in a highly-charged situation like the present, but there wasn't a better alternative to the fat, wheezing old king.

"I come from far away, that is true," the tall outlander said. His voice rang from the distant rim of the bowl. "But I am a prince among princes in my home, and if I buy and sell there—"

The Mirala kinglet scrunched away from the full shock of the foreigner's glare.

"—then some of the things I bought are the fifty warriors I've brought with me here. Can you say the same, *Master*—" the civilian honorific a deliberate insult "—Kawalec?"

A claque of warriors shouted bloodthirsty approval from the base of the Speaker's Rock. Kawalec must have had retainers present in the crowd, but none of them were foolish enough to call attention to themselves.

Lukanov waddled to the front of the rock. "I arranged, the order, of the speakers," he said. His shortness of breath broke the statement into three portions, but they were clearly audible.

He waved his heavy walking stick in the direction of the local kinglet, while the stranger stood coldly aloof. "Kawalec, milord," Lukanov said. "You've had your say and we've listened. Now be seated while others speak."

Kawalec nodded curtly to Lukanov and quickly took his stool again. He pointedly ignored the foreigner, but the incident had shaken a sense of self-worth Hansen would have judged to be impregnable. The mercenary claque had called for Kawalec's skull as a drinking cup, but the glance of the bearded stranger had an even greater impact.

"Lords of Mirala," the tall man said. "Lovers of freedom. I didn't journey from far Simplain to tell you of your rights, or of the wrongs that this upstart Venkatna has done others and plans to do to us. We all know that—that's why we're here."

He looked behind him at the seated nobles, then swept the crowd in the valley dished out of the mountainside by an ancient glacier. "I will tell you instead what we must do to safeguard our rights and end Venkatna's wrongs. If we wait here for the *emperor* to come in the spring, then we will win the battle or he will win—"

King Wenceslas leaped up from his stool. "We will win!" he shouted. "We will win!"

"And we will win *nothing*," the stranger continued. His voice carried over the shouts of a hundred warriors mouthing responses of rote pride and rote patriotism.

The shocked crowd quieted. "Because he will come again," the tall man resumed. "And again, milords and princes; and again, until finally he gains the day and we are all as dead as the defenders of Heimrtal. *That* is what will happen if we let Venkatna fight his war."

The Assembly Valley buzzed like bees swarming. The emotions were mixed, but no one cried a denial of what they all, warrior or civilian, knew in their hearts to be true.

"What we must do," the stranger continued, "is carry the war *to* Venkatna. Defeat his army beneath the walls of Frekka. Raze his palace, kill *him* before he can call upon the resources of his subject states to raise an army twice the size the next time. Venkatna has no son. If we break him and his army *now*, we break the West Kingdom back into a score of small states like our own."

"What's Simplain know about what *we* got to do?" Blood shouted unexpectedly from beside Hansen.

The tall man turned and looked down at Blood.

"What do I know?" he asked in a voice that crackled like a crown fire. "Then ask a warrior who has fought against Venkatna already, as none of you in Mirala have done."

He pointed into the crowd like a sniper aiming. "What do you think we should do, Lord Hansen?" he boomed.

Hansen met the cold gray eye of the figure on the rock above him.

"We should strike straight for Frekka," Hansen said. His voice seemed to fill the bowl of the valley. "Just as you suggest, Lord Guest."

≡ 25 ≡

SPARROW'S ARC WEAPONS, optimized for range rather than flux density, cut through Morfari and his crew like surf hitting a sand castle.

The arc from the right gauntlet caught the android at pelvis level. Morfari's bones were black from their stiffening of carbon fiber, but his blood was as red as a man's. His torso collapsed forward. The volley gun blew a crater in the mud, a centimeter short of the dog's forepaws.

There were risks to any endeavor.

Sparrow swept his gloves left to left, right to right, simultaneously, completing between them the semicircle of his unprepared opponents. The powerpack of a Lomeri laser exploded, spraying the molten plastic stock in all directions. Rifle ammunition, detonated by the arcs' fluctuating currents, crackled in bandoliers.

The squabble among the lizardmen had diverted the Fifth Plane female at the crucial instant. She tried to bring her plasma weapon to bear on Sparrow. A whipping arc sawed through her massive body at belt level, cutting to the spine.

Incredibly, the woman managed to squeeze the trigger. Her toppling body swung the muzzle so that the saffron fireball engulfed instead the lizardman she had just disciplined.

One of the slaves wore concussion grenades alternating with knives on his cross-belts. Three of the grenades went off in quick succession. The multiple blast staggered Sparrow and turned the slave's upper body into a soup distinguishable only by color from the thin mud of the swamp.

Sparrow's ears rang. Between his legs, the dog's mouth opened and closed as if barking. The sound, if there was one, did not reach the smith's shocked senses.

Two lizardmen still moved, but that was merely galvanic response to the high voltage which had lopped their bodies apart. The stench—of voided bowels and body cavities ripped open by the arcs—quivered over the scene like a bubble of green putrescence.

Sparrow sank to his knees. The dog leaped around him, yapping silently as she pawed muddy streaks onto her master's arms and shoulders.

The thumbs and forefingers of Sparrow's gauntlets glowed yellow; even the wrist flares had been heated to dull red. The smith tried to pull the overloaded weapons off with his hands. The heat and pain of closing his fingers to grip were too great, even for him.

At last Sparrow put his right hand on the ground. He stood on the gauntlet as steam spurted over him and the mud baked to terra cotta. He dragged his hand out of the metal by the strength of his arm. The relief was so dizzying that it was a moment before he was able to strip his left glove the same way.

The smith's hands were red and already beginning to swell. All the hair had been singed off them.

The smith laughed bitterly. He was used to pain, but he knew that pain didn't strengthen anything. Pain ripped a soul down to a desperate core in which the will blazed—if the will were strong enough.

Sparrow thrust his hands into the water, working his fingers into the mud past the horsetail roots. The cool fluids soothed his dry, throbbing skin.

Insects buzzed over the windrow of corpses. A pinkish slime overlaid the normal hues of the swamp. The arcs cauterized as they cut, but flash-heated blood ruptured vessels at some distance above and below the wound channels. Exploding ammunition, especially the grenades, did further damage.

Sparrow had butchered out mammoths. The aftermath of battle did not concern him; only the fact that he had survived.

He walked over to Morfari's body. The android lay face-down. His legs were beside the torso. The black-booted feet were planted firmly together, but the severed thighs splayed out to either side.

Sparrow rolled the body over. Morfari's muscles were rigid; the arms held their set as though they were welded steel. The smith wasn't sure whether that had something to do with the android's physiology, or if it was simply a freak result of high voltages blasting the central nervous system.

The dog, now confident that her master was well, sniffed the bodies. She bounced frequently as though threatened by some aspect of the cooling flesh. Sparrow could hear her barking again.

Morfari's mouth was drawn into a tight rictus. The lavaliere on his breast was undamaged. Sparrow let out the breath that he had held without realizing it. He needed the android's control device for the next stage of his mission . . . but in a wide-open battle that left a dozen dead, there was a limit to how much care Sparrow had been able to show.

The lavaliere hung on a ribbon of lustrous green synthetic. The material was non-conductive, which was lucky. Otherwise, the currents surging over Morfari's skin might have blown the circuits of the control device.

Sparrow activated the device in pre-set mode by keying one of the dozen buttons on its small control pad. A Lomeri corpse bent like a bow. The lizardman was dead, but his nerve pathways still passed the jolt of current which his slave collar applied.

So. The lavaliere was functional. More complex actions could be programmed through the keypad, but Sparrow had no need of those. What he needed . . .

He looked around him at mud and blood and stench. He would prefer a bench to lie on as he worked; but nothing outside the Matrix really mattered when the smith was working.

He lay down on the bank. The lavaliere was clasped in his huge right hand. The dog, familiar with the process, perked up her ears, but she didn't interfere with the smith's concentration.

Sparrow was a hunter and a warrior; and once, when he was a young man in the Open Lands, he had been a prince. Above all, and encompassing all, Sparrow was a smith. He slid into a state of half-sleep, half-hypnosis.

His eyes were open but glazed. The ball of the sun glowing through the mists swelled until its sanguine light filled all the universe. . . .

Sparrow's mind ranged the Matrix, searching through ideals without number, the basic substance of all objects existing in all times in the eight worlds of Northworld. Each a template, a mold from which a master smith could strike copies into matter in realtime.

The master of *all* smiths could strike copies: Sparrow alone.

Nothing changed visibly in the swamp where Sparrow's body lay, but crystals within the control device shifted their electronic pathways. A chip now resonated in tune with the smith's brainwaves rather than those of the android, who was slowly reaching equilibrium with the ambient temperature.

Sparrow blinked twice as his mind returned from the Matrix. He rubbed his eyes with the back of his hand, forgetful of the swollen flesh and the mud in which he had cooled it. The gritty shock brought him fully alert. He rose to a scene from a hotter Hell than Northworld's.

Dimetrodons—not a pack but rather a score of individuals lured by the reek of slaughter—swarmed over the recent corpses. A huge male, easily four meters long and a half tonne in weight, stood on the chewed remnant of Morfari's body and threatened the smith.

Sparrow's dog, snarling like a saw in knotted wood, stood between her master and the reptile's ragged jaws. She snapped every time the dimetrodon's tongue lapped the air. The big carnivore twitched out with a clawed forepaw, but the bitch dodged its clumsy blows easily. The dimetrodon was so disconcerted by the violent opposition that it didn't use its weight and scaly hide to brush past the dog.

Sparrow got to his feet. He was dizzy. His skin was cold and clammy in reaction to the time his mind had spent in the Matrix, but the swamp's oven temperatures and saturated humidity covered him like an avalanche of sodden clay.

The dog noticed that her master was up. She continued to snap and snarl at the monster. Her leg braces flashed like knives in the bloody sunlight.

There was an easy path of retreat along the stream bank. The other dimetrodons were wholly occupied with carrion, including the smoking carcase of their own fellow killed by Morfari's gang. The nearest beast would lose interest when its intended meal moved off with mammalian quickness.

"Dog!" Sparrow called. "Come away, you bloody fool!"

The carnivore lunged. The dog met the motion instead of retreating. Her canines scored two long gouges across the dimetrodon's snout.

"*Dog!*" Sparrow shouted, but the bitch's blood was up. If he tried to drag her off by main force, the carnivore would take them both while they struggled. The gauntlets lay beneath the dimetrodon's trampling feet, and even the thought of donning them again made Sparrow's punished flesh crawl.

He drew the knife from his belt sheath. It had a broad, 30-cm blade with a single edge and blood grooves to keep the suction of flesh from binding the steel during deep cuts.

Sparrow moved within a meter of the dimetrodon, then paused while the monster switched its attention from the dog to the dog's master. As if this were a planned maneuver, the dog leaped in and tore at the dimetrodon's ear hole. The dimetrodon snapped sideways with a wobbling undulation of its backfin.

Sparrow stepped forward. He slammed his knife home to the hilt in the dimetrodon's neck. Reflexively, the smith tried to throw his left leg astride the creature's back as his right arm ripped the knife downward against the resistance of flesh and scaly hide.

The sail blocked his motion. The tip of a spine jabbed his knee, and the creature's foreclaws tore the sandal straps and the flesh beneath. The reptile's stricken body writhed; Sparrow let the motion fling him away.

The dimetrodon waddled off, spewing blood and arping. The knifehilt wobbled in a wound that pierced the beast's throat and gaped to the breadth of the smith's own huge hand.

The injured animal blundered into one of its fellows which was snuffling at a lizardman's disjointed foot. With the suddenness of a trap springing, the second dimetrodon clamped its jaws on the other's neck wound. Three more of the big lizards immediately piled into the slaughter, ripping huge chunks out of their injured fellow.

Sparrow's dog turned and began to whine in delight as she licked her master's hand. The dog's rough tongue felt like a rasp against the swollen flesh.

Sparrow picked up the lavaliere, which he had dropped to draw his knife. He hung the ribbon over his own thick neck. The control device rode higher than it had on the android, who was classically proportioned except for his extra set of arms. That shouldn't make any difference to the unit's operation.

The killing frenzy directed at one of their own kind had dragged most of the carnivores twenty meters through the swamp before the victim finally collapsed to be devoured alive. They left Sparrow free to examine the cattle guard's paraphernalia.

Morfari's skimmer had been knocked over, but it appeared to be essentially undamaged. The vehicle was a control column on a circular plate a meter in diameter. It generated an electromagnetic field in the surface over which it rode and repelled that field by one of identical polarity in the plate itself.

The whole unit weighed only thirty kilograms or so. Sparrow righted it easily.

One of the knives scattered in the kill zone among the charred equipment and bits of meat—the dimetrodons were messy eaters—was the length and width at the hilt of the blade Sparrow had carried. The cattle guard's weapon was double-edged and tapered to a sharp point, but it fit the smith's sheath snugly enough.

Sparrow kept the knife. The rest of the weapons and equipment, including the arc gauntlets, he left for mud and the tannin-bitter waters to reclaim.

He touched the skimmer's controls. The little vehicle wobbled obediently.

"C'mon, dog," Sparrow said. When the animal stepped onto the plate with him, he reached down and tousled her ears again.

"You're not so bad to have around, you know?"

The dog barked. Sparrow rolled a handgrip, and the skimmer slid off toward the bower of Princess Mala, deeper in the swamp.

≡ 26 ≡

"IF YOU'LL STEP this way, milady," suggested the voice of Kumiswari, Hansen's new servant. "The tent with the *gold* battlesuit before it. And no finer suit in the host, not the armor of King Wenceslas himself."

Lamplight gleamed through the stitches of the pony-leather tent. Hansen bumped his head on the ridgepole while pulling on his linen breeches. The tent was twenty centimeters shorter than Hansen was, a hard fact to remember when he was in a hurry. He swore quietly.

Krita must have escaped.

The flap rustled as Kumiswari undid the upper set of ties. "Lord Hansen?" the servant called. He was one of the pair of slaves Wenceslas had assigned to Hansen—like the tent itself—from his own establishment. "There's a lady to see you, sir."

"All right," Hansen said, checking—not that there was the least danger—that the dagger with the spiked handguard was unobtrusively available in the sheath hanging from the head of his cot. A 'lady' looking for Hansen here had to be Krita— or a messenger from North, and North would not send an assassin.

Would North send an assassin?

The only light in the tent was a candle of mammoth tallow, held at reading height by a meter-long spike jabbed into the ground beside the cot. The wavering yellow flame had an animal odor which Hansen found surprisingly pleasant when he'd gotten used to it.

Kumiswari opened the tent with a flourish degraded by the fact that the woman still had to stoop to step past the end pole. This was too big a tent for one man's field use, but that didn't make it a palace reception room.

Backlit by the servant's lantern, the woman's hair glowed red/blond. She wasn't Krita, and she wasn't anybody Hansen knew—

Until she turned and said to Kumiswari, "You may go now—and if you know your master as well as you should, you won't linger too close."

Lucille. Lord Salles' . . . cousin, hadn't he said?

"Of course, milady," Kumiswari murmured. The light behind Lucille quivered as the servant bowed. His voice faded as he added, "Milord? If you call loudly, I will come."

She had only been around him for a few days, in the rebels' camp. Why had she put her threat to the servant in that particular way, as if she knew Commissioner Nils Hansen?

"Fine, that's fine," Hansen agreed. The woman bent forward to refasten the ties, reaching between the flaps.

He looked around the tent and grimaced, not that he'd asked for a visitor.

He wasn't really a hard-handed bastard like his reputation. He didn't lose his temper very often; and when he did, it was always a cold passion. As cold as Death himself.

The only furniture within the tent was the cot and the round of treetrunk that Hansen used as a stool. He'd been sitting on the wood, wrapped in a black bearskin and staring through the Matrix at distant places, when he was interrupted. A notebook made from thin plates of beechwood lay on the cot beside him, to explain to a servant or visitor what Lord Hansen was doing in his tent.

Lucille turned. Her head cleared the ridgepole by the thickness of the cowl which she had thrown back over her shoulders. Hansen, awkward because he had to hunch until he sat down again, gestured toward the stool and cot in a single sweep. "Please," he offered. "I'm not set up for this."

She settled, like a cat curling onto the end of the bed. There was no obvious hesitation. Hansen thankfully sat on the stool. He thought of flipping the bearskin over his legs again; but thought better of it.

"I . . . hoped you might know whether any of the others escaped from the—the attack," Lucille asked. She was minutely less self-possessed than she had been a moment before.

"Your cousin, you mean?" Hansen said. "No, lady. They all opened their suits and surrendered. I ran."

True enough, though not on his legs.

"Lord Salles was beside me when it happened," he said aloud.

Candid ignorance was the best choice. She could denounce him, if she chose.

"He shouted that we mustn't fight against the emperor," Hansen continued. "And he surrendered. I thought the servants and dependents had been captured also."

Lucille nodded curtly. "Most of them were," she said. "My sister is a lord's wife here in Mirala, and I—"

Her face was warmer and more textured than it had been when Hansen met her in the rebels' camp, but it suddenly went gray even in the candle's tawny light.

"—have had as much of the emperor's hospitality as my body could stand." She forced a smile. "Or my soul."

"I'm sorry," Hansen said truthfully. "I wish I could give you better news."

The woman wore a scarlet-lined cape of heavy blue wool. The dress beneath was brown and cream, with lace at the throat and bodice seams. Either her brother-in-law was wealthy as well as being noble, or Lucille had escaped from the wreck of the rebel cause with an unlikely quantity of belongings.

She had escaped because she had kin outside the West Kingdom. It was no treason to Venkatna that a woman visit her sister. The Web—and the slaves controlling the Web—carried out the emperor's instructions as precisely as a crossbow slammed its bolt down a trajectory determined by aim and physics when the trigger was pulled.

"It was the Web," Lucille said, correctly and to Hansen's surprise. Her fingers toyed with the bearskin Hansen had tossed onto the cot. "The thing in that demon's palace. There are rumors—"

She stared at Hansen, as if expecting confirmation or denial. "—and they're true."

He shrugged. *He was just here to fight.* "I'm sorry," he repeated.

"Did—" something changed in the woman's expression, though Hansen wasn't sure what "—Kriton escape also?"

"No," Hansen said flatly.

He'd been watching Krita when Kumiswari announced the visitor. She and the remainder of the Peace Rock rebels were imperial troops now. For the time being they carried out evolutions and battle training on the practice fields outside Frekka, but the real fight would come soon enough. . . .

"I asked . . . ," Lucille said to her hands. The fingers were so thin that the knuckles seemed unusually prominent, although they were not enlarged. "Because I know that she's a woman."

"I think," Hansen said quietly, "that you're mistaken."

"Oh, it's all right," the woman said hastily. "I won't tell anyone—I haven't, after all. But if Kriton was here, I wouldn't have . . ."

She looked up and met Hansen's eyes. He cleared his throat.

Lucille leaned forward and took his hands in hers. Her fingers felt cold even to him, sitting in breeches and a shirt of thin gray wool. "Will we defeat him?" she demanded. "The devil Venkatna?"

"I'm not the comman—" Hansen began.

"Don't!" Lucille snapped. "Milord, I don't know who you are, but you *know* things. I saw you in the camp, I *watched* you. You should be commanding this army and you're not, but you can tell me the truth!"

Hansen grimaced. At the direction of one part of his conscious mind, he began rubbing the woman's hands. "We've got enough troops to do it," he said. "A quick, straight shot at Frekka like we're planning—"

Thanks to the 'merchant prince from Simplain.'

"—could do the job."

"But," Lucille said. She shifted slightly, so that Hansen's right hand lay on her thigh and her own hand held it there.

He was a man, God knew. Whatever else he was, he was a man. . . .

"But," Hansen agreed, staring at the soft wool that bunched as his fingers kneaded gently, "we won't move fast. We've got twice the baggage and a quarter the speed of the same number of Venkatna's troops. We won't take them by surprise, and when we join battle—"

He raised his eyes.

"—*they'll* fight like an army, and we'll fight like a mob."

"Why are you here, Lord Hansen?" she asked softly.

Because I'm responsible for the problem. Because if I can't cure it, I can—

Die trying.

Die.

"I've fought enough battles," he said aloud, "to know that there's always a chance the other guy's going to fuck up bigtime. Let's hope, shall we?"

"I hope you survive, Lord Hansen," Lucille said as if she were replying to the words he spoke only in his mind. "But you may not—"

She lifted his right hand. He started to draw back, surprised and embarrassed, but the woman swept her skirt waist-high with her free hand.

"—and I've wanted you from the first time I saw you in camp." She smiled. Her eyes were unfocused. "It was like watching a leopard around those poor housecats my cousin led."

Her lips half-parted as she pulled Hansen toward her.

He wondered why he had thought her hair was brown. It gleamed golden in the candlelight, and the down above her thighs was pure blond.

≡ 27 ≡

FOR A MOMENT, nothing reflected back from the pool except cypresses and the stars above them. Planes shifted with the suddenness of prisms flashing. Nils Hansen stood on the bank. He wore boots, a jumpsuit, and a close-fitting helmet.

The smooth khaki surface of Hansen's garment was not broken, as it normally would have been, by a weapons belt.

A large, short-snouted tapir honked in surprise at the human's arrival, then galloped off through the forest. The beast vanished quickly among the undergrowth and the trees' outflung buttress roots. Its primitive hooves could be heard for another twenty seconds, splashing in the low spots and thudding heavily through the leaf mold on drier ground.

Bats chittered.

Hansen turned. The northern sky burned a cold blue, the corona discharge from the horizon-filling dome of Keep Starnes.

"You could have inserted closer to our objective," said the artificial intelligence in what Hansen's mind heard as a waspish voice. *"You could have inserted* within *our objective."*

"I could do anything I please, Third," Hansen said. "I'm a god, remember?"

As Hansen studied the huge fortress, he wiped his hands on his thighs to dry the sweat, then rubbed the palms together. The degree of care was worthy of volitional action.

"Besides, it's my legs that'll be getting the exercise." His fingers kept brushing back to where the pistol holster should have ridden, high on his right hip. "Maybe I wanted the exercise."

Sky glow penetrated the conifer needles and pin-leafed cypress foliage. The light illuminated the forest floor once Hansen's eyes adapted. Keep Starnes was its own beacon.

Maybe he *should* have entered Plane Five nearer to his objective. He'd always operated on instinct in a tense situation, though. This was tense, the good lord knew. Instinct warned Hansen to leave room for maneuver.

"Find us a good place to get in, Third," Hansen directed as he started walking north. "I kinda doubt they're going to roll out the red carpet for us."

The warning signal undulated through the Citadel like the tentacles of an octopus swimming.

Count Starnes lifted his head. "He's come?" he asked.

"He's come!" said Karring from an outstation in the rotunda. He shut off the alarm. "At any rate . . ."

The chief engineer paused to give APEX mental instructions. The numerical display above his console shifted to a panorama as it might be glimpsed from the exterior of Keep Starnes, hundreds of meters above their heads.

The trees were supported by bulbous bases or roots flung out from halfway up their boles. They grew on a surface that was as much shallow water as treacherous land. Over the next fifty million years, the present landscape would decay to peat and brown coal. For the moment, the site was notable for a stagnant purulence of vegetable life in which browsing animals seemed interlopers despite their considerable size.

Keep Starnes' sensor array extended kilometers into the sodden forest, but the thick growth shielded a man-sized target on many spectra. APEX formed the hints of mass, shape, and infra-red distribution into a figure on the display. The computer could have given it a face and mimicked expressions besides, but such details would have been wholly fanciful.

Karring limited the construct to what was supportable on

the evidence: a male of moderate height and a compactly-powerful build.

"He isn't armed," he called to the others. "Lena, seal all the keep's orifices as though we were under massive attack."

"Use proper respect when you address the lady!" bellowed one of the big woman's lovers. His hourglass shape was accentuated by a broad belt decorated with studs of electrum. The frames of his two holstered pistols were plated with the same rich, silvery metal; the black onyx of the weapons' grips matched the leather harness.

"Shut up, Plaid," Lena said as she watched her own display. "You're useless when you're using your tongue to talk."

Plaid straightened with an incredulous expression. His companion, Voightman, sneered and began to pose to set off his muscles. No one bothered to look at him, but the polished metal surfaces of the console provided a mirror.

"But Karring, dear," Lena continued, her tone smoother but far from agreeable. "I don't want to keep him out, this Hansen or whoever Fortin sent us. I want him inside where I can play with him."

Lena's display showed the network of all systems within Keep Starnes, overlaid in forty hues distinguishable only by an expert. As she spoke, the image rotated. The visual result suggested the peristaltic motion of an intestine digesting the animal's last meal.

"I want him inside also," Karring explained. "But for me to close his escape route properly—as I did that of his fellow—it's necessary that he enter through what Fortin called the Matrix."

"Oh, all right," Lena said. The pattern on her display changed. Sounds rang through the fabric of Keep Starnes, penetrating even to the Citadel. Shutters dropped; valves closed. The hum of the ventilation fans changed note as the system switched over to recycle the atmosphere, scrubbing poisons instead of sucking in large quantities of outside air to replace what was dumped in normal, total-loss, operation.

"I hear water," said Count Starnes. He lifted his helmet and rubbed his cropped hair.

"Back-pressure in the sewage lines," his daughter said with

satisfaction. "Waste is being pumped into the holding tank at ground level instead of being voided through the main siphon. We can go for three days this way."

Lena turned on her couch to look at Count Starnes. She moved like a whale basking. "Unless you want me to shut off water to everybody higher than Level K17? Or hold them to two liters a day? Then we could—"

"This will be fine, I'm sure, milady," Karring interrupted as he worked his manual keyboard.

He spoke more crisply than he should have done. Lena rotated her head, this time to look at the engineer. She did nothing further, but Plaid lost his pout and smiled again.

The external sensor trunks were conduits a meter in diameter. Lena's shutdown had severed them, so Karring shifted to induction inputs to regain data on the world outside the keep. The initial results were badly degraded compared to the images which passed through optical cables, but APEX used the baseline information gathered previously to enhance the new material to a similar standard.

"He's coming toward us," Karring said. He frowned. "But he's still walking."

"Some soldier," Lena said. "There's no more of this one than there was of the other. I've got room for his whole head."

She giggled and added, "Which might just be fun."

"Where's Lisa?" Count Starnes asked suddenly. He glanced toward the elevators as if expecting to see his younger daughter appearing from one of the cages.

"She is . . . ," said Karring.

His screen split. On the left half of the display, the blur-faced figure of the stranger walked among cypresses and bog conifers. On the right was a one-man armored vehicle gliding through the same forest on an air cushion pressurized by eight fans. From the center of the tank's turret projected the short, tapering barrel of a charged-particle weapon with a co-axial machinegun beside it.

"Lisa is outside the keep in her personal scout tank," the chief engineer resumed. A topographic overlay glowed in the air beneath the images of the two contestants, the man in khaki and the tank surrounding a woman. "She's moving to intercept our visitor."

"I didn't tell her to do that," Starnes muttered. There was both pride and concern in his tone. His hand idly caressed the bow slope of his own repulsion-drive tank. The frontal armor was of almost stellar density.

"She puts pressure on him," Karring said with satisfaction. "He'll have to do something, enter or flee back where he came from. Since he's come this far, I think we can expect him to come the rest of the way to where we want him."

Voightman and Plaid lounged and posed, bored by what was going on beyond their immediate presence. The other three humans in the Citadel watched the ill-matched contestants avidly.

In the corridor beyond, the Fleet Battle Director hummed as it gathered and analyzed and . . . waited.

≡ 28 ≡

VENKATNA FLUNG THE door open so violently that the single lamp in the audience hall guttered, stirring golden ripples across the brightwork of the Web.

The device was silent, the benches within its framework empty. No one was present in the hall except the armored guard at the entrance to the imperial suite.

"Where are they?" Venkatna shouted. His voice rang from the dome, rebounding like the raucous anger of crows. "Why aren't they here, the slaves?"

"S—your ma—" the guard stammered in surprise.

To stay awake, the guard had been watching the procession of ants moving under a leaded transom on the other side of the hall. His battlesuit optics were at $^{x}300$ magnification, giving him an unintelligible view of whiskers when he spun to face the emperor.

"Here they are, your majesty!" bleated the terrified underchamberlain responsible for the care and feeding of Venkatna's most cherished slaves. "Come along, you bitches, for North's sake!"

The guard muttered under his breath to the suit's AI, dropping the magnification to 1:1 while retaining a degree of light enhancement. What he saw *now* was even more of a shock.

Venkatna wore his night garb, a long linen gown with

flowing sleeves and a quilted cap. He was barefoot.

He held his wife in his arms. Esme's cap had fallen off; her face was gray. Her arms were stiff at her sides instead of hanging down as gravity should have drawn them.

Race and Julia stumbled from the alcove at the back of the audience hall where they slept and lived during the few hours a day they were not within the Web. Their tunics were clean enough, though rumpled, and they had been able to sponge their bodies off recently, but the women's hair was a dull mass of knots and matting.

Brett, the underchamberlain, wore court dress. His duties primarily involved the period the women were not entranced in the Web. The demands for his presence were uncertain, however, and the imperial focus was so close that Brett looked almost as worn as his charges.

"Here they are, your majesty!" he repeated. He tugged at the sleeve of Julia's shift. The Searcher, only half awake and ten kilos lighter than her normal weight, slapped Brett's hand away without being fully aware of the contact.

"She's sick!" the emperor cried, hugging Esme's stiff body closer to him. "I woke up and she felt—she felt—"

She felt cold as ice.

"—she didn't feel right. Make her *well,* damn you!"

Servants and officials in various stages of undress banged through the door leading to the apartments of the general household. Slaves began lighting additional wall lamps, adding to the illumination of the torches and lanterns the newcomers had brought with them.

"Let me see her," Race ordered, wakeful now if not entirely aware of her surroundings. She reached toward Esme's neck to check the carotid pulse.

Venkatna jerked back instinctively.

"Let me *see*—" Race snarled through waves of fatigue which corroded away the normal desire for self-preservation.

Race's fingertips brushed a cheek instead of the empress' throat. The temperature of the flesh, easily 15° below that of life, told the Searcher as much as she could have learned by searching for a heartbeat. "Forget it, she's dead."

"Make her well!" the emperor screamed.

Several of Venkatna's top advisors entered the hall. Baron Trigane saw what the emperor held, judged the potentials of the situation, and slipped back out hoping that he had gone unobserved.

"Your majesty," said Julia, "we can't do that. North himself, our master, can't bring the dead to life, not as flesh and blood. The Web affects only what is, not what once was."

"Your majesty!" Brett babbled. "It isn't my fault. Please, I'll have them whipped until—"

Kleber struck the underchamberlain with the butt of his dagger. Brett went boneless. He fell backward instead of on his face because Kleber's free hand tugged the back of the servant's collar.

Kleber flicked a smile of embarrassment toward the emperor. The advisor regretted that he hadn't acted more quickly, but he still hoped that Venkatna would not, in what was clearly an irrational moment, order the death of everyone in the audience hall.

"Your majesty," said Race with the power of simple honesty. "We will carry out your every order that we can. This we cannot do."

Venkatna's lips brushed the cheek of his wife. "Keep her, then," he said in a ragged whisper. His voice strengthened. "You say you çan preserve what is, so preserve her! I'll dress her in silks, I'll build her a couch here in the hall—but you preserve her!"

Advisors looked at one another and tried to wipe all expression from their faces.

"Your majesty, we've been in the Web all—" Julia began.

"Get in there!" the emperor shouted. "You bitch, you could have saved her but you didn't! I should have you—"

"You didn't tell—" Julia said, but Race gripped her shoulder with hard fingers and shocked her mind back to present realities.

"Your orders are our fate," Race murmured softly as she led her companion into the net of curves and crystal.

"What are you waiting for?" Venkatna demanded of the nearest servant, a night-duty usher. "Bring a couch! And where are my darling's maids? They should be dressing her!"

"Does this mean that your majesty will delay plans to bring Mirala within the Empire?" asked Bontempo from the open doorway. His age had delayed him, and he wore a full-length cloak over his nightdress and slippers.

"No!" the emperor said. "I'll rule Mirala or I'll kill every living thing in the district! I'll make my darling the queen of all the earth, and those pair—"

He glared at the Searchers as they settled themselves on the benches within the Web. Lamplight gleamed in his eyes like the fires of madness.

"—will preserve my peace and my Esme both, without fail!"

Race sighed softly. The universe trembled as internal lights began to play across the surface of the Web.

≡ 29 ≡

SPARROW'S DOG GROWLED deep in her throat. She was responding to the ultrasonics which, along with probes in a dozen other spectra, painted their skimmer.

"Steady . . . ," the smith murmured as he eased off the throttle. The skimmer slowed and dropped minusculy closer to the ground. "Steady now. . . ."

They curved around a spit where the land rose higher than most. It was covered densely with trees whose trunks were slender cones and whose branches flared into pompon tufts. Beyond the trees was a pond over which the sun drew mist like a bloody shroud. Across the water stood the stark black walls surrounding Princess Mala's bower, three meters high.

"Gee-*up*," Sparrow muttered reflexively as he dialed on more power and adjusted the skimmer's angle of attack. The little platform needed more speed to cross the pond. Open water dissipated the supporting charge more swiftly than dry soil would.

From the walls and the dome whose faceted curve could be dimly glimpsed beyond, scores and perhaps hundreds of weapons aimed at the skimmer. The lavaliere prickled on Sparrow's chest, seeming to burn him through the fabric. That was all in his mind—but Sparrow the Smith knew better than most the reality of a mind's images.

A large amphibian rose from the center of the pond with a

fish in its jaws. The broad skull turned. One of the beast's separate-focusing eyes started to rotate toward the skimmer a hundred meters away.

The motion brought the amphibian within the area protected against targets of that mass. The walls' automatic defenses went into action.

Vertical rods every two meters stiffened the black wall the way a bat's fingerbones brace its wings. Gun muzzles unmasked at mid-height on three of the miniature bastions.

A laser howled, pulsing its indigo beam across the amphibian's broad neck like a bandsaw. Explosive shells from an automatic cannon blew fist-sized chunks out of the creature's skull. Fléchettes from the third bastion drilled through the pond surface to the calculated location of the amphibian's body.

The shattered head sank and the beast's torso curved up convulsively. High explosive and the laser worked over the blotchy gray hide, while fléchettes now sought what was left of the skull. The weapons stopped hammering only when the largest piece of the luckless amphibian was the size of Sparrow's hand.

The reformed identification chip in the lavaliere had properly matched the brainwave patterns of Sparrow and his dog. Otherwise, similar weapons would have ripped them to patches of red mammalian pulp.

Spray lifted from beneath the skimmer. The spewing water caused further batteries to unmask and track the intruders, but none of them fired.

In order to reach the courtyard's single gate, Sparrow had to curve near the weapons which had destroyed the amphibian. The stomach-turning miasma of propellant permeated the humid atmosphere, mixed with the scaly odor of air the laser had burned to plasma.

The bitch rubbed herself against her master's legs, reassuring herself of Sparrow's presence and solidity. Her body trembled.

The gates were as wide as the wall was high. The double leaves were inset slightly between a pair of thick towers supporting multi-barrel plasma dischargers for high-altitude defense. Sparrow pulled up before them.

The strip of mud in front of the gates was the only bare

earth on the island outside the walls. It was broad enough, if barely, and Sparrow would have lain down in the muddy water if necessary. There was no discomfort that Sparrow would not accept if it was a necessary step in his path.

The smith arranged his equipment so that the weight of his body would not damage it. He settled full-length in front of the portal. One mark of a smith's skill was the distance from his entranced body at which he could affect the structure of molecules through the Matrix. Sparrow's powers of extension were unexcelled—but closer was better, and he wasn't involved in a contest.

The dog snuffled up along the smooth walls for a few meters, finding nothing of particular interest. The dense black plastic had no taste or odor, and the debris of years had been unable to cling to its waxy surface.

Insects hummed in clouds over the pond, settling on bits of the amphibian. Occasionally fish lifted through the greasy sheen to suck down carrion and carrion-flies together. The dog eyed the froth and the activity it drew, but she remained close to her master.

Sparrow closed his eyes. He slid into the Matrix like one of the pond's lungfish diving back for its burrow in the mud . . . but the water was warm, and the Matrix was a slime of cold light which froze the minds of those who entered it.

All templates, all realities, all time.

Princess Mala's dwelling had two layers of defense. The external band destroyed all targets which came within range. The targeting array plotted mass and proximity on a graph of death. Nothing larger than a thumb-sized beetle would be permitted to live within a meter of the black walls unless the creature was correctly keyed into the bower's identification system.

Within the gates, the defenses were simpler and still more stringent. Only if someone inside deliberately imprinted the visitor onto the system could that visitor enter and survive. Otherwise, blasting radiance would fill the courtyard, fusing the mud to glass and ripping all protoplasm into a haze which spewed upward toward the clouds.

But the controls were electronic, and their crystalline

pathways clicked into new forms under the smith's instinctual touch. Sparrow's body shivered on the warm mudbank, but there was never such a smith as he, never in the measureless eons of Northworld. . . .

Sparrow awoke from a shuddering nightmare in which he was one of the damned souls on Plane Four and crawled motionlessly across the endless ice. The dog barked fiercely as she pranced beside him, turning from Sparrow to the gates and back again.

The gate leaves were open. Their lower edges had planed arcs across the mud of the courtyard. The interior was virtually undisturbed, except by the daily rainstorms.

Sparrow started to get to his feet. He had to pause for a moment on all fours. His knees and knuckles sank into the wet soil.

The smith was still trembling from the cold of the Matrix, entered twice in an hour and either time on a task of utmost precision. His head ached from the grenade explosions, and his hands and forearms were swollen. He inhaled deeply, expelled the breath, and drew in another without yet attempting to rise further.

A fly, bloated with the meal it had made on the amphibian's remains, burred past Sparrow. The dog made a half-hearted snap at the little creature.

The insect zigzagged through the portal. When it was three centimeters into the enclosure, a spear of light from the inner surface of the wall made the fly vanish completely. Only the echoing thunderclap proved that the insect had ever existed.

Sparrow smiled. He rose to his feet. "Time for us to go, dog," he said, slurring the initial words slightly. "Inside, we will ask as guest rights that they feed us."

Dog and master stepped into the courtyard together. Their feet left deep prints in the bare mud.

Sparrow's stride was unsteady for the first few paces. For the rest of the way to the dome, his legs obeyed as though the smith were a creation of his own unsurpassed craftsmanship.

≡ 30 ≡

"THEY AREN'T GOING to wait for us to come to them," said the voice in Hansen's mind with what sounded like satisfaction. *"One of them is headed for us from the other side of the keep."*

Hansen jumped an open patch that he suspected was bottomless mud under a treacherous skin of cypress leaves. He was trying to pretend that the warning had not startled him, but he pushed off too hard and had to twist in the air to keep from falling.

"One?" he asked. He didn't have to vocalize questions to the AI, but it was natural to treat the command helmet as a person.

"One," agreed the helmet. It projected the ghostly monochrome of a hovertank into an apparent 20-cm circle a meter ahead of Hansen.

The image rotated, displaying the traditional three views. The hologram was bright enough for Hansen to pick out details if he so desired, but it didn't block his normal vision. He could continue moving forward if he wished.

"She is female," Third added. The tank was replaced by a view of a youngish woman in uniform. She had no particularly-distinguishing features, except that for Plane Five, she was very slender.

"Enough," Hansen muttered gruffly. Even as the image vanished from his field of view, he went on, "Vector and ETA?"

When he listened carefully, he could hear the roar of the tank's eight fans . . . or maybe that was his imagination.

The blue glow of Keep Starnes' protective field was occasionally visible through the trees three hundred meters away. The magnetic barrier didn't mean safety, but it was safety of a sort. The tank's co-axial machinegun wouldn't be affected, but the plasma weapon couldn't be discharged from or through that shield.

Third projected a schematic map of the immediate area. Hansen's position was a pulsing dot. A broken line worked around from the other side of the keep's huge bulk.

"Several minutes," the artificial intelligence said, *"but I cannot be precise. She is more constrained by the forest than you are, though of course the vehicle is much faster when it has a clear run."*

Hansen jumped, slipped, and dropped to mid-thigh in a pool so clear that he could see the bottom. He swore under his breath as he dragged himself out by a dangling tree root.

He *did* hear the fans.

"You could have entered the keep directly," the command helmet noted smugly.

"That's what they fucking expect me to do!" Hansen snapped.

Except that the woman in the tank either expected *this,* or somebody was playing a hunch. Fortin? That was possible.

"You are afraid that APEX will teach Karring how to use the Matrix and precipitate the Final Day?" the command helmet asked.

Hansen frowned. He hopped onto a fallen log. Rotten wood sagged beneath his boots. "Should I be?" he asked.

"Oh, yes, Commissioner," Third said. *"You should certainly fear that—if you care."*

The soil was firmer. Hansen could see the keep's shield regularly now. A pair of creatures with long, bushy tails chattered from a tree. Their slender bodies dipped forward and rose as part of their display behavior, while their forepaws continued to grip half-shredded pinecones.

"Are you ready?" Hansen shouted. He was three strides from the blue haze, light diffracted by the intense magnetic flux. If Third's electronics needed longer than an eyeblink to come into phase with the field, the command helmet was shit outa luck.

"*I am always ready.*"

Hansen sprinted between a cypress and a pine standing on gnarled black roots like a gigantic spider. His skin tingled at the field's plane of demarcation. The tank must be very close now.

"*To the right,*" the helmet ordered. "*There's a gully. Get into it.*"

"I can't hide from a damned thing with sensors like that bitch'll have!" Hansen shouted. He angled right anyway, running flat out though it meant he stumbled twice. He burst through a tangle of saplings—

And hurtled into a gully, all right, a fucking *river*bed— twenty meters across and five meters down. The bottom was soft mud, gleaming like black pearls because of water standing in low spots.

Hansen tucked and rolled. He was so pumped that he hadn't time to worry that a rock was going to smash his ribs.

You mighta warned me, he thought; but there wasn't much time, not for him or the command helmet. If they both survived, they could chew it over later.

Hansen used the momentum of his fall to fling him upright and running again toward the far bank. It was a perfect maneuver that he couldn't have duplicated in a thousand years on a gymnasium floor.

"*No!*" Third ordered. "*Follow the gully toward the keep. She has lost us for the moment, if you stay out of sight.*"

Hansen grimaced, but he obeyed. He felt as though he were jogging down a main highway on Annunciation at rush hour. The broad gully made him a perfect target if the tank forced its way through the screen of pines as Hansen himself had done.

"*Her sensors are not registering you,*" the command helmet explained in a tone of self-satisfaction. "*I can do nothing with simple optics.*"

Before Hansen could frame the next question—or as he did, thought replacing speech with the AI—Third admitted, "*If she realized what has happened, her vehicle's computer—*" the pejorative overtones the artificial intelligence gave to 'computer' were obvious "—*will be able to predict our course.*"

"Slick work," said Hansen aloud. If the tank driver had gotten this far, she *would* figure out where her quarry had gone; but at least he—he and Third—now had a chance to reach the keep before she caught up with them.

The gully had drained only recently. The bottom was soggy where it wasn't standing water. Rivulets flowed into the main channel from what had obviously been the overflow pools of previous periods.

"What the hell is this place?" Hansen asked.

"*The waste outlet for all of Keep Starnes,*" Third explained. "*They closed the gates when you appeared.*"

"Is that so . . . ?" Hansen murmured. Well, you expect a swamp to stink like a sewer. He had more important things on his mind just now than the muck clinging to his boots and the back of his jumpsuit.

For instance, the footprints crossing the gully ahead of him, left to right. They might have been bear prints, though they probably weren't.

For one thing, there weren't any bears on Plane Five. For another, bears didn't get this big.

Sewers meant nutrients . . . which meant life of all sorts in a concentrated food chain. The top of the chain here seemed to be a mesonychid carnivore. It was five or six meters long, with claws to match the size of its huge feet.

Hansen leaped for a root dangling down into the gully. He raised his grip with the other hand, then used the strength of his shoulders to twist his body back up onto the left bank. He vectored off at an angle to the left.

"*She is coming again,*" Third warned, but the remark was informational rather than a comment on the human's judgment. "*She is following the gully now.*"

They reached the outer skin of the dome. Hansen was breathing through his mouth. The humid air felt soothing to the roughness in his throat.

"*There is a personnel hatch twenty meters to our right,*" Third said. "*Or a vehicle hatch one hundred and seventy meters to the left.*"

Hansen jogged toward the right along the curving wall. Mosses and small plants grew in the detritus that had accumulated on the surface of the armor, but they did nothing to detract from the solidity of the dense metal beneath.

The air vibrated with the sound of the tank's lift fans, amplified by the gully walls. It was going to be close.

"Can she—" Hansen started to ask, then shut off the remainder of the question. Of *course* the tank could climb a five-meter bank. It had gotten down into there to begin with, hadn't it?

"The fans swivel," his command helmet explained without being asked to do so. *"They have sufficient excess power to lift the vehicle at a 70° angle, so long as there is a surface against which the plenum chamber can seal."*

He found the hatch, which was too fucking near the edge of the gully. Within what Hansen judged was a year or so, a maintenance crew had used defoliant spray to clear the immediate area. That looked like the last time the portal had been opened.

The hatch was sealed, as expected, a rectangle with radiused corners two meters by one.

There was no external latch or key plate.

"Put me against the power jack," Third directed crisply. *"At ground level beside the door."*

If the words had been human speech instead of thoughts generated by a machine, Hansen would have said Third was tense. Perhaps that was the listener's projection. . . .

The power jack was a three-prong outlet beneath a sprung cover, intended for the use of maintenance crews. Hansen tore off the command helmet. He felt naked without it.

The jewel on the helmet's forehead winked. Jointed arms extended the way iron filings grow into spikes in a magnetic field. The crystal appendages entered the jack. Hansen expected sparks, but there was no immediate response.

Hansen's body was trembling with adrenaline, but he had nothing to do except wait. A conifer uprooted in a storm lay tilted against several of its fellows nearby. Its sprays of needles were prickly brown; the bark had dried to a fungus-shot gray.

Hansen gripped a wrist-thick branch with both hands. The wood resisted, though fibers crackled as the branch bent. Hansen shouted and tore the limb away.

He turned, flushed with effort and triumph, to see how the helmet was coming with whatever it was doing.

The carnivore whose tracks they had noted lurched up from the gully. Its meter-long skull was almost all jaw. The beast straightened like a cat on a countertop, facing Hansen.

The beast had a brindled coat and legs that seemed rather short for its huge body. Its canines, upper and lower both, were the length of Hansen's index fingers.

Its snarl bathed the human with the effluvia of ancient death.

"Third," Hansen said in a lilting voice pitched to be heard over the predator's threat. "You'd best get that hatch open, or—"

He shouted and thrust out with the brush of dried needles. The beast, startled an instant before its own attack, snapped and caught the branch. Hansen tried to hold on. A quick jerk of the long jaws flung him sideways into the fallen tree.

The mesonychid worried the dead limb for an instant. Despite the size of its skull, the brain box was of reptilian proportions. Hansen staggered upright. The beast—

The beast turned in its own length and lunged toward the bow of the hovertank lifting up from the gully floor at a skew angle.

The carnivore weighed tonnes. The shock of its sudden mass overbalanced the vehicle and sent it skidding down the bank again. The tank's driver fought expertly to keep her vehicle from turning turtle. Her co-ax ripped the unexpected attacker.

Machinery shuddered somewhere in the dome. Third had penetrated the keep's control circuits by sending signals through the disused power jack, but the door was still set as firmly as if it had been cast in one piece with the armored dome around it.

"Third, damn you!" Hansen screamed as he tore off another treelimb, *useless,* even against the carnivore. He could flee through the Matrix and Starnes would win, evil would win, and that wasn't going to happen. Fuck 'em all!

The tank's co-ax used chemical propellant to fire ring penetrators, hollow tubes the size of a man's little finger that punched through armor more effectively than long-rod projectiles of similar mass and velocity. Continuous bursts raked whatever part of the mesonychid was in front of the gun muzzle at the moment. Some of them drilled the body the long way.

The beast continued to snap and struggle. Its snarls were as loud as the roar of the tank's eight lift fans.

The gate at the gully's head, twenty meters broad, rose majestically. Beneath it foamed the stored backlog of Keep Starnes' waste water. Hundreds of thousands of liters emptied into the gully as fast as the huge outlet could dump them.

The first onrush swept the predator's tattered corpse down the gully, biting at the foam. The tank lifted momentarily. When the flood poured over the vehicle's upper deck, the overloaded fans failed in a series of loud reports.

Hansen stared in amazement. Water boiled briefly over the tank's turret; then the flow sank back to a broad stream no more than a meter deep as the storage tanks emptied.

Hansen dropped the treelimb. He rubbed his palms against his thighs. They were sticky with pitch. He reached down for the command helmet and put it back on.

"*I thought,*" said Third, "*that it might be better to deal with what was behind us before we went inside.*"

"I don't second-guess my people," Hansen said. He rubbed his hands again, this time against one another. "So long as it works."

The tank's controls had fried when the drive motors shorted out. As Hansen watched, the turret hatch began to turn slowly open under the operator's muscle power.

≡ 31 ≡

"DURATION EXISTS ONLY in the eight worlds on the surface of the Matrix, Hansen," said Dowson in a sparkle of violet light. His curtained jar sat on the table at the head of the Prince of Simplain's couch. "Within, all times are one time."

Outside the richly-appointed tent, a draft mammoth shrieked to the moon and a dozen of her fellows echoed the call. From a lesser distance came another of the normal noises of an army in its marching camp: two gangs of servants raised their voices in a violent argument. There would be a riot unless nobles intervened quickly to damp down the anger.

"There aren't any guards posted," Hansen said glumly. "Venkatna could hit us with a hundred men, and there wouldn't be a Mirala Confederation left."

"Have some wine, Kommissar," North said, offering a ewer of agate glass. "Anyway, *I've* set guards. You needn't fear that we won't be able to escape into the Matrix if there's a surprise attack."

Because Dowson was present at this dinner in 'Lord Guest's' tent, North and Hansen served themselves. The chirp of female voices beyond a double curtain indicated that North traveled in the full state of a prince of the Southlands, with a harem as well as servants for all other bodily needs.

"What I'm afraid of," Hansen said, "is that there's no way this bunch of clowns can beat the imperial army."

His finger slid his cup of gold-mounted crystal a finger's breadth closer to his dinner companion, signaling North to pour. The serving table between the two dining couches was a round of mountain cedar, polished to bring out the prominent markings.

Very pretty if you liked that sort of thing; and Hansen did, more or less, though his mind didn't dwell on natural luxuries even when he didn't have a fight to prepare for.

"Win or lose," North said with harsh gusto. "It's more souls for us on the Final Day. We'll need them, Hansen."

"We will need," Dowson said in thoughts as cold as the Matrix, "more than we have. More than we can ever have, Captain."

"Excellent wine, this," North said as he swallowed the sip he had been savoring in his mouth. North wore the flowing silk robes suitable for a southern magnate, and he reclined while dining, though there was gray ice in his eye wherever it fell. "It comes from estates of mine near Simplain."

Hansen drank without finesse. Wine and beer were generally safer than water in the inhabited regions of the Open Lands. And they had alcohol in them, which was usually a bad thing . . . but not always, and not just now.

"Are you afraid of it?" he asked abruptly. "Of the end?"

"Not necessarily the end, Commissioner," corrected lime-green thoughts expanding from beside the shrouded container. "The end for us, perhaps, and we see no farther than we live . . . but the Matrix may exist beyond the Final Day, though we no longer observe it."

The sizzle of an arc weapon brought the men to attention. Flickers of light beat through the tent's silken weave.

The light died. An amplified voice shouted. A camp marshal was putting down the servants' quarrel, using his arc as a baton of office to get attention.

North chuckled. "Have you viewed your own death, Hansen?" he asked playfully.

"I don't look forward," Hansen said. He slugged down the rest of his wine, then refilled the cup.

"There is no forward or back in the Matrix," Dowson said in a soft mauve whisper. "There is no duration, Commissioner."

"You're a god," North said harshly. He fixed Hansen with his good eye and the milky globe of the other. "You can either accept that—"

"I'm a man, Captain," Hansen said. "I live life as it *comes,* because the line of it's important even if duration isn't!"

"Yes, you're a man," North sneered. "And by acting like a *man,* you've brought to life the monster that Venkatna's empire now is, haven't you?"

Hansen suddenly relaxed and sank back on his couch. There was a bowl of fruit on the table. He took a peach from the bowl. He toyed with it instead of biting through the soft skin.

"I'm not denying my responsibility, North," Hansen said softly. "I'm here."

North laughed. "You've come here to die, Hansen," he gibed. "You don't think these *clowns* can win. You've said it yourself!"

"You're here too, North," Hansen replied. His voice was toneless and still soft, but his face muscles were settling into planes.

"Oh, I'm here, Kommissar," the one-eyed man said lightly. "And my arc will lift souls from Venkatna's army for my Searchers to reap, never fear. But I won't stand and die when the battle is hopelessly lost."

"You'll stand on the Day, Captain North," Dowson said.

Hansen quirked a smile toward the curtained brain.

"You could bring down Venkatna, Hansen," North offered persuasively.

He lifted the ewer and noted from the weight that it was empty. A wine-thief hung from the flared lip of a footed forty-liter jar behind him, but for the moment the tall god remained on his couch.

"You could tumble the whole kingdom—the *Empire*—into the sea," North continued. "Flood it, shatter it with earthquakes, scour it clean with volcanos. I'd let you, you know. There'll be other battles, other souls than these."

"Never souls enough, Captain . . . ," murmured a bubble of tangerine yellow from the jar.

"When I do what a man does . . . ," Hansen said. He spoke slowly because he was articulating a judgment that he had never before formed in words, even within his own mind. "I make mistakes, I misjudge side-effects. But I can't not act."

He took a bite of the peach and chewed it carefully. Juice ran from the corner of his mouth; he wasn't used to lying on his side as he ate.

North watched him, half smiling.

"If I use the powers that I have *now*," Hansen continued, "my judgment doesn't get better. I do more harm, and more harm yet if I try to straighten out *that* mess. So I won't do that. I'll use what I know."

He set the peach down on the table and flexed his right hand as if there were a gun in it. He smiled back, a wolf to North's craggy eagle, and stood up.

North's laughter boomed out.

"Very well, Kommissar," he said as he rose also. He looked even taller than usual as his head brushed the lamplit expanse of the tent roof. "You follow your devices, and I'll follow mine. Who knows? We may find ourselves at a similar point in the future—"

North stepped toward the room's internal wall.

"—if you survive," he added.

"Thanks for dinner," Hansen said. He considered a moment, then picked up the peach again to finish on his way to his own quarters.

"Unless . . . ," North said as he paused with the silk brocade curtain half-raised " . . . you'd perhaps like another sort of hospitality also? I have one along who looks a great deal like Krita, I believe."

Hansen looked at the taller man; and, very deliberately, took another bite of peach instead of answering. He walked out of the tent, past the pair of guards in battlesuits.

"Surely," North said musingly, "he doesn't think he can correct *all* injustice here on Northworld?"

"He thinks," replied a shimmer of peach-colored light, "that a man could do worse than try."

North thought of Hansen's expression as he left. His face had been composed, his mouth vaguely smiling.

But Hansen's eyes were pits of molten fury.

≡ 32 ≡

HANSEN DIDN'T HAVE to speak aloud to the command helmet, but under the spur of tension he shouted, "Third! Hook to the antennas and take the bastard over!"

Then he jumped to the hovertank's back deck.

The vehicle was disabled; it wouldn't move anywhere under its own power until the burned-out drive fans were replaced. The tank's general systems were another matter.

The surge from shorting motors had tripped breakers and perhaps destroyed some of the circuitry itself, but a vehicle this sophisticated had redundant pathways. If the woman inside reset a switch or two, the automatic weapon which had sawed apart the mesonychid would be ready to repeat the process on Nils Hansen.

The tank was stranded in the gully. Hansen could avoid becoming a target simply by entering the dome through the personnel hatch—

But those who ran Keep Starnes would expect their visitor by that route. Avoiding the obvious was a survival ploy.

"*Staying home in bed is another survival ploy, Commissioner Hansen,*" Third commented acidly.

Hansen's boots hit and skidded sideways, both of them. Slime and water from the flood still pooled on the back deck, making the armor slick as glass.

Hansen snatched at the grab-rail welded to the turret side for the convenience of the crewman boarding through the single turret-roof hatch. His left-handed grip kept him from sliding completely off the tank, but his hip slammed the deck. The impact would have been disabling if his bloodstream hadn't been so charged with adrenaline.

"Sonuvabitch!" Hansen wheezed as he pulled himself up. He seized the hatch's outer undogging handle with his right hand. It rotated the last eighth of a turn to unlatch beneath his palm.

"*Put me down, then,*" Third ordered.

Hansen hung the command helmet from the stub antenna projecting from the top of the turret. He'd obeyed the artificial intelligence's directions without thinking about anything except how he was going to take out the tank crewman.

The club with which Hansen had faced the predator was up the bank, and he hadn't brought a gun or even knife through the Matrix with him. The hatch was a pretty good weapon itself for *this* purpose.

The armored disk started to rise. Hansen poised behind it. When the forward lip was twenty centimeters above the rim, he would slam it back down with the shock of all his weight. The armored bludgeon would crush the crewman's hands and maybe dish his skull—

"I surrender!" called a woman's clear voice through the part-open hatch.

Right. The crew *woman*, Third had said.

"You've beaten me! I'm completely at your mercy! I'm coming out!"

Hansen glared. The hatch was now vertical, his last chance to use it as a weapon, and he *ought* to . . . but instead he straightened and said, "Keep your hands high, and if you've got a gun, so help me—"

He swallowed the rest of the words. She didn't have a gun. She was stark naked.

"To prove that I'm no threat to you," the woman said demurely.

The command helmet clicked and sputtered. Antennas are designed to accept data and transmit it through a distribution apparatus. Third used the tank's common link to enter the vehicle's information processing network. The helmet now reset the operating system to suit Hansen's purposes. The tank was as thoroughly disarmed as if the component parts of its guns were slung out into the gully.

"I am Lisa, Lady Starnes," the woman said. "My father is the count."

Lisa looked like a parody of *The Birth of Venus* as she climbed from the hatch. She was a slight woman for Plane Five, though she would have passed for stocky in the Open Lands. Cropped brown hair, small breasts; pale lips and nipples.

A look of anticipation rather than fear, but maybe fear.

Hair-fine crystalline probes withdrew into the command helmet. Hansen donned Third again.

"*I have dealt with it,*" stated the cold machine thoughts.

"I'm at your mercy," Lisa Starnes repeated forcefully. "I can't prevent you from raping me. The others are waiting for you inside, but they won't be able to interfere with you here."

Hansen shivered. He'd once met—very briefly—a man who liked the bodies of those he'd freshly killed. That acquaintance had lasted little longer than the time it took to take up three kilos of trigger pressure.

Lisa turned Hansen's stomach about as bad, though he didn't guess she was hurting anybody else. . . .

"Let's go," he said mentally to Third. He jumped down from the vehicle's deck.

Waste water gurgled thirty or forty centimeters up the skirts of the disabled tank. It was a hindrance for walking but not a problem. Hansen could see an inspection way built into the side of the outfall line, above the current flow level. He'd follow that for a distance, then have Third find him an access hatch well inside the keep.

"Wait!" the woman shouted. "Where are you going?"

"Find somebody else, lady," Hansen muttered. "I'm not interested even a little bit."

The echoing pipe slurred and deepened his words; he doubted that Starnes' daughter could hear him.

"You should take the opportunity, Commissioner," the AI said. *"You may not get another one if you persist in this endeavor."*

"I'll want you to find us a way out of here in a hundred meters or so," Hansen said instead of responding to the—joke? Was the machine making jokes? "I don't want them to figure a way to flood—"

The tank's hatch clanged shut again. A mechanical whine indicated that the vehicle's systems had been reset.

"You *did* disconnect the armament controls, didn't you?" Hansen said.

He jumped onto the slimy metal ladder leading to the walkway. A blind man couldn't miss a target in a tunnel, even a tunnel this big. The walls would channel shots until they found flesh.

"Not exactly," said Third.

A breechblock rang as Lisa charged the tank's co-ax.

"Shit!" Hansen shouted and vaulted to the walkway. If he lay flat, he might be covered until ring penetrators chewed away the—

There was a flood of orange light and a huge explosion. The shockwave flung Hansen down, but he was already diving and the walkway's slickly-wet surface saved him from the pavement rash he would otherwise have acquired.

He looked over his shoulder. The tank's hull spewed flame from the turret ring and all eight fan ducts. The turret was gone, blown somewhere beyond Hansen's present field of view.

"I set it so that the whole power supply would short through the hull if anyone tried to close a gunswitch, Commissioner," Third said. *"Are you satisfied?"*

Hansen's ears rang. He got to his feet. "Any one you walk away from," he muttered.

He thought he smelled burning pork; but that might have been his imagination.

≡ 33 ≡

"HELLO THE HOUSE!" roared Sparrow in a voice loud enough to wake the stones from their rest. He waited.

The smith had regained his strength from proximity to his goal—and the momentary likelihood of action. He was living on his nerves and he knew it; but he knew also that he could go on like this with no degradation in his performance until he dropped.

For now, Sparrow stood with his muscular arms akimbo and his chin slightly raised. The dagger in his belt had scales carved from dimetrodon canine and wound with gold wire. The hilt made a show in the sunlight to rival the ovoid glitter of the probability generator on the other side.

Sparrow looked strong and smart and utterly confident. He was all those things, and ruthless besides.

The smith's dog walked an aimless figure-8 in the vicinity of the dome's entrance. She sniffed determinedly, but the mud was absolutely barren.

The door was pentagonal, a facet of the dome rather than a section of a facet. It opened abruptly, inward and down at a 30° angle because the side forming the jamb wasn't vertical.

The maid with her hand on the door switch stared open-mouthed at Sparrow. "Who are—" she began. Then she gasped and blurted instead, "You don't have a collar!"

She was a tall woman, only a hand's breadth shorter than

the smith. Her black hair was caught up with pins and ivory combs, and her fingers touched the black plastic ring around her own neck.

"I'm not a slave," Sparrow said. He stepped through the angled doorway before the maid took it into her mind to close the panel again. "My name is Sparrow, and I'm the son of a king. Who are you?"

"No!" the maid said and put her foot out. The dog followed Sparrow anyway, tracking footprints. Her tail wagged further speckles of mud across the antiseptically-white anteroom.

The woman grimaced in amazement, then looked at Sparrow. "I'm Olrun," she said. "I was captured when I was a child. But— you're from the Open Lands and you're not a slave?"

"I'm a messenger," the smith said as he looked around him. "From my master Saburo to the Princess Mala."

The anteroom was featureless—except for the mud, the dog's and that from Sparrow's own sandals. The ceiling and walls were of a thin material. It looked translucent, but it probably generated a soft illumination of its own rather than transmitting light from another source. For the room to stay this clean, most visitors must ride their skimmers directly to the dome's entrance.

Though mostly, Mala must not have visitors.

"Saburo?" Olrun said. "The *god* Saburo? But you—I mean, I don't dare disturb milady now, she's meditating."

Sparrow snorted. "Is she so harsh a mistress, then? Never mind. I'll protect you."

"No, she's very . . . ," the maid said. She patted a curl already precisely skewered by a pin of dark-veined wood. "She couldn't be nicer, really. Much gentler than anyone I knew before the slavers came . . . though I was very young."

Sparrow guessed Olrun was about thirty now, though it was hard to tell in the present context. She wore a robe of brown silk with a white sash, a careful centimeter or two shorter than her white undergarment. The fabric was of excellent quality, but its softness was out of place on a big-boned, strong-featured woman like her.

Olrun could have come from the kingdom of Sparrow's father. . . .

"It's just . . . ," the maid said musingly. Her eyes were on the visitor, but she hadn't fully comprehended his presence yet. "When we were at Nainfari's hold, there were lots of people around—and I was Princess Mala's maid, so nobody bothered me if I—"

Her smile was briefly tender.

"Unless I wanted it." The woman truly focused on Sparrow as a person. The smile that coalesced on her lips was frankly speculative. "But since milady had her bower built out here, three years and more, I . . . haven't seen many people."

The smith returned the smile, but anyone who could read his expression could hear a tree thinking. "That will change," he said and started for the rectangular doorway into the dome's interior.

"But—" Olrun objected. She stepped in front of Sparrow. The bitch barked happily at the movement. She trotted through the door, her nails clicking on the hard floor.

"Oh, North and Penny save us!" the maid cried as she turned to catch the dog.

Sparrow followed the bitch and the woman. He was smiling faintly again.

The center of the dome was a large room suffused with gentle light. A slender woman was seated cross-legged on a mat of russet fibers. She scrambled to her feet as the dog tried to lick her cheek. The dog's tail no longer slung mud, but its furious wagging knocked over foliage arranged in a vase on the low table.

"What?" Princess Mala cried. She looked shocked to the point of fainting. Her eyes stared from their black make-up like aiming circles on the pure white skin.

"Oh, milady—" Olrun said.

"Princess," Sparrow said in a rumbling voice that over-whelmed those of the women, "I bring you the greetings of my master, the god Saburo."

Mala straightened. The room's only furnishings were the mat, the table, and a featureless white cabinet behind the princess. Odd angles and the lack of shadows on the internally-lighted walls made it difficult to judge the room's size and shape.

"How did you get here?" Mala demanded in a shrill voice. The fabric of her robes grew brighter, layer by layer, from the olive-drab coloration of the outermost.

"I walked, princess, and I rode," Sparrow said. "My master sent me to bring you to his palace so that he can honor you by making you his wife."

Sparrow stood like a bear on its hind legs. His visage was neither angry nor threatening, but it was as coldly relentless as the advance of a glacier.

Olrun watched the big man without expression of her own. She knelt by the door, holding the dog with an arm around its chest. The dog licked the maid's wrist as Olrun picked dried mud from the animal's fur with her free hand.

"I don't want a husband!" Mala blazed. "Certainly not—"

Her face blanked. "Where did you get that knife?" she asked softly.

"I found it on the way," Sparrow said. His voice rumbled like steam building deep in the earth. By contrast, the android female chirped like a wren on the geyser's sulphurous rim. "Princess—"

"That knife was my brother's! You've killed my brother, haven't you?"

"Princess," the smith went on, "my master would like me to bring you willingly to him. But my *duty* is to bring you . . . and so I shall."

"How could you have killed Morfari?" Mala whispered in wonder. "And his whole band?"

"Saburo offers you wealth and power beyond your dreams, princess," Sparrow said. Her questions weren't really directed to him, and he had no intention of departing from the grinding certainty of his demands anyway. "He will—"

Olrun continued to stroke the dog as she watched Sparrow. The slight, crooked smile on the maid's face may have been unconscious.

"I don't want any man!" the princess said. "I'm happy here!"

She added with a vindictive glare at her visitor, "My father will kill you, you realize. You'll die in the way you deserve!"

Sparrow laced his fingers together and stretched his arms

toward the princess. The calluses on his palms were as coarse as treebark.

"Lady princess," the smith said, "my master is a *god*. The emissary a god sends will accomplish his task no matter what must be done along the way. Slave killed or prince, or—"

Sparrow smiled. His expression was not a threat, any more than the maelstrom threatens as it sweeps down a ship for all the screams and prayers of the crew.

"Or the king himself, princess."

Mala stared at the big man. The only sound in the room was the skritch of the maid's fingers on the dog's hide.

"*Watch*—" Olrun cried.

Mala turned like fluff spinning in the breeze. The cabinet behind her was the size and shape of a coffin on end. She stepped *through* its face—

And vanished, woman and cabinet together, as if there had never been anything between Sparrow and the white space of the wall beyond.

≡ 34 ≡

THE COURIER, PASSED by the guard and Venkatna's advisors, eyed the emperor hesitantly.

"Well, go on!" Kleber whispered hoarsely. "Deliver your message!"

"Your majesty," the courier said, running his words together as if he hoped they would prevent him from seeing what he thought he saw. "Duke Justin informs you that the Mirala kings are marching with hundreds of warriors maybe a thousand they're looting as they pass but they seem to be making for the capital Duke Justin thinks six days maybe less."

The man was no court messenger. He wore back-country garb, the cape of a dire wolf and aurochs-hide chaps stained by the froth of the ponies he had ridden hard enough to reach Frekka in a day and a half.

Venkatna's audience hall was like nothing the courier had ever imagined.

The Web's sweeping curves were meaningless to anyone who hadn't been told of the device's purpose. The courier's first thought was that it was a cage, a prison, for the two emaciated women who sat on benches within the construct. They were being fed milk and soup by palace slaves who reached within the glimmering loops. Though the Web had gaps through which those within could exit, the women looked barely able to stand, much less flee.

Other slaves cleaned with mops and rags the women and the benches on which they sat. The women had not been permitted to leave the enclosed area to relieve themselves.

That was disconcerting to find in a palace . . . and the fear which marked the imperial advisors made the courier uncomfortable too, though it was a normal enough attitude among those forced to stand very close to the great. Neither of those things bothered the courier as much as the emperor and his companion did.

"Your majesty," said Duke Bontempo. The fat old man faced Venkatna, but his eyes were almost closed. The clerestory windows had faded to gray bars and the lamps were as yet unlit. "Do you wish to accompany your forces to meet these . . . ?"

Bontempo spoke softly, as though afraid of rousing the emperor from his—reverie?

Venkatna sat in a cushioned armchair. A robe of marmot skins lay over his legs. His hair had been left untrimmed longer than had the courier's own, and the stringiness of the imperial beard indicated why Venkatna had always before gone clean-shaven.

He held his wife's hand and stroked it gently. The Empress Esme's cheeks were sunken and there was a bluish pallor to her skin. She was obviously dead.

Venkatna's eyes focused on Bontempo, then flicked to the courier with a frown, as if wondering who he was. The courier stood perfectly still. He stared at a point on the far wall, just above the emperor's shoulder.

The audience hall contained three broad fireplaces connected to flues and chimneys. No fires were lighted. The courier began to tremble at his first experience of the imperial court.

Venkatna looked at Duke Bontempo and said, "We'll meet them here at Frekka. Order the forces to marshal at the palace barracks."

"They're in poor order, the Mirala troops," Trigane offered. He based his statement as much on past experience as on his hurried questions to the courier at the door to the hall. "A bunch of farmers, really. I could lead the frontier levies in a night attack and settle matters quickly."

"No!" shouted Venkatna with unexpected violence. He half rose from his chair, and his left hand tightened on that of his dead wife. "I'll lead the army. It was while meeting that Mirala scum at Heimrtal that my Esme took cold, you know. She hasn't been right since."

Duke Bontempo's eyes squeezed firmly shut. From his expression, one might have thought the old man was being disemboweled.

The emperor settled again on his seat. A look of ordinary concern passed quickly across his face. He glanced—barely an eye-flick—toward the corpse on the bed beside him.

"That will give us the greatest time to gather our forces," Venkatna went on in normal tones. "We shouldn't be overconfident, even against Mirala farmers—"

His voice rose. Tendons began to show in his throat.

"—who will die to the *man* and the *slave*—"

He was shouting.

"—and the very beasts that they bring against me in their pack train! Die! And I will kill them!"

No one spoke or moved.

Venkatna relaxed again. He even managed a faint smile. "I . . . ," he said mildly. "Well, there's no advantage to us in stunts and night attacks. We will win as we've always won, through training and discipline. Until I've fulfilled my destiny. And laid the whole world at my darling's feet."

His hand stroked Esme's cold cheek, but he did not look at her.

Duke Bontempo bowed. "I'll see to gathering our forces, your majesty," he said. He strode out of the room, calling for his aides before he was through the doorway.

The courier winced. If he had been ready for it, he could have left the hall in Bontempo's wake. Now he wasn't sure if he dared walk out without asking permission. He was *absolutely* sure that he didn't want to open his mouth without a direct order to do so.

Venkatna suddenly lifted his hand and stared at the fingertips. He looked over at Esme. His complexion sank through sullen pallor before flooding back in an apoplectic flush. "Mold!" he shouted. "They've let mold grow!"

The emperor jumped to his feet. The fur slipped, tangling his legs but ignored. For the first time Venkatna seemed to notice that the women within the Web were awake and the device's fabric did not glow with its own power.

"Get back!" Venkatna screamed. "You're letting her—you're—*get back*!"

"Excellency . . . ?" one of the women begged. Some of the milk she had drunk dribbled from the corner of her mouth. "Please, we must have rest, just a little rest."

"So cold . . . ," whispered the other woman. Her eyes were glazed and unfocused.

"Get back to your work!" the emperor cried. "I order you! I *order* you!"

The face of the woman who had been able to plead slackened. "Your orders are our fate," she said. Her voice was so soft that the courier would not have been able to hear except for the breathless silence in which all others in the hall held themselves.

"Your orders are our fate," repeated her companion. They lay down on the benches as though they were entering their tombs.

"WHO WOULD HAVE thought it?" Lena murmured in a gluti-
nous, good-humored voice.

The image of Lisa's vehicle exploding rolled in looped
slow motion on a corner of Lena's screen. The tank's outline
brightened and blurred as current surged through it. Steam
bubbled from the water flowing around the skirts.

"Karring!" Count Starnes snarled. "Did Lisa get out? She
had plenty of time to get out, didn't she?"

The image of the hatch blew off, puffing a perfect smoke
ring into the sky. A heavier explosion bulged the hull's armored
flanks. The turret lifted a hundred meters in the air, spinning like
a flipped coin. The solid casting came down in the distant forest,
while steam roared to cool and shroud the glowing hull.

"Who'd have thought it?" Lena repeated, chuckling over the
utter dissolution of her sister.

"Milord," said the chief engineer in a distant voice, "we'll
be able to determine casualties when we've accomplished our
purpose. For the moment, the target is still loose."

Karring sat at an outstation in the Citadel's rotunda instead
of his normal lair deep within APEX. The device he had
created to modulate the Matrix hung in the air above him.
On the chief engineer's console, the Fleet Battle Director used
color and three dimensions to stimulate the greater ambiance
in which the intruder could move whenever he chose—

But he *didn't* choose. Without further data, not even APEX could make Karring's trap perfect.

"Another skinny one," Lena said. "But a clever little bastard, isn't he, boys?"

Her console displayed a full groundplan of Keep Starnes at the intruder's present level. Overlaid on the schematic were visuals of Lisa's death and—across the main screen—an image of Hansen in the waste outlet. The fabric of Keep Starnes was woven with sensors to determine the health and status of every portion of the keep's systems. A Fleet Battle Director was capable of converting heat, pressure and vibration into a three-dimensional picture—

So Lena could watch a stocky, filth-smeared man advancing relentlessly into the heart of the keep.

"I'm sure she got out before the—the explosion," Count Starnes muttered.

"What's he doing now, Lena?" whispered Voightman, the lover in iridescent posing briefs, in the ear of the count's surviving daughter.

"What are you going to do to *him*?" asked Plaid from Lena's other side. As usual, his costume involved studded leather and decorated pistols.

"Watch and see, dearie," Lena said as she reached up without looking to massage Plaid's bulging groin. "First we close the outflow again . . ."

Plaid hooked his thumbs in his groin cup to evert it and display himself to his mistress, but Lena's attention had returned fully to her workstation. The shudder of the waste gate slamming at the woman's direction could be felt through bedrock to the Citadel if one knew what to expect.

"I don't see why it opened in the first place," said Count Starnes. Starnes shook his head at memories which replayed as surely in his mind as they did on Lena's console.

"Because . . . ," said Karring. The chief engineer was so concentrated on his own screen that he didn't recognize his master's question as rhetorical. "All the keep's systems are interconnected. A power cable, a door control—APEX itself, though APEX is protected. He's using the system's own pathways to introduce commands."

The intruder stopped. He leaned his helmeted forehead against the tunnel's dripping wall. The waterlevel in the main channel was rising, though it was still well below the walkway.

"What's he doing?" Lena muttered. "There's nothing there but blank concrete."

Voightman preened and nuzzled closer to his mistress. Lena appeared oblivious to Voightman and the fact she had echoed his words of a moment before. Sweat gleamed on his body, from anticipation and the heat which radiated when the console worked at full capacity. Droplets splashed onto the gleaming rhodium plate of the workstation.

APEX threw the answer across Lena's display as a line of lime-green block letters which contrasted with both underlayers:

SUBJECT'S COMMAND HELMET IS EMITTING ULTRASONICS AT THE SYMPATHETIC FREQUENCY OF

Hansen's image stepped back. He kicked the tunnel wall with a bootheel. A one-by-two-meter section of cast plastic collapsed into powder.

"What?" cried Starnes' daughter.

THE POLYMER PLUG WHICH WAS INSERTED INTO THE OUTFLOW PIPE AT THE CLOSE OF KEEP CONSTRUCTION.

"That's not on my plans!" Lena shouted. "How did he know that there was a sealed tunnel there? His plans can't be better than mine!"

"Perhaps he's echo-sounding," Karring murmured as the shape and colors on his display changed almost imperceptibly.

THE SUBJECT IS NOT ECHO-SOUNDING, replied the Fleet Battle Director.

Lena angrily stabbed at her manual controls. She was too angry to limit herself to mental input. Though her wrists were bloated white sausages, her fingers were surprisingly delicate. They shifted the layers of schematic and simulacrum to follow the intruder through the ancient construction boring. Hansen's image lost some definition.

Karring's face suddenly froze. "For god's sake, woman!" he blurted.

He caught himself and resumed, "That is—milady? You've opened the outlet gate again, haven't you? If the level in the tunnel rises much further while this hole is open, it will drain down. We don't know precisely down *where*."

Lena swore. A fleck of light on her schematic switched from yellow to green, lost in the mass of detail to anyone but an expert like the huge woman herself. The vague ringing of the pumps changed.

GATE IS OPEN, APEX responded across Karring's display in response to the chief engineer's surreptitious question.

The emotional temperature in the Citadel had changed. Plaid and Voightman were nervous. They didn't understand what was happening, only that something had gone wrong for their mistress; and they knew Lena well enough to understand how dangerous she could be when she was angry.

"I don't see how you can raise a door through a power socket," Count Starnes muttered as he wrung his hands together. "And Lisa . . ."

"If there weren't a connection between the electrical system and the gate motors, the motors wouldn't *work*, would they?" Karring snapped. Only the fact that his master listened with no more of his brain free than the chief engineer spoke saved Karring's life at that moment.

"Now, the computing power that can trace the pathway and counterfeit the proper instructions, *that* is very interesting," the chief engineer added more calmly.

"He's reached Level FF," Lena announced. "He's coming out through a ceiling vent in the main auditorium on that level. Now I'll get him."

"Now!" Voightman repeated in a husky whisper. Plaid didn't speak. He was slowly masturbating himself through his leather briefs.

The image above Lena's schematic sharpened: there were visual inputs in the large room as well as the wide variety of other sensors by which APEX had tracked the intruder thus far.

A grating fell away. Hansen followed it. He landed on his toes and kept his balance after the drop.

Moving swiftly but with no sign of panic, the intruder crossed to a door and left the auditorium. The cameras tracked him down a corridor of closed doors.

"Where are the personnel?" Count Starnes asked in surprise. "FF40 is troop leaders' quarters. There should be someone out, surely?"

For a moment, no one answered. Lena hissed a curse and made a manual correction with her controls.

"Ah . . . ," said Karring. He nodded cautiously toward Lena. "Your daughter has ordered all personnel to their quarters and locked them in. I'm not sure . . . ?"

"Now!" Lena snarled. Blast doors slammed down to seal off the hundred-meter section of corridor through which Hansen strode. The ceiling vents pivoted shut. Dense yellow gas poured from the floor louvers.

"Halons to suffocate flame," the fat woman chortled. "They'll suffocate him, too!"

"His helmet has provided him with filters," Karring noted in a distant voice.

The intruder rested his helmeted forehead against a switch-plate controlling the corridor lights.

"He won't be able to—" Lena said. The blast door slid sideways, delayed only by the inertia of its great mass.

The Fleet Battle Director followed Hansen as he slipped through before the barrier was fully open. Water gurgled from a 10-cm wall outlet, onto the floor of the next section of corridor.

"What are you doing, Lena?" Count Starnes asked in puzzlement.

"I'm not doing it!" his daughter replied. "This *bastard* has opened the standpipe valves! The vents will flood if I don't keep them closed. I'll kill him for what he's doing to my system!"

The intruder entered an elevator, then brought his helmet in contact with the controls. The cage began to drop. It wasn't coupled, as it should have been, to another cage. This bank of elevators stopped two levels up from the Citadel.

"Wait," the count said sharply. "He's coming this way. That's what we want him to do. We'll simply let him come."

"I want him to come here through his *Matrix*," Karring objected. "Remember, we haven't had half a dozen visits from this one to refine our calculations, as we did with Fortin."

The chief engineer licked his lips nervously. "I think we need to release the personnel and set the mechanical locks. No matter how powerful his command helmet's computing capability, it won't be able to work a manually-set bolt on the opposite side of a barrier."

"No," said Lena as her schematic shifted to a new level.

"Milady, we *must*—" Karring began.

Lena moved with the sudden smoothness of a whale broaching. She drew the pistol from the holster slung to her couch and sent a bolt of charged particles toward Karring's head.

The chief engineer ducked at the first motion. A bank of imaging controls behind him went white and slumped as the bolt's thunderclap rocked the Citadel.

"Daughter!" the count snapped.

Lena dropped her pistol onto the floor of her console. The weapon's glowing muzzle discolored a patch of the plating. The air was sulphurous with the reek of the discharge.

Lena resumed tracking her target. "*I* will kill him," she growled to herself. "When he leaves the elevator. I will!"

"Yes . . . ," Voightman purred as he rubbed his groin against the back of his mistress' couch.

≡ 36 ≡

OLRUN'S FACE WENT white when her mistress disappeared. Sparrow began to chuckle.

The maid was already on her knees. She bowed her forehead to the floor and said, "Milord, milord! I wasn't a part of that. I didn't help her to, to . . ."

Sparrow's dog whined. She licked the woman's cheek and ear in concern.

The smith bent and touched Olrun's shoulder to guide her upright. "I didn't think it was your doing, lady. Do you—"

He smiled as Olrun rose at his touch. She was very nearly as tall as he was; and solidly built for a woman—though Sparrow was massive for a man.

"—know where it is your mistress might have gone, though?"

The maid shook her head miserably. "I'd never asked about the cabinet," she said. "It came from Nainfari's palace with us, but I'd never seen it do anything. It was just—"

She waved at the blank white walls and the overturned foliage. "Just decoration, I thought. I don't understand why she lives in a place so bleak when she's a princess."

Sparrow laughed again with grim amusement. "She'll get along well with my master."

Olrun raised an eyebrow.

"Oh, yes," Sparrow said. "She'll come to my master. I was sent to arrange that."

The maid smiled minusculy. "That will be a change for Princess Mala," she said with a perfect absence of inflexion. "She has always done what she wishes . . . and only what she wishes."

Sparrow touched Olrun's shoulder again, the way he might have petted his dog in affection or for reassurance. "Do you think you could find us some food, lady?" he asked.

"Of course," Olrun said as she started out of the room. She paused. "But it won't be real food like you're used to," she warned. "The meat hasn't any proper fat to it."

"That's all right," the smith replied. "In hot lands like these, you couldn't keep rich food down anyway. You'll learn that when you travel more."

The maid left the room with a vague smile playing over her lips. The dog followed her to the open doorway, then turned back to Sparrow and whined.

Sparrow got out his mirror. After a moment, the bronze face clouded. It cleared in a view of Princess Mala, huddled against a background of gray mist.

The vectoring bead on the mirror's rim was green. The smith walked slowly around the spot where Mala had vanished. The bead rotated around the metal rim, indicating a point in the center of the empty floor.

Sparrow chuckled again. He lowered his bulk onto the table carefully to be sure that the flimsy-looking piece of furniture would support him. The legs and paper-thin surface were stronger than they appeared. It was like sitting on a solid block of glass.

There was nothing wrong with the craftsmen here on Plane Three, though their techniques were not those the smith himself used.

Olrun bustled back with a platter. On it were a stew of boiled roots and a rack of edaphosaur ribs from which ladylike portions had already been carved. "What sort of utensils do you want, milord?" she asked.

"Nothing wrong with my fingers the last I checked," the big man replied. "You've been living among frogs in a swamp for too long, my girl."

The maid blushed and set the platter down beside him.

Sparrow gripped adjacent ribs with either hand and broke off the endmost. He tossed the smaller portion to his dog, then began gnawing the remainder of the roast himself. "It's hungry work, the job I've been doing," he commented to Olrun.

The maid's eye fell on the seeming handmirror which rested on Sparrow's lap. Mala's face stared from the bronze surface. The black eyes of the princess were calm but unfocused.

"Oh," Olrun cried. "You've found the mistress! Where was she?"

Sparrow cracked the rack's chine with a thrust of his thumbs. He dropped the rib that he had mostly cleared. The dog sniffed the new offering, then returned to the meatier portion she had started on.

"The princess is in the Matrix," the smith said. "Between planes. She hasn't traveled anywhere, she's just crawled into a hole."

He snorted. "To think that anybody would try to hide from *me* in the Matrix! Me, Sparrow the Smith!"

A tag of flesh hung down from the end of the roast Sparrow was worrying. Olrun tugged the bit of meat loose between her thumb and forefinger then dropped it into her mouth.

"Would you like to bathe?" she asked without looking at the smith directly.

Sparrow shrugged. "It'll be the same mud going in the opposite direction. There'll be time enough to clean off when I have the princess in my master's hands."

He glanced sidelong toward Olrun. "There'll be time enough for a lot of things, I think."

Olrun smiled without meeting the smith's eyes. "You'll go after her, then, Master Sparrow?" she asked.

Sparrow set the meat back on the planter and picked up the container of vegetables. They were still hot, hotter than comfortable. He slurped a little of the broth from the edge of the container.

He grinned at the maid. "No," he said judiciously. "I'll bring her back here. In good time. But first I'll give the princess a lesson about running from *me*."

The bitch looked up at the note she heard in Sparrow's voice. When she was sure nothing was intended for the immediate present, she went back to her bone. Her back teeth splintered the edaphosaur rib with a series of short, crunching sounds, like the *clock/clock* of a mason's hammer.

When Sparrow had finished his meal and washed it down with drafts of brandy distilled from cycad hearts, he lay on the cold stone floor. His eyes glazed.

Beside him, Olrun began to groom the dog.

Time meant nothing to Mala *here*. Often she entered this state to meditate in perfect nothingness. Some day, she thought, she would decide to remain forever in this gray perfection, free of the nagging asymmetries of present existence.

The stranger's intrusion, the *smith's* intrusion, was intolerable. It should not have happened, so here in the featureless realm of the ideal it had not happened. Nothing could touch her. Nothing existed outside herself, nothing moved—

Something moved.

At first Mala thought it was her hammering heart that caused the sensation. Nothing *could*—

But the grayness had shape now; beyond the strait confines of her cabinet was a plain of stark outlines.

Icy stalagmites rising from an icy floor. Slime molds the size of men, motionless all around her. Mala stared. On all sides the same.

Her feet edged to the center of her immaterial enclosure so that no part of her body was closer to the edge than any other.

The figures shifted at the infinite slowness with which constellations wheel in the heavens, turning their faces toward the girl in their midst.

A mountain loomed on the distant horizon. Mala stared at it for an unimaginable time in order to avoid watching the nearer figures; but as she looked, the crags and fissures ceased to be geological occurrences. The mountain wore the lineaments of a human face.

She gasped and spun around. A stalagmite of blue ice was pressed toward her. She started backward.

It was her brother, Morfari. Half his skull had been burned away.

Mala shrieked and closed her eyes. Her universe dived, then spun vertiginously. Light flashed. She threw herself forward, screaming, and sprawled onto the floor of her bower on Plane Three.

Olrun, her fingers tangled in the neck ruff of a brown dog, stared at her mistress, while Sparrow the Smith groaned as he returned from another frozen plunge into the Matrix.

≡ 37 ≡

HANSEN PAUSED A half second after the elevator door purred open. The air was muggy—warmer than expected in the climate-controlled keep, and very humid.

He stepped into the corridor. It was empty, as usual.

"*Wait*," Third ordered.

Hansen's feet held in place as though tack-welded to the dull blue carpet. His mind was balanced on a glass spike, tilting at the weight of a thought and prepared to free-fall if the support shattered. Hansen's head continued to swivel as he absorbed sensory cues.

All the hard surfaces within Keep Starnes vibrated to a single frequency, as though they were parts of a living cell. The residents must grow used to it; Hansen, coming from outside with his senses stropped to a fine edge on adrenaline, was constantly aware of the greasy quiver.

Air moved up from the floor vents and down again through intakes offset in the ceiling. The ventilation system was working normally, so the raised humidity didn't result from a malfunction there.

Hansen wasn't about to believe in a normal glitch in the keep's infrastructure anyway. Not now.

There wasn't a soul walking the halls. A child's ball lay near the edge of the carpet, abandoned in the owner's haste to get under cover.

"*She is raising the humidity to provide a proper ground,*"

Third said with obvious satisfaction. *"The door at the end of the corridor is connected to a high-amperage four-kilovolt line."*

Hansen sauntered forward. The rotunda and the elevators that served the Citadel were on the other side of that door. "Suggestions?" he asked.

"She expects me to enter the control system through the switchplate at the end of the corridor," the artificial intelligence replied. *"It is electrified also. Bring that toy ball close to me."*

Hansen obeyed without comment. The ball was hollow plastic and the size of a grapefruit. Swirls of pale green and pale blue patterned its surface. The toy was the first sign of frivolity he had seen within the arid corridors of Keep Starnes.

"She?" he asked.

A crystalline blade, as narrow as a hair, extended from the jewel over Hansen's forehead. Its tip probed the ball. *"Her name is Lena,"* Third said. The mental voice lacked any of the overtones which would have suggested interest. *"She is a daughter of Count Starnes."*

The helmet offered at the corner of Hansen's view the hologram image of a woman. Lena did not so much look fat as she appeared to be a sea creature, rolling on a self-shaping couch which supplied the support of a fluid medium.

The blade finished its operations. The ball was slit two-thirds of the way around its circumference. The halves flopped loosely, though they were still joined.

Hansen suddenly laughed. "Are you a weapon, Third?" he asked. "Did I cheat the terms Count Starnes set?"

"Is your brain a weapon, Commissioner Hansen?" the artificial intelligence responded tartly.

"On a good day, Third," Hansen said. "On a good day."

He bent down and added, "Help me get this floor vent loose. It's graphite. It'll conduct just fine."

Hansen tugged against the louvers to stress the patches of hardened adhesive which attached the vent to the ducting. The command helmet extended a probe to touch the composite material, then fed in pulses of high-amplitude ultrasound. As the harmonics reached critical frequency, the adhesive vibrated into dust motes. The tacks failed one after another.

Hansen lifted the grate. It was rectangular, a meter by twenty centimeters. Long enough to reach from the door to the switchplate, and massive enough to carry the current for at least a time.

Hansen shifted so that he held the grating with his right hand alone. He gripped the graphite composite between insulating layers of the sectioned ball.

With that much current connected to the switchplate, Third couldn't use it for access to the door controls. The AI hadn't explained its plan to Hansen; but as Hansen had said, *on a good day*, and this was a day that had waited too long.

Using the ball as an insulating mitt, Hansen extended one corner of the grating so that it touched the metal-faced blast door. The fat blue spark and *pop*! made Hansen jump even though he knew to expect it. He swung forward to bring the far corner of the meter-long plate in contact with the switchplate on the corridor wall.

Electricity roared like the sky tearing open.

Hansen stepped back. His hair stood on end.

The grating remained in place. Current had welded the ends into the structure of the door and wall. The remains of the plastic ball stuck to the louvers, melted there by resistance-generated heat in the first fraction of a second. The graphite fibers glowed white, and the epoxy which they stiffened sublimed off in the black curls.

There was a bang from inside the heavy door. A rectangle of foul-smelling smoke spurted from around the panel. It mushroomed upward.

The snarl of electricity died as suddenly as if a switch had been thrown—as, in a manner of speaking, one had. The enormous wattage had burned through its conductor in a fashion that neither Third nor Starnes' daughter could bridge.

A yellow-orange ball about the size of a man's head sprang from the switchplate. It rolled down the center of the corridor, hissing and emitting faint blue sparks. After a few seconds, the ball turned 90° and vanished through a closed door.

Hansen let his breath out. The circulation system was running at full capacity, but the hall was gray with bitter smoke.

"You'll have to slide the door open manually, Commissioner Hansen," Third said.

Hansen gripped the handle and braced himself. "Don't s'pose you've welded it shut, do you?" he muttered.

"I do not. Anyway, we could go around."

Hansen straightened the leg he had braced against the corridor wall. The blast door moved suddenly. Only inertia had held it in place. The grate, burned to ash and hairs of graphite, fell to the carpet when its corner broke free of the door.

A gush of air from the rotunda—scrubbed and textured by machines, but fresh as a sea breeze compared to the throbbing hallway behind—massaged Hansen's lungs. His legs felt suddenly weak.

"Have you had enough of this gaming, Commissioner?" Third asked coolly.

Hansen leaned against the wall of the rotunda. A stench of ozone and superheated polymers drifted from the corridor. He hadn't had enough ambition to slide the blast door shut behind him.

He walked toward the elevators in the center of the circular room. Every step away from the poisoned atmosphere brightened his mood and strengthened him.

"Yeah," Hansen said. "End it now."

He didn't have to be told the drill. He knelt with his head close to the elevator call-pad. His eyes roved around the empty room.

There was nothing to see. The carpet had been replaced in sections, leaving some patches brighter than others. The walls' luster had dimmed from ages of use and washing.

Above Hansen's eyes, limbs extended from the gray jewel and passed signals into the controls of Keep Starnes.

The elevator cage opened. *"Time to go, Commissioner Hansen,"* the command helmet said.

Hansen got into the cage. "What did you do?" he asked as the elevator began its long drop to the Citadel.

"What you said to do, Kommissar," replied Third. *"Precisely what you said."*

The display above Lena's couch showed the ball lightning trundling away from the intruder before disappearing into a residential suite. Hansen entered the rotunda, paused for a moment, and then strolled toward the elevators.

"How did he make the fire go down the hallway?" Plaid asked, staring at his memory of the *Kugelblitz.*

"Shut up!" Lena snarled as she stabbed at the manual controls. "If anyone says another word, I'll *kill him!*"

Count Starnes opened his mouth, then closed it. He walked toward the tank that fitted his powerful body like a glove. With its mass between him and his daughter, Starnes said, "I'm going to get ready. Karring, see to it that you're ready also."

The chief engineer nodded without taking his eyes off the display before him.

The intruder's image bent down beside the elevators. "Fine, that's fine . . . ," Lena hissed. "I'll let him get halfway, and then we'll see how well he eats his way through—"

The display above her console went fluorescent white and vanished. A blue aura played over all the workstation's conductive surfaces. Lena and her two lovers froze in the postures they occupied when the current gripped them. The woman's mouth was open to scream, but her paralyzed diaphragm couldn't force the sound out.

Components within the console banged loudly as they failed one after the other. A panel blew open but stuck midway when its hinges welded. Rapid puffs of smoke poured out of the console's interior.

Plaid fell sideways onto the concrete floor of the rotunda. His legs from the knees down remained stuck to the console's metal floor. They had burned to matchsticks of carbon. Voightman's body twisted in on itself. No human features remained. He looked like an outcrop of coal.

Count Starnes and Karring watched with amazement that was too shocked for horror.

"APEX is protected . . . ," the chief engineer repeated to himself in a whisper.

The current roaring through Lena's workstation cut off abruptly, but smoke continued to stream through the seams and connectors.

The grease fire on Lena's couch continued to burn as well.

≡ 38 ≡

"Now, LET ME scout the lay of the land," Blood said, pausing at the edge of servants and retainers around King Wenceslas, "before you shoot your mouth off."

"Fine with me," Hansen agreed mildly. The sun was well up, but the king's tent had not yet been struck—and Wenceslas' contingent was farther along than were some of the others in the Confederate forces.

"A' course," Blood admitted, "I don't really understand the crap myself. But fuck it, I guess it's a good idea. Let's go."

The red-haired warrior strode forward, muscling servants aside. Two senior warriors, Garces and Hopewell, discussed with the king the prospects for hawking this close to Frekka. They, with Blood, were Wenceslas' chief aides—bodyguards—and drinking companions.

"Vince," Blood said to the king, "I need t' talk to you without all these chickenshits around, okay?"

"Who you calling chickenshit, buddy?" said Garces, a black-bearded man whose beer gut did not keep him from looking both powerful and dangerous.

"Hey, not you guys," Blood explained hastily. He pushed at Wenceslas' secretary, a freeman wearing a cloak trimmed with beaver fur. "You know, the *other* guys."

Wenceslas looked around the chaotic camp. The Simplain mercenaries under Lord Guest had marched off an hour earlier.

Some of the smaller contingents had followed, in no particular order; though by this time in the invasion, an order of march had been established in practice if not by formal agreement.

"Oh, all right," the king said. "Go on, give us some room, you all!"

Hopewell looked hard at Hansen.

"Not him," Blood said. "Look, it's his idea. It's about—"

He looked around. The servants moved away, chattering among themselves. A few of the more cultured—the secretary among them—glared disdainfully at the crude warriors whose inferiority was a secret article of faith in the servants' hearts.

"Right," Blood said. "Look, Hansen, you understand it better 'n me, so you tell them. It's about winning the battle."

"Damn right we're going to win the battle!" Garces growled. "Assuming they come out 'n fight us, leastways."

"I don't think there'll be a problem with that," murmured Wenceslas.

It struck Hansen that the king was by no means a stupid man. It was even possible that he was smart enough to agree to Hansen's plan. . . .

"When we meet the imperial army, your majesty," Hansen said, "they'll be better disciplined than our troops. We'll have some edge in—"

Hopewell, a blond man in his twenties, built like a demigod, spat noisily to the side. "Discipline is a lot of bullshit," he said. "What wins battles is good armor and good men—and *we* got that. Venkatna's pussies, they have t' ask permission to wipe their ass. Fighting's for one man at a time—if he's a *man*."

Hansen remembered:

The Easterner's armor is dark green, with chevrons of lighter green across his back and chest. His battlesuit is of royal quality. It absorbs all the power Hansen can pour into it, while the Easterner forces his own arc inexorably down toward Malcolm's helmet.

Needles of ozone jab Hansen's lungs. He stretches out his left hand slowly, fighting the drag of his battlesuit's sticky joints. The stress of the duel has drawn all power away from the suit's servos. The soil under the combatants' feet has been cooked to brick.

Hansen's groping fingers jerk open the Easterner's suit latch. The armor switches off. Malcolm strikes upward with the fury of a man who saw his own death in an arc weapon approaching millimeters at a time. He burns away the chest of the opponent whom Hansen's trick has left defenseless.

The Easterner's intestines balloon for an instant before they burst. . . .

"You need men and armor, no argument . . . ," Hansen said softly. His eyes took a moment to refocus on the present. The king was looking at him in surprise, while Garces blinked with a new respect.

What the hell did his face look like when he lost himself in a past he'd rather have forgotten?

"Right, okay," he resumed. "I want to lead off a good chunk of Venkatna's army. Enough to give the rest of our people the margin they need to crush what's left. If you'll give me ten men, I think I can do it."

"Give *you* ten men?" Wenceslas said in puzzlement. "And why should *I* do anything like this?"

The king looked from Hansen to Blood. Blood grimaced fiercely as though he hoped by wrinkling his face to squeeze understanding of Hansen's lengthy explanation the night before back into his awareness.

"Me, because I know how to work the identification circuits in the battlesuits to give a false report," Hansen said. "I'll tell them that there's a hundred-man battalion working around their flank, and they'll send out a force to block us."

He raised a finger to forestall the question none of his listeners were sophisticated enough to ask.

"I know," he went on. "If Venkatna's people go beyond the IFF signals—which they can—then they'll realize it's a trick; but I'm betting that they don't *understand* their hardware, they'll just say, 'Mark hostiles,' and not check they're getting suit locations instead of just identification codes."

"But they'll see you," Hopewell said. "Can't they count?"

"Negative," Hansen explained. "We'll keep behind cover with a good screen of horsemen. They'll have to hit us with warriors to learn that there's nothing there to hit."

He grinned. He saw in the king's eyes the realization that

when fifty or a hundred imperial warriors realized they'd been duped by a handful of the enemy, it was going to be very hard on that handful.

"And it's you," Hansen went on, "because you're my liege . . . and because you're smart enough to make a decision. If I tried to bring this up to the Confederation council, nobody'd listen. And there's not a snowball's chance in Hell that word wouldn't get out to Venkatna besides."

Only Hell wasn't hot on Northworld . . . and it wasn't just a theological concept. Not to someone like Nils Hansen, who had seen the damned souls frozen to the ice of Plane Four. . . .

"We never done this sorta crap," said Garces. He wasn't so much hostile to the idea as baffled by it.

"No, it's a ruse," Wenceslas said with a frown of concentration. "Ruses are proper. Only—"

He stared very hard at Hansen. "You can make ten men look like a hundred?"

"Yes," said Hansen. He'd qualified his statement before. Now it was time to state probabilities as facts.

A female mammoth began to bleat in high, piteous notes. She'd made a friend among the baggage train of another princeling. She was not yet loaded, but her friend was padding out of the camp, carrying heavy battlesuits in rope slings on either flank.

. . . good night, Irene, Hansen thought inanely, *I'll see you in my dreams. . . .*

Maybe not so inane.

"Then why don't other people do it?" Wenceslas pressed.

Because I didn't teach them how when I put the West Kingdom army together four generations ago. "Because nobody thinks about it," Hansen said aloud. "But I do."

"Look, is he just trying to stay outa the fight?" Hopewell said to the king in genuine puzzlement.

"Are you questioning my honor, friend . . . ?" Hansen heard his voice lilt, as lightly as a nightingale calling from a distant hedge.

Hopewell turned and looked at him. Hopewell was the larger man by 10% in height, 20% in bulk; and Hopewell's bulk was muscle also. But a duel in battlesuits wasn't muscle against muscle; and anyway, Hansen wasn't the sort of fellow you chose to fight under *any* circumstances.

"Naw, that's not what I meant," the bigger warrior said. "Look, I just don't figure it, all right? Why don't we just, you know, fight 'em? That's what we come t' do."

"What about five?" the king asked. "All told."

Kingship, business—and love, however you defined it. They all required trade-offs, and you never had all the data that you needed for a decision. Like Dowson had said in another district of All Times. . . .

"Five should work," Hansen said aloud. "Ten would work better, and it wouldn't be much degradation of the Mirala main force."

"But it would degrade *my* contingent, Lord Hansen," Wenceslas said with a tone of equality that the king would never have used to address one of his bodyguards on a point of strategy. "I've brought seventy-three warriors to the fight . . . counting yourself."

Hansen understood the implication. "As you are right to do, your majesty," he said.

His mind spun in a montage of kings and slashing arcs and the way the Lord of Thrasey's battlesuit lost its gleam an instant before Golsingh's weapon ripped off the head in bubbles of glass and blazing metal and blood, blood flashing up as steam.

"If you so order," Hansen's voice continued, "I will stand by you as I have sworn; and fight in such a way that when Venkatna's men put us both down, as they surely will, you will say with your last breath that never did a warrior die better for his liege. . . ."

King Wenceslas touched the back of Hansen's wrist. When he saw that Hansen was alert in the present again, he said, "You're sure of yourself, aren't you, Hansen?"

Hansen managed a poor smile. "Of nothing else, your majesty," he replied. "But of that, yeah. I'm—all I've got."

"All right," Wenceslas said. "I'll give you three men, they won't be much but that shouldn't matter for your purpose."

He raised an eyebrow in query. Hansen nodded agreement.

"And I'll give you Blood," the king continued. "You'll

need somebody that the back-rankers'll take orders from. They
know Blood, and Blood knows you—"

The king grinned harshly. "As I hope that *I* know you, Lord
Hansen."

The lovesick mammoth, laden at last, jingled past at a pace
in advance of what the mahout on the beast's humped neck
desired. He cursed, but the mammoth gurgled and strode on.

Hard to quantify emotional factors; hard to *identify* emotional
factors. But they were what made the world work like it did,
not the hardware and not even skill.

"You know the important part, your majesty," Hansen said.
*You know as much as I do; and what the hell, it might work.
Surely nothing* else *could possibly work.*

Blood clapped Hansen on the shoulder. "I told you he'd
explain it!" the bodyguard caroled to his king and companions.

Blood didn't understand a thing about Hansen's plan or the
necessity for it in the coming battle . . . but as King Wenceslas
had said, Blood knew his man, and nothing else mattered.

≡ 39 ≡

HANSEN STEPPED FROM the elevator with a smile and the nonchalance of a cat entering a familiar room, but his eyes were wells of green fury.

"*Hel*-lo, Count Starnes," he called to the Citadel. No human being moved within Hansen's line of sight, unless you counted the curl of smoke rising from Lena's couch. "You know, I could complain about the hospitality you show your guests, if I had a mind to."

Besides Lena's shattered console, one of the three outstations in the rotunda was live. The unit's seat had been spun to the rear when the user left in a hurry. The display was full of colors flowing in patterns. It could have been abstract art, for all it meant to Hansen.

"*Chief Engineer Karring is trying to display the Matrix in three dimensions,*" Third explained with a hint of mechanical amusement. "*When the power surged in Lena's workstation, Karring decided that he would be safe only in one of the bays of APEX proper.*"

"*Could* you get to him there?" Hansen asked as his eyes searched the portion of the rotunda he could see from where he stood. The haze of burned insulation and burned meat was familiar, God knew; but familiarity didn't make the reek less sickening, mentally as well as physically.

He'd known what he was doing when he gave Third the

order. Not the technique, not exactly; but Hansen had ordered
enough killings that he didn't kid himself when he had to—
chose to—do it again.

"*I haven't had occasion to determine that,*" the AI responded
coolly.

Hansen sauntered around the column of elevators in the
center of the rotunda. "Count Starnes!" he called. "Hey, Count.
Come out, come out, wherever you are!"

He could see the single corridor which led off the rotunda at
this level. The mass of the Fleet Battle Director almost filled it,
and Hansen knew the installation led back hundreds of meters
into the bedrock.

A short man, balding and powerfully built (as were virtually
all the inhabitants of Plane Five), sat in the nearest bay. He was
dwarfed by the mass of the computer on three sides and above
him. The device hanging over the mouth of the alcove had a
noticeable similarity to the Web North gave King Venkatna;
but the Web was static, and this unsupported ovoid spun in
a pattern more complex than Hansen had thought at first
glance.

"Count Starnes?" Hansen asked as he walked toward the
corridor.

"*That is Karring,*" Third said.

"I am Count Starnes!" boomed an amplified voice.

"Welladay!" said Hansen brightly. He turned to face the
repulsion-drive tank a hundred meters away across the rotunda.

Despite the vehicle's mass, it was as much an article of dress
as the battlesuits of the Open Lands were. The operator reclined
in a couch with all the tank's controls at his fingertips—and no
room to move more than those fingers. There was no rotating
turret: the tube of a railgun extended from the frontal armor
like the blade of a push dagger in an assassin's fist.

"Good to see you at last, Count. I was worried that I'd come
all this way and missed you," Hansen said.

"*Are you mad?*" clicked the icy thoughts of the command
helmet.

"Very, Third," Hansen said in a clear voice. "Very angry
indeed. But I don't think he'll shoot when his computer's
behind us, will he? How far through APEX do you suppose

a slug from that gun would travel, eh?"

"He's right, milord!" Karring shouted from the bay. "There needn't be violence."

"Don't tell me what I need to do," snarled the speaker on the tank's roof. "Either of you!"

"They expected you to slink in here the way Fortin did," Third commented. *"They don't know how to react to Nils Hansen."*

"They'll know soon enough," Hansen said/thought.

The tank shuddered into motion. It slid forward at a barely-perceptible pace, the railgun centered on Hansen's chest. The hum of the vehicle's drive was almost hidden by the subliminal hugeness of the Fleet Battle Director, poised like a couching lion.

"You invited me to use APEX," Hansen said. He grinned and put his hands on his hips with the elbows flared out. "That's what I was told, anyhow. I think you ought to know that when I was Commissioner of Special Units back home, no place you ever heard of . . . but back on Annunciation— when I ran into somebody like you, Count Starnes, I kinda made it my job t' take care of things."

"Milord!" the chief engineer called desperately. "He can vanish faster than the bolt even!"

"Why would I want to do that?" Hansen lilted. "Now, you've nothing to fear, milord, not from me, so long as you keep your part of the bargain. I came to you unarmed . . . and you'll let me ask a question of APEX, now, won't you?"

"What question?" the tank demanded.

"Nothing to affect you," Hansen said. "Nothing to affect Plane Five, not really. I'll take off my helmet here—"

He touched the black plastic case above his temple with the pad of his right forefinger.

"—and it'll connect itself to APEX. Then I'll go home, and you'll go on with your—"

The air of mocking insouciance slipped. "—nasty little games that somebody oughta stop. But it won't be me. Unless."

"The locked sectors can't possibly be breached!" said Karring. The chief engineer was too aware that he was in the line of potential fire to listen to the nuances in the intruder's voice, nor was he in position to see the threat in Hansen's eyes. "Let him bring his helmet over here."

"He wants to bring you close to the device he built to control the Matrix," the command helmet observed.

"I know what it's like to have a new toy," said Hansen, pivoting smoothly though not particularly fast. "With me, it was mostly a gun, though, or a battlesuit later on. Let's go give Karring something to play with."

He walked across the rotunda with his back to Count Starnes. He could hear the tank behind him. Its drive sputtered like bacon frying, though the vehicle had stopped and was merely hovering a hair's breadth above the concrete floor.

The chief engineer's expression was a mixture of fear and exaltation. Karring remained in his seat, but he looked ready to jump up and run. His hand dipped occasionally toward the pistol he wore as insignia of his rank within Keep Starnes' hierarchy, but that was just a sign of nervousness.

"Karring is summoning additional troops," Third warned. *"Count Starnes is not aware of this."*

Karring was no gunman. He perceived war as a chess game, while Nils Hansen saw it as muzzle blasts and men's eyes rolling up into the whites as their bodies toppled backward.

Hansen smiled. The chief engineer squeezed against the back of his chair. He spread his hands at the level of his mid-chest. The posture was an unconscious attempt to prove that he was harmless, no threat at all to the predator who walked toward him, grinning like a skull.

The twenty bays were inset 90° to the right or left from the axis of the corridor which APEX occupied. Hansen walked under the spinning ovoid at the head of the first one. He looked up and winked.

This close, the Fleet Battle Director was a lowering presence, not a machine.

"Have fun, Third," Hansen said. He took off the command helmet. "Karring, isn't it?" he went on. "And your APEX takes mental input?"

The chief engineer nodded tightly. A skein of colored fibers showed on the display which covered the inner face of the bay. The strands knotted down to opalescent white. Karring was afraid to look at the pattern lest Hansen understand and attack while he and Karring were within arm's length.

"Then it'll take mine, I'm sure," Hansen said. He stepped past Karring and placed the command helmet on the coaming in front of the holographic display.

"Purty thing, isn't it?" he said to the chief engineer as he walked back out of the bay. Probes extended from the moonstone-gray crystal on Third's forehead.

Hansen sauntered back across the rotunda without looking behind. The tank swiveled to track him with its railgun. Hansen was headed toward the wrecked console and the corpses still smoldering on and around it.

"It's worked, milord!" Karring shouted. "He can't flee into his Matrix now, I'm sure of it!"

"Tsk!" said Hansen. "I just got here, Karring m'boy. Why would I want to leave?"

"Try it!" Karring said. "You're so sure of yourself, you bastard—but *try* your Matrix!"

Hansen shrugged. He continued strolling toward the destroyed workstation. His fingertips, then his right hand, vanished into a shimmer not of Plane Five.

"Not much of a trick, is it?" he said with a supercilious frown. His hand reappeared. The fingers, long and tanned and callused, flexed as though they held a weapon.

"He's yours, Count Starnes!" the chief engineer cried. "He's your slave, completely at your mercy!"

Hansen bent down and drew one of Plaid's pistols. The leather holster had insulated the weapon from the current which burned off the owner's legs.

"The man who killed my daughters," boomed the speaker on Count Starnes' tank, "can scarcely expect mercy!"

The railgun fired.

≡ 40 ≡

"PRINCESS," SAID SPARROW the Smith. His face was as bleak as cliffs at sunrise, and his voice rasped like tangled briars. "You will do. What I say. Or I will punish you in ways you will never forget."

"Kill me, then," Mala whispered, sprawled face-down at the feet of the huge, implacable man. "If that's your will."

The dog growled softly in Olrun's arms. The bitch's claws clicked on the floor, but the stone was too smooth to give her purchase. She felt the tension rising, and she wanted to be close to her master.

"Death would be a release, lady," Sparrow said.

He unhooked the small probability generator from his belt. It began to spin between the tips of his forefingers. When the ovoid settled into a rhythm, it hung in the air unsupported.

Sparrow's expression was too tight for certainty, but there might have been pity in the set of his mouth. "And *my* will," he went on, "is only that you do my master's bidding. I am the tool of my lord Saburo. But you *will* do as he requests."

The probability generator continued to spin at the same moderate velocity. The coils of its structure changed from wire and fine-drawn crystal to bands of rich indigo light.

"No," Mala said. She raised her face from the pale stone. "No, I will not."

Sparrow smiled. The ball of spinning light expanded away

from him to engulf the princess in a web of alternate probabilities.

Reality shifted.

"Have you got the rest of the prisoners?" demanded King Stengard's two outer heads together. His middle head twisted to look into the hold his forces had just captured.

Stengard's androids and armed slaves wandered across the courtyard. The defensive wall was half melted, half blasted, into a thirty-meter gap, but the attackers had then opened the main gate for King Stengard to enter.

The party sent to the outlying hold dismounted from their individual skimmers and the heavy truck which carried the wall-breaching armament as well as a dozen personnel. The slaves, Lomeri and humans both, chattered with delight as they described to one another their recent victory.

"Got one," said the leader, Stengard's son Stenred. "The other, she was too close to the door. When it went west, so did she . . . but that was just the maid."

"Fishfood, that's all she was!" chortled a human slave who had been burned horribly some time in the past. His eyes winked out of masses of keloid, and his nostrils were slits in a smooth, pink surface. "But we got the main one!"

He jerked his electronic noose. The prisoner writhed at the jolt of fluctuating current applied to her tender throat.

"What you want done with her?" Stenred asked.

Stenred's head and torso were those of an ordinary human, save for their android pallor, but he walked on four legs. Because of the limbs' close placement on his modified pelvis, the prince looked less like a centaur than he did a spider lurching upright on two hind pairs of legs.

His genitalia hung down beneath a tasseled fringe intended for emphasis rather than concealment.

In the courtyard, the victors played with the control devices they had found in the hold. The game was to punch in random settings, then twist the control to full power. Each time, a captured slave bent backward, screaming until contraction of his or her muscles choked the throat silent. Occasionally, the victim's neck broke during the convulsions.

Stengard's troops were placing bets on which captive would die next. Whoever won crowed and demanded payment from the others. Occasionally, vicious fights broke out among Stengard's personnel, but those were minor incidents in the general bloody apathy.

"You captured her," said the king's left head.

"Whatever you please," agreed the center head.

"Though if *you* don't have an idea," leered the right head, "I sure do. Tasty little morsel, isn't she?"

Stenred grinned. "Hold her down!" he ordered.

"Seconds!" cried the slave with a face of scar tissue.

Princess Mala tried to struggle despite the pain that surged from the noose. It was no use. Slaves gripped her limbs and spread-eagled her on mud reeking with slaughter.

King Nainfari had been impaled on a stake in the gate of his hold. He stared through sightless eyes as Stenred knelt on his four knees to be the first of the conquerors to rape Nainfari's daughter.

Reality shifted.

"Where have you been?" croaked Mala as her husband's figure darkened the mouth of the cave. Behind him, red sand skirled on the wind. It filtered the light and made each breath taste dry.

"Keep your pants on!" snarled Offut in reply. He laughed at his own accidental joke.

The male android set down a container made from the hollow stem of a giant horsetail, a meter long and a quarter meter in diameter. He began to unwind the scarf with which he protected his face from the omnipresent wind.

"You've been gone all day!" Mala shrilled. Her fingers twitched, remembering the pain of weaving the coarse, cycad-leaf fibers into cloth. "And where's the water?"

"I brought water," Offut said, "but I had to go nearly five klicks to get it. Both the nearer holes were clogged deeper than I could dig."

Offut's left leg was shorter than his right. Both his left arms were withered, and the left side of his face looked as though it had been poured from wax which was still too hot when the mold was removed. He leered at Mala.

"Food?" Mala asked, trying to keep the desperation out of her voice.

Offut grimaced and turned aside. "There's still some of the Gulper hide, isn't there?" he said apologetically.

"That had been dead weeks before you found it!" Mala shrilled. "That's all we've had to eat for three days, and *it's* almost gone!"

"Well, tomorrow I'll find something better," her husband promised without confidence. He poured water from the pipe into a slab of rock polished concave by the wind. It was the cave's only furnishing. "Here, drink some water and you'll feel better."

Mala's stomach growled. She muttered a curse, but she knew from long experience that water really was better than nothing. She pulled herself to the rock with the fingers of her four hands. Her legless hindquarters dragged behind her.

"It's not, well, the clearest water I've ever seen," Offut admitted with his face turned away.

The brackish fluid stank, even in the dense fug of the cave.

Mala closed her eyes as she bent to slurp water from the hollow. Otherwise, she might catch sight of her own hideous reflection.

"And then," said Offut, limping around behind her, "we'll fuck before we finish eating the hide."

His misshapen hands gripped her. Mala whined in familiar desperation.

Reality shifted.

There was light but no sun and no movement, and the cold cut Mala like a thousand knives.

The plain might either be endless or straitly bounded, but all she could see was a single stalagmite of ice like those she had glimpsed when Sparrow sent her cabinet briefly to Plane Four.

This time Mala was one of them, and 'this time' was eternity.

She felt tides at her frozen core, but if there was any change in the round of her existence, she was not conscious of it. Pressed against Mala's being was the rigid soul of her brother

Morfari. His mouth was twisted in an echo of her own eternal silent scream.

Reality shifted.

Princess Mala's gang yipped in delight. They grounded their skimmers in a circle around their quarry, a desperate male slave.

One of the cattle guards snapped his electronic noose about the escapee's neck from behind. The captive was naked except for smeared mud. His throat bore the calluses of servitude but not the collar itself.

"Hey, how did he cut the collar off?" demanded one of Mala's crew.

The princess shrugged. "How the fuck would I know?" she said. "I figure somebody fucked up welding it on, but it don't much matter. *He's* not gonna tell anybody else how t' do it."

She prodded the captive in the belly with her volley gun. "Is he, now?"

"Lookit that!" cried the Fifth Plane female who acted as adjutant of the cattle guards. "Lilius! Give 'im another jolt!"

The captive was sitting on the ground. "P-p-plea—" he whimpered uselessly.

The guard holding the noose twitched his end, sending surges of electricity through the captive. At each fresh shock, the victim's legs splayed and his penis pumped erect.

A Lomeri female chirped in her own language. She stepped toward the captive and started to crouch.

Mala knocked her reptilian subordinate sideways. "Who died and made *you* queen, Ssadzeril?" she demanded. The princess tugged down the sweat-blackened elastic briefs which were the only garment she wore apart from her harness.

"Nexties!" the Fifth Plane female cried in delight.

The princess stepped forward and squatted over the captive. The knives dangling from her harness jingled as the cattle guards cheered.

Reality shifted.

Princess Mala lay on the floor of her bower. The probability generator was a cold ball of wire hanging from Sparrow's belt, but the reflection of its blue glow colored Mala's memory of possible truths.

"Please . . . ," Mala whispered. Her eyes were open but glazed. "Please. Don't."

"Princess," said the smith, mildly for a man so big and so relentless, "my master Saburo is a gentle man. He loves you as ever a man could love a woman, and he will treat you as a goddess yourself."

Sparrow cleared his throat. He did not raise his voice as he continued, "But lady, *I* am sworn to bring you to my master. I wish you no harm, but there is nothing to which I will not subject you in order to gain your agreement to wed my master."

The menace was not in the statement but rather in the flat certainty with which Sparrow delivered it.

Mala began to sob. Olrun looked from her mistress to Sparrow. The maid's face revealed nothing. Her fingers continued to hold and stroke the dog.

"Lady," said the smith, "Saburo would never put you through tortures and misery to bring you to his palace. But I am not my master, and I will do whatever I need to do."

"Mistress," Olrun said quietly. "Go with him. This one will do whatever he says."

"I will go with you," Mala said, her lips so close to the floor that her breath fogged the cool stone.

≡ 41 ≡

THE DROP OF clear matter oozing from Esme's right eye twinkled as the opening door made the lamps gutter.

There was a brief discussion. Baron Weast turned from the messenger. "Your majesty?" he said. "Lord D'Auber is here. He says that the Mirala forces are marshaling and the battle will surely begin at dawn."

Venkatna made no response. The only sound in the audience hall was the hiss of the lamps and D'Auber's harsh breathing. Rather than send a courier with this warning, D'Auber had run from the palisade marking Frekka's municipal limits.

Weast's face twisted into a caricature of pleasantry. "Lord D'Auber is of course concerned that your majesty be with his armies during the battle. . . ."

No response. It was like talking at a *pair* of corpses. The emperor's chief aides rotated night duty in the audience hall among themselves, but each further exposure to silence and the glittering Web was a closer approach to Hell.

"Or that you depute the command to, ah, one of your companions, your majesty."

He heard low voices out in the corridor, Bontempo and Kleber and the rest—being careful not to enter the presence unless they were summoned.

The presences. Weast wondered how the guards stood it. Perhaps their battlesuits protected them from the miasma that permeated the audience hall. More than death and madness; but certainly *including* death and madness.

Emperor Venkatna roused suddenly. His eyes had been open, but he blinked to clear them. Venkatna's cheeks were hollow and his eyesockets looked bruised. "No," he said wearily. "I'll—"

He shook himself and stood up, kicking aside the rug that humped at his feet.

"But perhaps we won't have to fight," Venkatna resumed. He spoke in the strong, determined voice of past years. That was the part that Weast found most disconcerting: the real man, the king and emperor, was still present—the way a skeleton lurks within a liquescent corpse.

The emperor walked over to the Web. Instead of boots, he wore felt slippers, like those a warrior dons before getting into his armor. "You there!" Venkatna called. "Slaves! Rouse and listen to me!"

An underchamberlain sat on the stone floor beside the Web, cradling his head in his hands. "Race and Julia," the man muttered in a sing-song. "They have names. Julia and Race."

Nobody paid any attention to him. The guards and councilors rotated night duty in the audience hall. This underchamberlain, Brett, had somehow gotten a permanent assignment, and by now he was quite mad.

Despite that, Brett's plight was less horrific than that of the slaves within the Web.

"Your orders are our fate . . . ," Race whispered from her bench as light faded from the device she used and which used her up. She had been a tall, muscular woman. Now she looked like something found in an unsealed sarcophagus. Her joints stood out from spindly limbs, and for some moments she was unable to lift herself upright.

Servants with milk and sponges scuttled to the women's sides. Brett watched the activities apathetically. Julia did not speak or rise. The violent shudders which shook her emaciated frame indicated that she too had returned from her trance within the probability generator.

Weast could not keep from glancing toward Empress Esme's bier. He trembled and locked his attention back on Venkatna.

The Empire had remained in perfect internal peace since the two slaves were put to work in the Web. The processes of corporeal decay, however, were more difficult to chain than those which afflicted political entities.

"This will be simpler than fighting them," Venkatna said confidingly—to Esme. "I won't need to leave you after all, my dearest."

Venkatna's expression hardened as he returned his attention to Race and Julia. "You two," he said crisply. "I want you to pacify the Mirala confederates. They're right outside the city. Make them all surrender."

"We can't do that, your majesty," Julia said. She managed to wipe her mouth. A palace servant, his fear overcome by pity, reached through the series of looped crystals. He held the woman upright while another servant fed her spoonfuls of thick gruel.

"You must do it!" Venkatna shouted. "I order you to do it!"

"M-m-mirala isn't part of your domains, majesty," Race whispered. Her tongue slurred through a mouthful of warm milk. She seemed unaware that droplets spattered as she spoke. "We cannot affect that which is beyond your rule."

"What use are you, then?" the emperor screamed. He spun on his heel. "Go on back to your work. I'll take care of these scum another way. Somebody bring my armor, but—"

A look of forceful cunning claimed his pallid face.

"But I won't leave here, ah, just now," he continued. "I'll stay with, with, *here* until later. Weast, you take care of the army."

"*Him?*" blurted D'Auber, the first words the warrior had uttered since his whispered conversation with Weast at the door to the hall.

"Please, your majesty," Julia said. Her eyes were closed. Servants held a bison robe around her, but its thickness could not prevent the tremors shaking her wasted body. "We will do your work, but give us a little peace, just an hour . . . ?"

The clerestory windows of the dome brightened with a hint of dawn, though they did not yet illuminate the hall below.

"We are your slaves," Race echoed, "but give us peace. . . ."

"You'll have no peace, none!" shouted the emperor. "You let my darling *die,* you bitches!"

"Your majesty, you didn't tell—" Julia said. Her voice was too weak and toneless to be called a protest.

"No peace!" Venkatna cried. "Get back to your work, I order you! No peace!"

The slave women sighed together. The sound was like that of the last breath oozing from a dead ox.

Servants scrambled to get out of the hemisphere of the Web. Race and Julia lay back down on their filthy benches.

And there, in accordance with the orders of Emperor Venkatna the First, the two Searchers began to grind out No Peace.

≡ 42 ≡

"AMBUSH BATTALION, FALL in!" Hansen ordered on the general frequency as the eastern sky hinted the first pale warning of dawn. As far north as Frekka, the sun made a long production of rising.

'Ambush Battalion' was boast and a chance of confusing the enemy, in the unlikely event that Venkatna's forces monitored enemy transmissions. Mostly it was a boast, a proud name with which to encourage Hansen's own four underlings.

They needed encouragement. They sure needed something.

Blood had a good battlesuit, about second class, decorated with large red drops on a silver field. It wasn't quite true that a warrior was only as good as his armor; but the armor was important, and in this case there was a good match between the man and his hardware.

Blood was better equipped than nineteen out of twenty men he would meet on the field of battle. After sparring with him repeatedly in the past several weeks, Hansen knew Wenceslas' bodyguard was a man he would be happy to have backing him in any fight.

The other three were named al-Hauk, Empey, and Brownow. They were warriors by virtue of the fact they wore battlesuits. Hansen wouldn't trust the armor any of the three wore against a shower of crossbow bolts, much less the cutting arc which sprang from the gauntlet of another battlesuit.

The men were what he'd expected the king would give him; and for present purposes, they would do.

"Suit," Hansen said, switching on his AI, "battalion push."

Using encrypted transmission that could be heard only by the other members of the Ambush Battalion, he continued, "Boys, what we're going to do is win the battle if it can be won. It's absolutely necessary that you follow me and that you keep your intervals. I'll lead, Blood brings up the rear. Ten meters between each man and the next."

Hansen looked over the four faceless battlesuits that were his force. Empey's must have been made by an apprentice smith who never rose to journeyman status. Brownow and al-Hauk wore armor compiled from bits hacked off various suits in battle. The parts fit poorly together. Even when the welds were done expertly—most of these were not—there would be a noticeable degradation of performance compared to that of a battlesuit whose parts retained their integrity.

"Now, I realize you don't understand what all's happening," Hansen continued grimly. "But you can understand this: if any of you hangs back or runs away, I'll kill him. No matter what I'm doing at the time, I'll manage to kill him. Understood?"

"Less'n I get there first," Blood boomed, using his external speaker instead of the spread-transmission radio. "Then *I'll* kill ye."

The Confederate army marshaled around them with shouts and clashing. Warriors tested their arcs. The weapons picked threads of static from the radios despite the work of suit AIs to synthesize perfect reception.

"One more thing," Hansen said slowly. He hadn't meant to go on, but the words came out nonetheless. "I don't know that it matters to you—I don't know that it *ought* to matter. But if you follow me, boys, I'll make you heroes. They'll sing about us around banquet tables for generations to come."

He smiled. The other warriors couldn't see his expression, and they probably wouldn't have been encouraged if they *could* see.

Hansen's battlesuit was gold and of royal quality. The suit was as good as any armor in either army, and it was an article of Hansen's faith that he was better than any other man of war.

He couldn't fight a whole army himself, or even two first-class men, not and hope to win; but Nils Hansen would do what he could, as he had always done. . . .

"Let's go, troops," Hansen said. "Let's kick some ass."

He led his four men out of the camp in a wide sweep to the left, moving at a fast walk. The pace would be bruising to his subordinates, since there was considerable lag time before their suit servos responded to the movements of the users' legs and bodies.

That wasn't the worst punishment the poor bastards were going to get this day.

Forty pony-mounted freemen conformed to the warriors' movements as Wenceslas had ordered them to do. It was crucial that Venkatna be forced to send armored warriors to develop the threat to his flank. The crossbows and lances of these Mirala freemen would keep imperial scouts at a distance.

On the map overlaid across Hansen's electronic visor, Venkatna's army was a mass of red specks falling into line at the edge of the built-up area. There were many hundreds of them, though still fewer than the amorphous blue mass of the Confederates rousing themselves for battle. Numbers weren't the whole story. The sharp-edged imperial divisions would punch through the Mirala army like an awl through leather.

Hansen headed out of the camp along a swale so slight as to go unnoticed by a strolling pedestrian. A slope of two meters in a thousand would hide a suited warrior from sight; that was all that Hansen needed. There were no trees within fifty klicks of Frekka, not with the population increase the capital had seen and the slow growth of vegetation in these latitudes.

"Suit," Hansen ordered as he moved. "Project a battalion IFF by ten times. Scatter the unit distribution according to friendly forces, plus ten—plus *twenty* percent in quality."

He couldn't pretend to be a force of a hundred warriors: the suits' Identification, Friend or Foe, circuits couldn't achieve the necessary separation to make more than a plus-ten magnification believable. Hansen was doing the next best thing by pretending to be a picked unit: fifty men wearing battlesuits

of unusually high average quality, but of *believable* quality
nonetheless.

The battalion's outriders reached the squatter dwellings on
the outskirts of the Mirala encampment. Whores, gamblers,
thieving traders—trading thieves; but of the low-level sort who
preyed on the servants. They were debarred from entering the
camp proper, as did the better sort of grifter who dealt with
the nobles.

Hansen's freemen yipped and charged, knocking down leather tilts and swinging lance butts and sword flats at whoever got
in the way.

The technique wasn't as mindlessly brutal as it looked. The
mounted men cleared a path for the warriors; and most warriors
would use their arcs as quickly on a slave as they would a clump
of brambles that got in their way.

"Hey, Hansen," Blood called. "Boss."

"Go ahead," Hansen said. He had to watch the deployment of
imperial forces, but the map overlay was a serious distraction.
Not because he couldn't see his footing through a 30% mask.
Rather, it was because the perfect discipline of Venkatna's
troops drew Hansen's eyes the way he had once seen a victim
staring at his blown-off foot.

"We gonna get any fighting ourself?"

"You bet your ass." Literally.

"That's good," Blood said.

And meant it, the damned fool . . . except he *wasn't* a fool.
Blood was a warrior, and this was what he did.

Hansen barked out a laugh that the compressed transmission
made even harsher than it sounded in his own ears. This was
what Nils Hansen did too; and he did it very well.

"Hey, boss?" Blood again. The other three didn't have the
breath to talk at the present pace, and chances were that they
didn't have the stomach for it either.

"Go ahead."

"That girl of yours. The blond bint? I haven't seen her in
camp."

Lucille.

Nils Hansen had been a fighting man in two cultures over
a lot of time. Men whose business is death don't have a lot

of delicacy about the various life-affirming activities in which
they indulge.

"She's got kin in Peace Rock," Hansen said. "I sent her back
there to them. She's a good lady. I don't need a piece so bad I
want her t' get hurt."

"You sent her into the *Empire?*" gasped one of the other
three; Brownow, Hansen thought it was.

"If we take Venkatna out," Hansen said, "then there's no
problem. If we don't, the bastard's going to kill everything in
Mirala down to the mice."

Blood chuckled. "My old mom's back t' the farm, not ten
klicks from the valley mouth. Guess we better win this one for
her, huh?"

Hansen's breath quickened. "Keep moving," he said. He
hoped he sounded calm. "There's an imperial section changing
front. I think we're going to have company soon."

They passed a trio of small houses with separate stables,
built around a spring-fed pond. Perhaps the rural retreat of
some court officials; as probably, one of Venkatna's marcher
dukes lived in this isolated setting during his infrequent visits
to the capital. The buildings were empty now.

Empey switched on his arc. Its sudden power drain made
the warrior stumble. He slashed his weapon across the shingled
front of the nearest house anyway. Before Hansen could object,
Blood got the stables of that house and extended his arc an
impressive four meters to torch the next dwelling as well.

"*Hold* your fucking formation!" Hansen snarled. "Move!"
He increased the pace by a half beat as punishment.

His bloodstream was already roiling with hormones. The
surge he got from the vandalism made him almost sick. Nils
Hansen, *Commissioner* Hansen, had spent his former life putting down—literally—the forces of destruction. He hadn't been
choosy about his methods, preferring something fast even if
it made a lot of noise to letting a situation drag on; but his
long-term purpose was always to lessen destruction and stress
on the society he was paid to protect.

Now he was leading a gang whose first thought when they
passed a wooden house was that they could make it burn like
a box of matches.

"Hey, boss?"

Blood. "Go ahead."

"If we're s'posed to look like an army all by ourse'f, then we gotta do what an army does, right?"

Blood was either smarter than Hansen had thought . . . or he was psychic. "Right," said Hansen. "There's a stock barn or some damn thing up ahead. The walls're stone, but there'll be fodder and the roof'll burn."

Some of the Ambush Battalion's outriders were engaged with imperial freemen half a kilometer to the right. A number of the riders nearer Hansen's warriors spurred their ponies to join the fight, though others hung back.

Nobles tended to ignore the mounted scouts. It was a wonder that the freemen had the amount of discipline and élan which they regularly displayed.

The main armies were moving. Hansen needed more than dots on a topographic display.

"Suit," he said. "Upper right quadrant. Remote me the view from K—"

He'd started to request that his suit echo the images from King Wenceslas' visor.

"The view from Lord Guest," Hansen finished instead.

Better see what a real professional was looking at. Captain North was that, the good lord knew.

The stockyard was on the outskirts of Frekka proper. Immediately beyond it were the new barracks whose construction Hansen had watched from a loggia of the imperial palace.

"Suit," he ordered, "*cut!*"

He slashed his arc, drawn thin as a king's honor, across the roof trusses projecting from the loft eight meters above. Masonry cracked under the tongue of high voltage. The building's roof of ancient thatch burped flame.

I am the best!

The viewpoint in the upper right quarter of Hansen's visor advanced by long, powerful strides. North was leading his Simplain contingent toward the imperial flank exposed when a section marched off to meet Hansen.

The Confederate army was ill-organized, but it was composed of *fighting* men. At the present juncture, the Mirala warriors' instinct was precisely correct. The whole mass swept forward to support North's calculated attack.

North was the point of the wedge into which he had formed his mercenaries. The front rank of Venkatna's troops had extended to the right to cover the detached section. The imperial warriors were featureless within their battlesuits, but their line bunched and gapped nervously.

It momentarily occurred to Hansen that his plan, his *feint*, might just succeed as a real thrust. What would the imperial forces do if the palace exploded into flame behind them? Were they disciplined enough to hold their impeccable formation and win the real battle before worrying about events among the civilian installations in their rear?

Probably; and anyhow, the question was moot. An imperial section fifty warriors strong was bearing down on Hansen's poor handful like the Wrath of God.

≡ 43 ≡

THE RAILGUN'S COLLAPSED uranium slug was invisible, but behind it followed a track of fluorescing plasma: the driving skirt, stripped of electrons and heated sun-heart white by the jolt of electricity which powered the bolt.

The streak ended a centimeter from Hansen's smiling face. There was an almost-visible blotch at the point the hypervelocity shot vanished, the hint of a fracture in reality. The shimmer was no larger than a hole that would permit a man Nils Hansen's size to thrust his hand through to the wrist—

But that gap in normal spacetime was more than large enough to engulf the railgun slug. The projectile snapped across the Matrix with its velocity and momentum unimpaired.

A fluting, birdlike cry burbled up the ten-meter throat of a distant sauropod. The call rang through the forest. The carnivorous mounts of the Lomeri turned their heads toward the sound like six questing gun turrets. Lizardmen spurred the beasts' off-side flanks and tugged fiercely at their reins.

After brief struggles, the ceratosaurs settled down again. Under other circumstances the carnivores might have been more difficult to control. Now, poised on the edge of the Open Lands, they knew they would soon have ample opportunity to kill and feed.

The Lomeri captain chirped a sharp order to his subordinates. One at a time the lizardmen racked back the bolts of their weapons to load them; switched on, then off again, the force screens which would protect them against both arcs and projectile weapons in the event that the victims mounted a defense; and held up the bundle of self-looping nooses that each slaver was to bring.

The nooses were metal fiber and extended ten meters when thrown. They goaded their victims with low-amperage shocks and attached the fresh-caught slaves securely to the lizardmen's saddles.

The Lomeri carried twenty nooses apiece, but a ceratosaur dragging such an entourage was likely to turn and rend half the slaves before the rider could whip the beast off.

Smoke drifted from the eave openings of the houses in Peace Rock. It was midmorning across the shifting discontinuity. Folk sat on the benches in front of their dwellings and enjoyed the winter sunshine while they knitted or worked on harness.

A woman with brown-blond hair wove on a hand loom in front of the lord's thatched hall. She was working the figure of a warrior in gold armor onto a white field.

The humans were not consciously aware of the disaster being prepared for them across the Matrix, but occasionally a child or an old woman stared at the sky and frowned. Hobbled mammoths blatted nervously to one another as they foraged among the stubble in the fields.

The Lomeri captain gave another order. His team jockeyed their mounts into line facing the discontinuity. Even at this juncture, the lizardmen snapped and kicked at one another with clawed, narrow feet over questions of precedence and perceived insult.

When the captain was satisfied, he took his place at the head of the line. He gave the final command and spurred his mount forward.

The railgun slug, moving at a substantial fraction of the speed of light, entered and exited Plane Two a millisecond later. The bodies of the six Lomeri, decapitated in a fluorescent streak, pitched out of their saddles.

The ceratosaurs, maddened by the spray of blood, began to fight as they devoured their late riders.

• • •

On a plain that stretched without curvature or horizon, cones
of wrinkled ice crept with sidereal sluggishness. Light bathed
them from a point source that was not a sun. It penetrated the
crawling figures and drove the utter cold still deeper.

A streak of excited plasma appeared and vanished across the
waste in front of the hill that was the only terrain feature for as
far as an eye could see.

The hill suggested a human face: a man with prominent
cheekbones and a mouth as ruthless as a bullet from his gun.

If one spent long enough staring at the stalagmites which
crawled across the plain on their damned rounds, one might
imagine that many bore the distorted visages of those whom
Nils Hansen had slain.

A lichen stared up at the red, swollen sun which could no
longer bring it comfort. The corniche cracked away, sliver
by sliver. There was no other movement in the airless void
overlooking what had been a beach.

The lichen had endured, starving more slowly than the rock
eroded around it. In the ordinary course of existence, the lichen
would continue to endure for countless eons; helpless in the
grip of entropy and a pain no less real for being visited on a
lifeform little more complex than a bacterium.

A streak, especially vivid for occurring in a void where no
gases diffused its light, flashed across the landscape. Rock
smashed to vapor at the touch of the hypervelocity slug. A
patch of corniche vanished in the cleansing flare.

The glow faded, leaving the scene much as it had been
before. The sun's dull red eye remained—

But the lichen had found peace at last.

Saburo knelt on the roof courtyard of his palace, facing
a table. On the table's surface were sand ridges and three
irregular bits of tuff—ash blown from the vent of a volcano
to harden in the air. The eyes of the slim god were open, but
his expression was blank. His mind was fading to gray void.

Above the crag-top palace, clouds boiled in a storm lighted
opalescent by internal lightning strokes. The rain lashed down

to within meters of the courtyard, then sluiced sideways against an invisible barrier. Droplets from the heavens mingled with spray kicked up against the rocks; fresh water with salt, neither penetrating the limpid perfection of Saburo's mind.

If he could clear his mind completely, then he would be above existence—even the existence of a god. He would be worthy of the Princess Mala. When he had made himself worthy, then Mala would come. When—

A lambent streak ripped across a short distance of the courtyard. The sand table shattered.

Saburo shouted and hurled himself backward. Servants poked their heads up the staircase, then ran to help their master.

Saburo stroked his tingling face in wonder. His fingers felt gritty and glittered when he stared at them.

His cheeks were covered with microbeads, like the tektites formed by a meteor strike. The uranium slug on its track through Plane Seven had friction-heated the sand on the table to glass.

Fortin stood in the hall of his ice palace. His upper lip quivered with ecstasy. He stared through the milk-streaked discontinuity toward the lowering splendor of Keep Starnes.

Fortin could not see what was happening within the keep, but he could guess. Hansen had gone straight ahead in his pride, in arrogant *certainty* that he was better than all the forces Count Starnes could range against him.

That he was better than Fortin . . . though Fortin knew a truth that Nils Hansen would die rather than learn. Fortin was as low as the algal slime on stagnant pools—but for all that, Fortin was as good as any *man,* human or android or self-loathing halfling like himself. . . .

Because of Hansen's pride, Hansen would die. Was dying *now.*

Fortin quivered before the dark mirror of the discontinuity. If he dared, he could watch the event rather than the exterior of the city/building in which the event occurred. He could see the vain struggles, the blood; the *screams,* perhaps, as the victim learned there was truly no escape.

To become a spectator meant becoming a victim as well. Fortin understood perfectly how Count Starnes' mind worked, and how little mercy Starnes would show if Fortin returned to the keep. But it would almost be worth that to watch Nils Hansen humiliated in the final degree.

The handsome half android paced by habit around the facets of the discontinuity, but his mind was caught in the vision of what he could not see. *The pain, the terror. . . .*

Fortin's servants stood in plain sight at the arched entrances to the central court. They were afraid to be accused of hiding if their master needed them, but they desperately avoided looking at the court. When Fortin was in this mood, he was less predictable and far more dangerous than a wounded sabertooth.

"What are you doing now, Commissioner?" Fortin whispered as he stared toward the facet showing Keep Starnes. His voice was thick with gloating and self-disgust.

The discontinuity shattered. Eight simultaneously co-existing images of the same uranium slug ruptured its fabric from within. The mirror through which Fortin viewed life vanished with the slap of air rushing to fill hard vacuum.

Eight glowing tracks hung in the courtyard for a moment before they dissipated.

Fortin stared at empty air.

And began to scream.

The Citadel of Keep Starnes rocked with the whiplash *crack!* of the railgun.

The track that vanished a finger's breadth from Hansen's face reappeared a meter to the rear of Count Starnes' vehicle. The projectile retained the same heading and virtually the same velocity as when it left the muzzle of the count's gun. The only difference was that it now was behind him.

The slug hit the tank with the sound of a hammer on an anvil, magnified to cataclysm by the velocity and densities involved.

The vehicle lurched forward despite its mass. The frontal slope bulged. A white glow marked where it took the slug's impact on its inner face. The side and roof armor, relatively thin, ballooned outward.

Everything in the projectile's path inside the tank had been converted to gas at a propagation rate faster than that of high explosive.

The hatch through which Count Starnes had entered his vehicle flew back across the rotunda. The slug's entry hole was a neat punch-mark in the center of the panel. Orange flame, then a perfect ring of black smoke, spouted from the opening.

All the tank's systems were destroyed. The vehicle's carcase crashed to the concrete in a dim echo of the impact which had gutted it. Anything flammable within the tank began to burn.

Hansen grinned. He held Plaid's pistol in his right hand. "Your turn, Karring," he called in a clear, terrible voice as he sauntered toward the Fleet Battle Director.

≡ 44 ≡

OLRUN FOCUSED HER gaze on a corner of the white wall beyond Sparrow. She asked coolly, "How will you take us to your master's home?"

At the word 'us,' Sparrow quirked a taut grin at the kneeling maid. "The way I came," he said. "A place where the worlds rub together, yours and Saburo's; a discontinuity."

He looked down at Mala. The princess lay limp as a sea creature brought from such depths that its cells burst from internal pressure. "You'll ride with me on the skimmer, princess," he said gently. "There may be some mud and discomfort. But as soon as you reach my master, he will dress you in gold and diamonds—or in flowers, if that's what you wish."

Mala groaned. "I *wish*," she murmured, "to stay here and live the life I choose to live."

"When we get back, Mistress Olrun," Sparrow said, as if apropos nothing, "I'll remove your slave collar."

Olrun released Sparrow's dog and stood up. The bitch ran to her master, yapping excitedly. She calmed almost at once when she had sniffed the backs of his knees.

Sparrow reached down to scratch her ears, but the dog had already trotted off to resume the course of exploration interrupted by the events in the bower's central room.

As she passed the theatrically-sprawled princess, the dog snuffled Mala's outflung hand. Mala shrieked in despair and

flailed blindly. The dog woofed and left the room, her claws
clicking.

Sparrow's face was without emotion. Once he too had hidden
himself from the world . . . but the world had found him. As if
idly, the smith's fingers touched the top of the leg brace he had
made with such cunning that he could walk almost as well as a
man with uncut hamstrings.

He hadn't made the world; he only acted a part in it. If
sometimes he regretted that part, well, there were many things
he regretted in life.

Mala got up from the floor. She had no taste for playing a
role in a farce.

"What sort of transportation do you have here?" Sparrow
asked Olrun.

The maid grimaced. "None," she said. "We never go out.
Sometimes Prince Morfari comes by, or the king. . . ."

She let her voice trail off, glancing with concern at her
mistress. Mala did not appear to have heard the accidental
reference to her brother.

Or perhaps she had. "I want time to see my fam—my father,"
the princess said with her face averted. Her right index finger
stroked the perfect, pumpkinseed nails of her left hand. They
were painted a green identical to her innermost garment in hue
and metallic luster.

"No, lady," the smith said quietly. "You will come with
me to Saburo. My master may allow your kin to attend the
wedding—I don't know. When I've delivered you to Saburo,
he will choose how you are to be kept. Until then . . ."

Mala covered her face with her hands.

"Why?" asked the maid unexpectedly. "Why don't you let
her see Nainfari? You'd bring her back again, wouldn't you,
whether he let or no?"

Olrun's face was expressionless, but her eyes reflected the
vibrant animation Sparrow heard in her voice. He didn't answer
for a moment. The dog returned to the central room, brushed
by the maid in friendly fashion, and tapped over to her master
to be stroked.

"I would find her if she hid," the smith said carefully. He
watched Mala from the corner of his eye.

"I would bring her though she resisted," he continued. His voice was taking on the harsh sense of purpose that Sparrow could not avoid when his mind turned toward contingencies and the ruthless certainty with which he would deal, had always dealt, with obstacles.

"If others tried to stop me—"

His hand played, perhaps unknowingly, on the ivory pommel of the dagger he had taken from a waste of muck and blood.

"—then I would take her anyway. But not even the gods, milady, can bring the dead to life. And that . . ."

He looked squarely, appraisingly, at the princess.

" . . . is why I do not choose to leave your mistress to her own devices. Until I've accomplished the task my master set me."

"Your *duty,*" Mala sneered. "A slave's duty!"

"My task, lady," Sparrow said. He smiled, a slowly-mounted expression which finally enveloped his whole bearded face. "A man's task."

Mala turned abruptly away.

The dog whined softly. Sparrow reached down and rubbed the animal's ears.

"We'd best go, now," he said in a detached voice. "I have no wish to harm your kin."

"What should I pack?" asked Olrun. She forced a bright smile to meet Sparrow's eyes, but the smith knew the maid was still afraid that he was going to leave her behind.

His smile and face softened. "All will be provided. There's nothing you'll need, Olrun, you or your mistress either. And besides, the skimmer that we have for transport won't carry but two as it is."

Sparrow gestured abruptly with his chin. "Come," he said. "We need to be going."

Mala said nothing. She remained stiff as a statue, facing the empty wall. Olrun looked from her to the smith.

"Shall I take your arm, lady?" Sparrow asked in a voice as soft as the creak of a catapult being twisted to lock.

The princess turned like a marionette and walked toward the dome's entrance. She took short, precisely-measured steps.

"She will find that Saburo shares a heart and soul with her," the smith said conversationally to Olrun as the two of them followed the princess. "She'll actually be happier than she is now—"

Mala, moving like an automaton, touched the door switch. The panel began to swing down from its housing.

"—but I don't expect anyone to like being coerced," Sparrow continued. "Any more than I did, in my time."

Warm, fetid swamp air oozed through the open doorway. Mala shuddered uncontrollably. She tried to force herself to step into the muddy courtyard. Her dainty foot hung, quivering above the surface.

"I'll fetch the skimmer, lady," Sparrow said with a certain degree of pity. "You and I will ride."

The princess edged aside so that Sparrow could get past her without contact. The dog brushed between the man and android, barking joyfully to be outside again.

"When we reach my master's palace," Sparrow continued over his shoulder, "you'll have luxury that you've never dreamed of."

"I am a king's daughter!" Mala said.

"Ah, but there'll be flowers," said Sparrow from the courtyard gate. "You'll like them."

He got onto the skimmer and lifted it from where it had settled. Mud curled and spattered from the repulsion surfaces. When the vehicle had cleaned itself, Sparrow guided it through the gateposts and up to the dome where the princess waited.

"Milady," he said, grounding the vehicle again.

Mala broke from the doorway. She ran around Sparrow, headed toward the gate. The dog barked and gamboled alongside her.

"Lady!" Sparrow cried. He blipped the twistgrip, lifting the skimmer again. It would be hard to chase the girl down on the vehicle without injuring her, but she was too fleet for him to catch on foot. . . .

"Sparrow!" Olrun screamed. "Get out of the courtyard! She's going to clear the defense controller!"

Mala snatched open the access plate in the back of the left gatepost. Within were banks of touch-sensitive switches and two large red handles.

The upper handle disconnected all the weaponry which

defended the courtyard. The second handle, intended for use after the first one had been pulled, cleared the defensive unit's memory completely.

Mala looked at Sparrow. Her face was a skull mask. She reached for the lower switch, knowing that the blast would vaporize her even if Sparrow and the maid managed to fling themselves back into the enforced exile of the dome.

Sparrow's hands were on the ends of his probability generator. It pivoted between his index fingers, glowing indigo and violet.

Mala touched the switch.

A slug of collapsed uranium, moving at the speed of a meteorite, ripped across the courtyard. The gatepost disintegrated with an electrical crash that echoed the thunderclap of the railgun bolt's own passage.

The blast hurled Princess Mala onto her back in the mud. The wall's tough plastic drank the energy from multiple shorts within the weapon-control circuits and melted in on itself.

The black wall lost the threatening glimmer which bespoke weapons live and prepared to rend intruders. The dog was angry and frightened. She barked and feinted attacks in the direction of the smoking, spluttering gatepost.

Sparrow began to laugh. He grounded the skimmer. Olrun looked at him in a mixture of fear and wonder.

"I think . . . ," he said, " . . . that we'll go in a different fashion for safety."

He put his broad right hand on Olrun's waist and guided her onto the skimmer.

≡ 45 ≡

THE CORRAL FENCES were of strong posts on masonry foundations a meter high. They were meant to hold aurochs and, in a pinch, herds of half-tamed mammoths. The barriers weren't proof against men whose battlesuits could shatter rock and sheer through any weight of wood. Even so, the rubble and flaming debris would be some protection for the outnumbered defenders.

Better than nothing.

"Battalion!" Hansen said. He lumbered through a gate left open. Stockmen had driven their herds to yards near the port, safer when the Confederate army arrived. "Hold up here and form close order!"

Five men in close order. Well, you did what you could.

Horsemen bolted past the gate. Hansen's men had been overborne by imperial riders backed by the section of battlesuited warriors. A few scouts carried crossbows that they weren't delaying to reload.

Blood paused at the entrance to the corral. His weapon licked out to its maximum length and touched a lancer wearing a quilted jack. The shock threw the man off his mount. His linen armor was aflame. The arc didn't have the amperage at five meters' range to detonate the victim's own body fluids, but he was certainly dead for his presumption in coming too close to a warrior.

Hansen wasn't absolutely sure that the rider was one of

Venkatna's troops. *What the hell, he wouldn't be the last man to die this day.*

"Ever'body take it easy," Blood said calmly. "The boss, he's the left end and I'm the right. You other three, you just stay in the middle 'n back us the best ye can."

"How many of 'em are there?" gasped al-Hauk. Jogging in a poor-quality battlesuit left the user feeling like he'd run the gauntlet. Hansen knew that very well.

"Don't ye worry about it," Blood said. "When they see the whole army eat up behind them, they'll run like lizard slavers're on their tails."

Did Blood believe that? Did he even care?

The images echoed from North's battlesuit were a-dance with the light of arc weapons. Three imperial warriors braced themselves to stop 'the Simplain prince.'

Hansen had never measured himself against North in a battlesuit. Captain North had seen his share of hard places before he came to this world and to godhead. His battlesuit was the template from which smiths forged other armor in the Matrix, and North was an artist in its use.

The center man of the imperial trio thrust. North stopped dead. Instead of crossing his arc with the threatening one, he slashed left-handed at a sideman and cut off the fellow's feet at the ankles.

The leading imperial glanced reflexively toward the toppling victim. *Then* North thrust home, striking at the junction of helmet and plastron. The remaining sideman bellowed in rage and stepped into the sparks streaming in ropes from his leader's short-circuited armor. North's backhand cut was almost contemptuous in the way it ripped the third victim's arm off at the shoulder.

Three men were dead in dazzle and fury, and North was through Venkatna's front line. The defensive screen of his battlesuit had not been required to block a single hostile arc.

"They're coming by the gate," Brownow noted in a high-pitched voice.

He must be using an order-of-battle display like the 30% mask across Hansen's own field of view. That was more initiative than Hansen would have expected from somebody wearing a piece of junk like Brownow's suit. If he survived this fight, Hansen would see to it that Brownow went into the next one better equipped; but there wasn't a chance in hell of that happening, so fuck it. . . .

"They're coming *to* the gate," Hansen said aloud. "Back me, boys, I'm going to handle this one myself."

Imperial warriors had swept around the corral in both directions. Nobody'd cut a path through the fence; a facet of Hansen's mind realized that they must still think there were fifty hostiles within the 500-meter stone and timber circuit.

The gate was wide enough to pass two bull aurochs side by side, but the beasts would be rubbing against one another. The four armored warriors who burst through together were cramped as well, to a slight but fatal degree.

Hansen stepped forward. He thrust high at the cerulean-armored man on the left of the line. The fellow wore a royal suit, and his nearest companion was nearly as well equipped.

Cerulean blocked Hansen's arc expertly. His companion's nervous slash flicked Cerulean's helmet in a hasty attempt to strike Hansen. Cerulean's armor failed under the double load. His voice screamed through a last blast of static on his external speaker.

Hansen used the upright dead man as a shield to block the imperial warriors pressing from behind. He stabbed Cerulean's companion in the groin, toppling him against the men bound by the right gatepost. Hansen's arc extended across their plastrons.

The armor of the last pair was of only moderate quality. It failed with two quick *cracks* and a gout of orange sparks.

Hansen stepped back. High-density arcs had burned air to ozone. His lungs throbbed as though he had been breathing vitriol. His gauntlets were hot, both of them. He hadn't been conscious that he was striking the last pair with his left hand until after they died. *Something unplanned, something instinct had suggested and reflex had put to lethal effect. . . .*

"Mine," said Blood. He lunged forward to meet an imperial warrior trying to clear the sudden windrow of bodies with a desperate leap.

Hansen swung to back his man, but Blood didn't need the

help. His arc crossed the imperial's while the latter had both feet in the air. The power draining to the arc weapon froze the imperial's knee joints. He crashed down on his face with his limbs splayed.

Blood hacked off his head. The three other members of the Ambush Battalion ripped the legs and belly armor. The victim didn't need it, but perhaps Hansen's men did.

"They're breaking through the sides of the corral," wheezed Brownow.

"Right," said Hansen with the exalted calm he always got at the killing times, *as he ought to know by now.*

Venkatna's men bunched outside the open gateway. Cerulean had probably been the section leader. Dust swirled over the scene like a stripper's last veil, drawing attention to the bloody tangle that it did not conceal. "Not yet, when I tell you to move."

The Order of Battle display showed a blue wedge cutting into a red block, and a smaller red block shifting from the reserve to meet the point of the wedge. On the visuals relayed from Captain North's suit, twenty imperial troops double-timed to stop the Simplain charge—

And Krita was one of the imperials.

Arcs sawed into the corral fence at a dozen locations around the circumference. Blue-white electrical flux flickered viciously through the orange flames springing from the wood. Where imperial weapons touched the masonry, rock shattered and the yellow-white glare of superheated lime dimmed the rising sun.

An imperial stepped toward the gate. Hansen spread the thumb and forefinger of his right hand. His arc leaped out between the gateposts and kissed the imperial's frontal armor.

Defensive screens flared but withstood the arc. The imperial staggered; his fellows wavered back with him.

"Now!" Hansen shouted as he wheeled toward the most serious of the assaults on the corral fence.

A three-meter section of wall collapsed in a heap of blazing timbers. The imperials had severed tie-beams at the top of the fence as well as carving through the uprights. Some of the poles fell into the corral. The shattered foundations were a sea of white fire.

Hansen had thirty meters to run. He reached the gap in the fence as the first two imperial warriors struggled out of the flames. They swept their arcs widely in order to drive back opponents for the instant they were blinded by the inferno of their own creation.

Hansen thrust like a surgeon lancing a boil. His arc ripped the inside knee of the left man of the pair. The second warrior stumbled over the toppling body of his companion. Hansen stabbed through his backplate, where the neck joined the shoulders.

Another warrior bulled through. His arc met Hansen's, held for a moment. Two more imperials crashed into him from behind. Hansen and Blood—*only a stride behind, but so much heat and glare and fresh, stinking death*—cut the trio apart before they could disentangle.

The wood fire roared, supercharged by misdirected arcs.

"They're behind us!" Brownow said/screamed.

Hansen drew a deep breath. His arms to the shoulders felt as though they were being squeezed in red-hot iron. He turned.

Venkatna's warriors had rushed the gate after Hansen's force withdrew. Other imperials straggled through gaps they'd blasted in the fence at points the defenders couldn't reach.

Empey, Brownow, and al-Hauk lunged at the nearest of the oncoming enemy. They struck simultaneously, luck aiding desperation. The imperial warrior threw up his arc to block Empey's cut, but al-Hauk's thrust sizzled on the fellow's helmet. The paired arcs drew enough power that when Brownow slashed low an instant later, the imperial's suit failed in a spurt of glass, steel, and pelvis burned to carbon.

Other imperials hit the Confederates from both sides and the front. Brownow's cry of triumph was a one-syllable squawk as all three of Hansen's men died. Hansen took an imperial from behind while the fellow concentrated on Empey, but then he and Blood were back-to-back in a ring of hostile warriors.

The main Mirala onslaught was drowning in its own blood against Venkatna's army.

North's viewpoint danced like a dervish. Each shift was accompanied by a cut from one hand or the other. Many of the cuts went home.

It wasn't enough, just as North's disciplined wedge of

mercenaries hadn't been enough—quite—to rip the fabric of the imperial line. His force had melted away under assault from all sides, as soon as the imperial reserves managed to slow the initial impetus.

The Mirala Confederates had started the battle with superior numbers, but their opponents fought as three-man units instead of being a mob of individuals. Trebled strokes would overload any battlesuit, even the best. Trying to overwhelm with mere numbers a force so disciplined was like trying to quench a fire with naphtha.

Captain North was almost alone, but his opponents gave him a wide berth. One of the suits at North's feet had a blue plastron and silver limbs. The helmet lay a meter away, burned black by the arc that had severed it.

Lord Salles had met his match at last.

"Try *that* again, fuckhead!" Blood shouted as he thrust at an imperial who'd made a distant pass at him. The man lurched back to the safety of his companions; but it wouldn't be long now.

"Hey, boss?" Blood gasped.

They were both breathing through their mouths, gasping in deep lungfuls that still weren't enough to fuel the needs of battle. The mucous lining of Hansen's nose and throat had been eroded by the trickle of ozone which leaked through his battlesuit's filters.

"Go ahead."

"D'jew see the way Brownow sold that bastid a farm? Suit as good as mine, too! You know, I—"

Two imperials came at Hansen's front while a third poised to the left. Hansen feinted left with his arc a long whip. One of Venkatna's men lunged a half-step ahead of his comrade, just in time to catch the full density of Hansen's weapon switched to the right hand.

Hansen's thrust penetrated the plastron. The latch gave. The whole frontal plate flew open, driven by the victim's exploding chest.

"—didn't think they'd keep *up* with us, let—"

Both the surviving imperials hopped back into the circle.

"—alone fight. But they sure—"

On the remote display, Krita in her black armor stepped
forward. Her arc crossed North's. That quadrant of Hansen's
visor flared into white static. The roar of the huge outrush of
power made the air quiver even in the corral half a kilometer
distant.

The Searcher's suit was as good as that of the master she
long had served—

North's viewpoint suddenly cleared. Krita fell backward.
Her helmet was the gray and black of fiery disaster instead
of paint.

Should have been as good.

"—did that bastid up a treat!" Blood concluded as six of
Venkatna's men rushed him together and he lunged a pace
forward to meet them unexpectedly.

The remote transmission disappeared from Hansen's visor.
North had vanished—into the Matrix, and into the legend of
the Open Lands. His godlike laughter boomed in Hansen's
ears; then it too was gone.

Blood's attack caught the imperials off-balance. They fouled
one another. One went down and a second, arcs and overloading defensive screens tearing across the sonic and visual
spectra. Hansen's quick pivot and swipe cut an imperial's legs
off at the knees.

The man fell forward, covering the corpse of King Wenceslas' bodyguard. The backplate of Blood's garish armor had
been blasted by the weapons of at least three opponents. Both
his gauntlets glowed from the arcs they had been directing till
the moment he died.

*If Blood's mother was anything like her son, she'd tear the
throat out of the first of Venkatna's men to come to her farm.
But they would come. . . .*

For a moment, only the crash of the burning fence broke the
silence within the corral.

Nils Hansen knew that even gods had to die some day.

And he knew that he wasn't going to run from the battle in
which Krita had fallen.

≡ 46 ≡

DEEP IN THE Web, Race and Julia ran the figures of warriors through the icy fingers of their minds. Sorting, choosing; plucking one here, another there.

The terrible weight and chill of the Matrix impinged upon the Searchers, but they no longer felt its crushing burden as they had on their previous journeys into the frozen heart of probability.

Race and Julia were carrying out orders, as they were sworn to do. If the results were not what Venkatna desired, then he should have thought of that before he screamed his orders. This day he would get precisely what he asked for—

To the hilt.

Figures moved in two discrete settings, dwarfed by the vastness of infinity. The Searchers merged portions of one parcel with the shrinking remainder of the other; picking and choosing; using the power of the Web, but working with a subtlety that only the knowledge they had gained as humans made possible.

No peace? Then war would continue.

Warriors disappeared from North's battleplain. Their figures reappeared in the stinking, smoke-shrouded corral outside Frekka, at the side of Nils Hansen.

A warrior in red-and-gold armor; a warrior in horizontal stripes of black and yellow; a warrior in armor burnished to

*the bare metal, save for the chevrons of a marshal on the sides
of his helmet. . . .*

There were not so very many of the warriors who joined
Hansen: a handful, a score; perhaps as many as a hundred at
the end.

*A warrior in lime green with a gold phoenix on his breast;
a warrior in red and white; a warrior whose battlesuit had a
blue torso and limbs of gleaming silver. . . .*

Not so very many warriors; but they all wore armor of royal
quality, and they were all very good men.

*A pirate with bronze wings welded to the sides of his helmet;
a warrior in orange swirls; a warrior in gleaming silver with
no other marking. . . .*

Or they had been good men, in the days they lived and
walked the Open Lands.

≡ 47 ≡

LIFE WAS GOOD, now that it was about to end, but Nils Hansen stepped forward anyway.

Imperials in front of him retreated, but he heard the rasp of weapons at his back—

And knew that he was dead—

And charged the clot of hostile warriors, watching them shout and stumble over Blood's body. Hansen's arc flicked like a viper's fang and lopped off an imperial's wrist.

He wasn't alone any more. Taddeusz strode at Hansen's right hand in red-and-gold armor.

Whatever you said about Marshal Taddeusz—Hansen had said plenty—no one had ever denied he was a bad man with whom to cross arcs. A pair of imperials were too startled by Taddeusz' sudden appearance to react intelligently.

They see-sawed. One of them backed a step, then lunged forward to support his fellow who had tried for a moment to guard himself but retreated a heartbeat later.

Both imperials wore decent armor, suits in the third- or fourth-class range. There was no armor better than that of the dead warriors on North's battleplain, and few warriors ever with more experience than Taddeusz had of killing in a battlesuit.

The red-and-gold figure struck alternately, right gauntlet and left; into one opponent's hip joint, through the other's guard and into his throat with fireworks of molten metal.

"Follow me!" boomed Taddeusz' amplified voice, but only because that was the sort of thing leaders were supposed to say. The warrior who had in life been warchief of Peace Rock didn't care if others followed him, so long as he himself was able to stride into the midst of blaze and slaughter.

"I'm closing your left, Lord Hansen!" called a once-familiar voice over the Ambush Battalion push. Hansen cut at an imperial. The man parried Hansen's arc, but the power drain froze the joints of the fellow's armor and heated the outer skin of his gauntlet bright red with the current of only a fraction of a second.

Shill, painted like a bumblebee—

Shill, who had closed Hansen's flank until he died, doing his job—

Shill stepped forward to lop off the imperial's head. He used the training Hansen had hammered into him, and the splendid battlesuit his soul wore since Nils Hansen got him killed. . . .

There were a dozen beads of gold light on Hansen's Order of Battle overlay, covering the sides and back of his own solitary blue pip. More joined every moment, though he didn't—couldn't—didn't *dare*—look around to be sure there was hard metal and ceramic backing the signals on his helmet screen.

"All friendly units!" Hansen ordered. He didn't know what to call the force now at his disposal. *Men he had killed, men he had gotten killed . . . and men no more.* "Rush the gate!"

He didn't want his troops to struggle over walls reduced to blazing rubble, the way the imperials had done. These were Nils Hansen's men *now,* for whatever reason. He would spend them if he had to, but he wouldn't throw them away.

Taddeusz was in front of the line, the way the self-willed bastard *always* was. For a change the big warrior's lack of discipline worked better than any plan could have done. His berserk fury hit the clump of six imperials—half-arrayed, half-retreating—in front of the gate. Taddeusz shattered them.

Hansen's screen blanked the sparks and purple coruscance to save his vision. He paused, then lunged forward seconds later when the glare of arcs and screens faded.

Four of Venkatna's men were down. Two got through the gateway ahead of Taddeusz' ravening arcs, but the red-and-gold figure was right behind them. He cleared the gateway that would have been too strait for even a pair of warriors advancing deliberately—

And Hansen was behind *him,* with Hansen's two sidemen following at a half-step's distance.

He'd never known the name of the warrior on his right. He'd been bodyguard to one of Frekka's Syndics—a century ago when Nils Hansen killed him.

The imperial section didn't know what had hit it. For that matter, neither did Hansen, but he'd learned long since not to slack off when his opponent stumbled. He crossed arcs right-handed with the nearest of Venkatna's troops. Even as Hansen spread his left gauntlet to stab home from an unexpected direction, Shill took the fellow's knees from under him.

"Suit!" Hansen said. He was gasping, but it didn't seem to slow him down. He was burning adrenaline in place of oxygen, he guessed. "Where the fuck's Venkatna? Gimme a—"

His right sideman engaged an imperial warrior. Hansen spun and slashed by instinct, overloading the enemy's carapace armor with a bang that blew the dead man forward in a cloud of steam and vaporized steel.

"—vector!"

A bead of imperial purple gleamed on Hansen's map overlay, amid the other Order of Battle information. "In his palace," said the suit AI.

It spoke in a sweetly feminine voice that Hansen hadn't heard it synthesize before. A comment on Hansen's lack of courtesy or he missed his bet. Even the machines were getting smart-ass.

"All units," he called. "Toward the palace!"

He doubled Shill's stroke on a warrior in green and blue—needless, the imperial was already toppling, his suit dead and the man too almost certainly. The rhythm was the thing, though, get into the rhythm of slash and lunge and the fighting would take care of itself.

Taddeusz' suit failed with a thunderclap.

There had been at least six of Venkatna's men surrounding

Taddeusz. It was possible that every one of them had managed to get an arc home simultaneously. No battlesuit was capable of withstanding such abuse. The shockwave of ceramic components converted to gas lifted dust from the trampled soil.

Nothing remained where Taddeusz had been. No ashes charred from blood and bone, not even an empty battlesuit.

"Let's go!" Hansen shouted as his arc rocked an imperial whom his sidemen lopped to collops.

Taddeusz had done them another favor in his last instants by concentrating the attention of Venkatna's nearby troops on himself. When Hansen and the rest of his line hit the enemy, they went down like barley before a scythe.

There was nothing closer than the main imperial army that could stop Hansen now—

And the main army wasn't going to do the job either. Almost a hundred warriors followed Hansen, spreading out to either flank. Enough when they were as good as they were . . . and as well equipped as they were . . . and when Nils Hansen was leading them toward the spot the enemy was most vulnerable, as he always did.

The straight line toward Venkatna's palace led through a jumble of shanties and cribs which had serviced drovers and troops from the nearby barracks. The Strip had caught fire earlier in the day—earlier in the *morning,* it was still morning, even though a thousand men or more had died since the sun rose.

The flimsy buildings had too little substance to long sustain a fire, but as Hansen's armored boots stirred the ashes, they kicked orange tongues to life.

"Golsingh and Victory!" Shill called, a battlecry dead almost as long as the man who shouted it.

"Frekka and Freedom!" boomed Hansen's other sideman. Top-ranked warriors were by definition competitive. From the way they'd sliced through Venkatna's men, Hansen knew the troops he now led were the best.

From their performance today, and from their performance in the days that Nils Hansen watched them die.

The palace was in sight. Half a dozen imperial warriors braced themselves across its entrance. Their arc weapons licked in and out to maximum distention.

The display was probably meant to be threatening. Instead, it painted Venkatna's men with a look of nervous indecision. That emotion was just what the poor bastards were feeling, if they had the sense God gave a goose.

The buzzsaw shriek of arc weapons sounded to the east. What had been the imperial right flank stumbled down onto the right flank of Hansen's force. Venkatna's men were confused and shaken already by hard fighting, but they were professionals and still three hundred strong.

The imperials in the palace entrance hunched instinctively lower. They knew that if they held for as little as three minutes, the weight of their fellows could win the battle for Venkatna after all—

And incidentally, save the lives of the remaining guards.

The threat was the imperial main body. If Hansen ignored that mass of troops to crush the entrance guards, the chances were very good that his whole force would be cut down from behind.

He opened his mouth.

"Maharg to Hansen!" crackled a voice on the command channel. "Take what you need, buddy, and let me handle the rear guard. Over!"

"Suit," Hansen ordered because there wasn't time for hesitation, wasn't *ever* time to look gift horses in the mouth, "pick six, they're Blue Group. Other units, form on Marshal Maharg."

He was gasping, but the air his lungs dragged in burned and his arms burned back as far as the shoulders while his gauntlets glowed. Pain wouldn't matter until afterward.

"Blue Group, *follow me!*"

The seven warriors hit the entrance guards like a broad-headed arrow; six warriors who had been men, and Nils Hansen at the point. Light ripped across the sky and the building's facade of colored marble.

Two of Venkatna's men hacked together. Hansen's right sideman vanished with a blue-white glare and a dull implosion. The men who—killed?—him were dead, and their fellows were dead.

Sections of battlesuit bubbled white and jounced to the flagged courtyard. The larger chunks of torso, some still attached to armored legs, fell more slowly because of their greater inertia.

"Up Wenceslas!" bawled the warrior now guarding Hansen's right side. "Gut the bastards!" His suit had a silver ground, decorated with painted drops of blood.

The palace doors exploded. Arc weapons shorted one another in their wielders' enthusiasm to slash through the obstacle. Gilt straps riveted to the wood as decoration curled back like honeysuckle, burning green and purple.

On Hansen's schematic overlay, seventy-odd gold dots met the rush of three hundred red markers. The red mass recoiled. The scattered Mirala army was streaming back to catch the imperials, now, in the rear.

God have mercy on any poor bastard who thought he could power through a force Maharg led.

And God have mercy on Emperor Venkatna, for Hansen would show him none.

"Follow me!" he shouted through a throat rasped raw by ozone and more subtle poisons.

The stride of Nils Hansen's armored boots cracked delicate mosaics as he ran to bring an emperor the reward his actions had earned him.

≡ 48 ≡

CHIEF ENGINEER KARRING leaped from his seat in the nearest bay and turned to run down the corridor housing the rest of the enormous mass that was APEX.

"Help!" Karring screamed as he rounded a corner that hid him from Hansen. "All troops to the Citadel! We've been—"

His direct voice faded. Speakers in the rotunda—speakers in every room and hallway in Keep Starnes—relayed the chief engineer's commands.

"—invaded!"

Hansen's head rang from the impact which had demolished Count Starnes' vehicle, and afterimages from the flash still danced across his retinas. His throat burned with combustion products of both organic and synthetic origin, fused at near-solar temperatures—

But he felt alive in a way that happened only in battle. He viewed his surroundings in crystal perfection through a template of experience and adrenaline and instinct.

Especially instinct. Without that killer instinct, Nils Hansen would not have been the man who could exist *here*.

Did Karring think to run from *him?* At fifty meters, Hansen could have emptied the pistol into the back of Karring's skull, and the tenth shot would hit before the shattered body slumped to the floor.

Hansen whistled between his teeth as he entered the bay the chief engineer had just vacated. *"This hard-liquor place, it's a lowdown disgrace. . . . "*

APEX was above and around him on all sides. Three-meter displays looked huge when attached to the outstations in the rotunda. The one in the alcove was dwarfed by the Fleet Battle Director. Lines of shifting color knotted themselves on the holographic screen.

"The meanest damn place in the town. . . . "

Karring's device spun above the entrance to the bay. Hansen swatted the hollow ovoid casually with the barrel of his pistol. Fragile connections shattered. The construct's off-balance rotation spun it across the corridor to flatten against the wall.

There was a green flash. The remnants of the delicate object drifted away as fine dust. The holographic screen blanked to an expectant pearl gray.

In the ambiance of the bay, Hansen understood better why Count Starnes—and Karring, still more Karring—had tried to trample down everything around. Living within APEX would be much like being immersed in the Matrix. Here were powers beyond the conception of a normal human; powers that could mold a human mind into something inhumane that thought itself above humanity.

Hansen understood; but he'd never been good at pity, and mercy was for after the job had been completed to full, ruthless perfection.

The Citadel trembled with unfamiliar stresses. Karring's alert—the words were little enough, but the Fleet Battle Director had certainly amplified them—had stirred up this anthill, no mistake.

Hansen's smile was instinctive. He hadn't come here to kill Count Starnes' common soldiers—

But he didn't have any objection to doing that too.

Third remained on the console. The helmet was connected through the jewel on its forehead to APEX. Hansen reached for Third with his left hand. As he did so, the huge display lighted with violet letters: NO DATA TO YOUR QUESTION.

Hansen lifted the command helmet. Crystal fetters reabsorbed themselves into the jewel with series of jerky movements, the way lightning moves across the sky when viewed in slow motion.

He settled the helmet onto his head. "*You took your time about it,*" Third commented acidly.

"Are we in a hurry?" replied Hansen in a mild voice. His eyes were as restless as wood flames, flickering across the bay and the corridor beyond, searching for dangers.

"*They'll attack us, you know,*" said Third.

Hansen snorted. "They'll do wonders!"

He dodged out into the corridor. His eyes swept left—toward the rotunda—to right, while his body moved right to follow Karring. The bays of the Fleet Battle Director alternated like the teeth in a crocodile's jaws, ready to scissor together and trap whatever entered them. . . .

"*Karring dropped the Citadel's defenses when he summoned help,*" the helmet said with electronic smugness. "*He was in too much of a hurry to be careful. He lifted the interlocks from APEX, as well. I now have full access to APEX.*"

Hansen spun into the second bay, offset from the first on the left side of the corridor. It was empty. The holographic display showed a schematic of the Citadel. Blue carats marked the elevator bank, the drain beneath the elevators in the center of the rotunda, and three of the Fleet Battle Director's twenty bays.

"You've blocked the elevators?" Hansen asked as he scanned the vast cable trunks in the shadowed darkness above him.

"*Of course,*" Third replied. There was a click of thought that would have been a sniff were there nostrils to deliver it. "*I sealed them to the shaft walls by firing the safety girdle intended to prevent the cages from free-falling.*"

Something crashed loudly in Bay 1. Hansen swung back into the corridor. As he moved, his gunhand stretched upward like the trunk of an elephant sniffing for danger.

Part of the base section had fallen from the meter-thick conduit which normally fed Bay 1 with sensory data. The edges of the metal glowed from the saws which had cut the opening. A soldier was crawling out of the hole with a short-stocked energy weapon in his hand.

Quick work, that, even though the conduits had already been gutted to trap Fortin.

Hansen fired at the soldier ten meters above him. The pistol's *blam!* and the *snap!* of its explosive bullet were almost simultaneous.

Hansen's finger twitched a second round to follow the first by reflex, but the target's chest had already vanished in a dazzling flash. The bullet had struck one of the spare energy cells in the soldier's bandolier. The cell shorted and set off at least a dozen additional charges.

The command helmet blinked to save Hansen's sight. When the visor cleared an instant later, he could see that the conduit was bulged and wrinkled all the way to the dense cap of the Citadel roof. The chain explosion had traveled up the tube like powder flashing across the ready charges in an artillery magazine. It had wiped out the whole attacking force.

You have to be good; but it helps to be lucky.

"They're cutting through by way of the elevators as well," said Third, *"but I'll see to it that it takes them some time. Did they think we came here without knowing how to use a Fleet Battle Director?"*

Hansen ran back past Bay 2 and around Bay 3 on his right again. They were not among those by which the keep's defenders were entering the Citadel.

A tremendous explosion from the rotunda shook Hansen despite the corridor's baffling. Third giggled obscenely in Hansen's mind. *"I detonated the safety charges in only one of each pair of cages. I held the rest until the fools lowered an assault gun and its caisson through the hole they'd cut in the cage floor."*

Bay 4 was another of—

Gunfire ripped and ravened in Bay 4. Hansen's command helmet projected a miniature image of what he would see when he swung into the alcove behind his gun. A dozen of the keep's soldiers had spilled out of a hole in the data feed conduit. They were shooting down into the empty bay.

Hansen moved. One shot per target, not great because they were in body armor, so he was aiming for heads and he wished he had a mob gun or a back-pack laser, something to *sweep,* but they were going down, four of them, six, and the last was the only one who saw Hansen and aimed but it was too late and the soldier's cheeks bulged as the bullet exploded in the spongy bone behind where his nose had been.

The console was slashed and punctured by the volume of fire the soldiers had directed down into it. The holographic display was still live. On it capered a life-sized image of Nils Hansen. The hologram winked and thumbed its nose at the real gunman, then vanished into electronic limbo.

Equipment and bodies dribbled from the top of the bay like water overflowing a sink. Hansen thrust the pistol's smoking barrel through his belt. He snatched up a grenade launcher.

NO DATA TO YOUR QUESTION, said the display in blocky saffron type before it went blank.

Hansen fired two grenades into the hole from which the soldiers had entered the Citadel, angling the bombs upward. They burst within the conduit. There were no secondary explosions or sign of further attackers. The weapon's original owner had already expended the other three rounds in the magazine.

Hansen tossed the launcher away. He took an energy weapon from the hands of a soldier who'd been too nervous to slide up the safety before he squeezed the trigger in vain.

Keep Starnes rocked.

"*I'm firing the main missile batteries,*" Third explained. The helmet's titter/giggle/electronic squeal scraped its nails across Hansen's mind again. "*But I haven't raised the shutters of the launch tubes. Karring really should have thought before he dropped the interlocks.*"

Fallen soldiers lay on the floor of the bay like piles of old clothes. One of the men was on his back. His eyes were glazed, but the lids blinked and blinked again, despite the bullet hole in the middle of the forehead.

Stick grenades hung from the bandoliers crossing the victim's chest. Hansen pulled two grenades off and stuffed them into his left cargo pocket.

"What type are they, Third?" he asked. The folk of Plane Five fought in armored vehicles, so standard-issue grenades were likely to be smoke for marking rather than anti-personnel.

"*Non-fragmenting assault,*" the helmet responded promptly. "*You're dealing with internal security teams. Until Fortin arrived, they hadn't been deployed operationally in the past three generations."*

"They sure kept their fucking training up," Hansen grunted. He looked at the weapon in his hands, still on Safe when its owner died. He smiled a shark's smile. *Mostly* they'd kept their training up.

The display had showed another team entering the Citadel through Bay 18. They were going to have plenty of time to prepare before the intruder reached them.

"Six men have entered the rotunda from the drain system," Third noted with thin exasperation. *"More are making their way through the elevator shafts."*

"No rest for the wicked," Nils Hansen said. He bent and took a third grenade from the bandolier. Aiming his energy weapon toward the crook in the corridor, Hansen held the grenade against the floor. He stepped on the safety ring, holding it while he drew the bomb away, armed.

"They're fanning out in the rotunda," Third reported.

Hansen threaded the corridor quickly, back to the edge of the first alcove. He tossed the grenade into the rotunda and darted back.

He wasn't left-handed, and the throw had to be side-arm anyway. For this purpose it didn't matter—and the bastards *were* good; a streak of focused plasma released its snarling fury against the corner of the bay only a fraction of a second after Hansen's hand curled back to cover.

A series of six rhythmic shocks made the whole fabric of Keep Starnes vibrate.

"Mine," the command helmet noted with cold pride. *"I overloaded the magnetic shield generators one by one. Next I will short the keep's power supply into the dome itself. It will glow like the sun before it weakens enough to collapse, Commissioner."*

The stick grenade went off in the rotunda with a triple *crack!* and a series of white reflections down the corridor instead of a unitary explosion. The bomb was designed to blind and stun defenders without fragments to endanger the assault force running toward the blast.

Hansen jogged back down the corridor. He ignored the ruin

and corpses in the bays he had cleared. That was the past, that was over.

The massive Fifth Plane bodies looked utterly inhuman in death. . . .

Hansen didn't expect the ill-flung grenade to kill or injure any of the Keep Starnes troops. It *was* likely to hold them in the rotunda for a time, though. Heavy gunfire—some of it from an automatic cannon like the one Third had blown up earlier—ripped the mouth of the corridor in confirmation of Hansen's assumption.

Ghostly holograms, a 20% mask, glowed at the lower left of Hansen's field of view. They showed a schematic of Bay 18 from which advanced six rosy beads: Keep Starnes soldiers. They were rushing in pairs.

Hansen jogged past Bay 10. He'd meet them at about 14. *They* would meet Nils Hansen, because he knew exactly how his opponents were deployed. To the soldiers, the intruder they sought was only a lethal ghost.

"You're not bad backup to have in a firefight, Third," Hansen said/gasped. He didn't notice how his lungs were burning until he tried to speak.

"*I was thinking the same thing of you, Kommissar,*" the helmet replied.

Hansen paused in Bay 12. He dragged in breaths as deep as his lungs could hold. His legs trembled. He sat in the console's chair for a moment and let his feet dangle as the muscles cleared themselves of fatigue poisons.

The trouble with living on nerves and hormones was that you could never be quite sure when you were about to exceed the mechanical limits of your body's framework.

Hansen didn't want that to happen five meters in the air.

Out of the line of Hansen's necessary vision, beads representing two soldiers flung themselves into the schematic of Bay 15. The Keep Starnes troops were alternating at point. They knew that the pair who first contacted the intruder had no purpose but to target Hansen for their fellows as they died.

Hansen slung his energy weapon. He jumped onto the console and groped within the pale glow of the holographic screen. Hansen's arms cast dark streaks when they interrupted one component of the three which gave the display solidity and color. He found the projection head and used the wrist-thick conduit which fed it as a pipe up which to shinny to the top of the alcove.

Soldiers rushed Bay 14.

"*They're trying not to damage APEX,*" Third noted in amusement. "*Karring warned them not to.*"

"Karring's a fool," Hansen gasped as he lifted himself to the platform where the thick sensor duct spread its optical cables throughout the alcove.

He unslung the energy weapon, then took the grenade sticks from his cargo pocket. There was no cover on the platform, but the shadows were thick.

The pistol barrel was so hot from rapid fire that he'd burned a blister where the muzzle lay against his thigh. He hadn't noticed it till now; and anyway, it didn't matter.

"*Karring thinks he faces only a gunman, Kommissar,*" the helmet said.

"*Though I admit . . . ,*" the mental voice added judiciously, "*he faces that too.*"

NO DATA TO YOUR QUESTION, glowed the display in orange as soldiers threw themselves around the corner into Bay 13. Their weapons swept, side to side and upward, trying to cover every nook before the intruder's snake-swift trigger finger cut them down.

Hansen pulled the safety ring from a grenade. The other four members of the Keep Starnes team joined the two scouts. A new pair poised on the edge of Bay 12.

Hansen threw the grenade stick back the way he had come. It bounced off the corridor wall and detonated within Bay 11.

The blast jolted the pair picked to clear Bay 12 into action an instant faster than they otherwise would have moved. That broke their rhythm and robbed them of concentration on the task in hand. The first two men flopped onto the floor of the alcove beneath Hansen. Two of their fellows rushed past them screaming and shooting—at Bay 10, from which they assumed the bomb had come.

The remaining pair of soldiers were also drawn off-balance by the break in routine. They jumped from cover and hesitated.

Their gun muzzles were lifted so as not to aim at the backs of their enthusiastic teammates.

One carried a grenade launcher, the other an energy weapon like the gun Hansen had appropriated. Hansen shot them, then shot the pair rising from the floor of Bay 12.

His gun fired bolts of saturated white, like bits clipped from a stellar corona. The weapon had considerable recoil. Though the plasma released could be measured in micrograms, it was accelerated to light speed by a miniature thermonuclear explosion.

The two standing soldiers flopped backward when their chests vaporized. The other pair were on their knees and twisting to scan the top of the bay as they had failed—to their cost—to do initially. The bolts slapped them against the floor again.

Hansen drew the safety ring of his remaining grenade. He lobbed it into Bay 10. The two soldiers who had rushed ahead of their companions launched themselves into the corridor before the bomb went off. They were trying to look everywhere, but the ten-meter height advantage gave Hansen the fraction of a second he needed. He dropped the men with two dazzling bolts.

One of the victims flew back into Bay 10 just as the grenade stick went off. It couldn't have mattered much to him. The bolt didn't penetrate his body armor, but its cataclysmic energy dished in what remained of the breastplate so that it was virtually a coating on the inner side of the back piece.

There were still four charges in the energy weapon's magazine, but its barrel glowed white. If Hansen tried to climb down with the gun slung, it would burn him to the bone as it oscillated on the sling. He tossed the weapon to the alcove floor.

"Karring has a pistol," Third warned.

"Karring doesn't have any balls," Hansen grunted. "Not for this."

He lowered himself hand over hand through the blank screen. His soles gripped the conduit until they swung free. "How about the guys from the other end, from the drains?"

The command helmet flashed him an image. A gang of twenty or more red beads clumped together in Bay 4. From the look of the schematic, the Keep Starnes soldiers were gnawing their way through, straightening the corridor with heavy weapons.

"*Tsk,*" chirped Third. "*They needn't destroy APEX.*"

Hansen stepped over a headless body and trotted toward Bay 20. He didn't bother to rearm himself. There were ten rounds or so in the pistol's magazine; that would be quite enough.

"I'm not going to leave APEX for another Karring to conquer the world," he said.

"*That is correct, Kommissar,*" the command helmet said. "*We are not going to leave APEX.*"

Keep Starnes shook.

"*The dome is sagging,*" Third explained. "*Its weight is buckling the internal structures of the keep. I don't believe that even the Citadel will survive. Still, I've initiated the self-destruct sequence implanted in all Fleet Battle Directors to prevent them from being captured by an enemy.*"

Hansen reached the corner of Bay 20. He paused, breathing deeply. He was not so much catching his breath as controlling it.

Hansen laughed at his own vanity; the command helmet echoed the human sound with a trill of thought.

Pistol still thrust through his belt, coveralls torn and muddy, face blackened by metal vaporized from the energy weapon's bore and recondensed on the shooter's face—Nils Hansen strode into Bay 20.

"Hello, Karring," he said. Some of the syllables caught in his throat, making them a crazy half stammer, half lilt. "Not much point in running, you know. Not from me."

The chief engineer backed against the console. The display behind him writhed in an iridescent maelstrom. Hansen couldn't guess the question which APEX was trying to answer in its last moments of existence.

Karring's pistol was in his right hand, but the muzzle trembled toward the floor. This was a man to whom war was a game won by cunning strategy and superior weapons. Not a gunman; not a killer to face Nils Hansen.

"Go away . . . ," whispered the squat, bald man.

"You *brought* me here, Karring," Hansen said as he walked closer. "I would've told myself you were none of my business, but you and your boss insisted that I *make* you my business."

The air was hot. The cable ducts feeding Bay 20 were red where they passed through the ceiling. The glow brightened the alcove.

Karring looked upward despairingly. He let the pistol slip from his fingers. "Please," he begged. "Please. Take me away with you."

"You made your bed, friend," Hansen said. "Now lie in it."

The cable duct ruptured. It began to spurt smoke or steam across the ceiling of the alcove. "Time to go, I think, Third," Hansen said.

"*Yes*," agreed the command helmet. "*But I'll make my own way back, Kommissar.*"

Hot, dry air puffed across Hansen's bare scalp. "Goodbye, Karring," he said and vanished into the Matrix himself.

NO DATA ON YOUR QUESTION, read the vermilion letters which crawled across the bottom of the huge display.

Karring's eyes opened wide. "You think you're gods!" he screamed to the empty bay. "You're not, you know? The *world* is a god and you're only its pawns! Paw—"

The roar of the ceiling's collapse drowned the last of Karring's words an instant before it crushed him into the ruins of APEX.

≡ 49 ≡

THE METAL FACING ran as Hansen's arc licked the doorleaves ahead of him. The audience hall's barred entrance tore apart in a blast of fire, charcoal, oak splinters, and the blue-white electrical tongue which flashed the portal into an orgy of self-destruction.

"There's troops comin' down the hallway towards us!" warned Shill behind him.

Hansen kicked at the center of the shattered doorleaves, where he thought the bar ought to be. He hoped Shill wouldn't decide to give the door an extra slash and get Hansen's boot instead, but at this point most actions had to be reflexive and you took your chances.

Something clanged away from the kick, an arc-severed bar or twists of decorative strap. Nothing that would have hindered the onrush of Hansen's close-coupled body wrapped in a hundred kilos of armor, but he was back on trained reflex. He hadn't worn a battlesuit until he arrived on Northworld—

A couple lifetimes ago.

Hansen crashed into the hall in a cloud of sparks and splinters. His AI instantly adjusted the visual displays to a pre-set 100% of normal daylight intensity, brightening the dim room.

"Blue Group," ordered Nils Hansen, "keep the rest of them off my back. I'll handle what's in here."

"Who are you?" boomed the Emperor Venkatna. His battlesuit was decorated in royal blue with ermine trim.

Venkatna stood at the right side of his wife's bier; behind him, Race and Julia stirred from their trances within the Web. Half a dozen slaves and palace functionaries cowered where the irruption had caught them in the large room, but there were no armored warriors except the emperor.

"I'm the guy who's come for you," said Nils Hansen as he eased forward. Arcs sputtered between his thumbs and forefingers. The flux was so dense that its color verged on the ultraviolet. "I'm what you earned for yourself."

"I earned glory!" Venkatna shouted. "I earned honor and worship!"

"Oh, no," Hansen said. His amplified voice rasped like a tiger's tongue. "That's not at all what *I* bring you, Venkatna."

The arc from Hansen's right gauntlet flicked four meters toward the emperor's helmet. Venkatna parried expertly. Madness hadn't destroyed his warrior's skills, and his suit was of royal quality.

Illumination by the snarling discharges lighted Esme's face deeper into the bluish glaze of death. Venkatna glanced aside at the corpse. As if the sight shocked him back to memory and reality, the emperor shouted, "Slaves! Make my enemies go away!"

Race's mouth gaped as she settled back. Julia had not risen from her bench. Her eyes closed, but her lips murmured, "Your orders are . . ."

Hansen lunged. He had to get past Venkatna to disrupt the Web before—

A railgun bolt, invisible save as a track of fluorescent plasma, lighted ten meters of the audience hall. The bier and the empress' corpse disintegrated under the impact and hypersonic shockwave.

Bits of the Web, shattered when the slug clipped through them, danced down on the Searchers like crystal rain.

"I wanted peace for the West Kingdom," Hansen said as he advanced slowly. "You turned it into a cancer."

His paired arcs extended twenty centimeters or so, killing range against anything short of another royal suit. When he struck home, it would be with one gauntlet or the other, not both.

The weapons pulsed slightly, forming a wave like the kerf of a metal-cutting saw.

"Who *are* you?" Venkatna screamed. He lunged, his arc extending in a sudden thrust.

Hansen parried with his left hand. He swiped at the emperor's helmet with his right. Venkatna's screens held in a roar and a momentary nimbus filling much of the hall. Paint scorched; bits of plaster dropped from the decorated vaults.

The emperor stumbled backward. Hansen continued his slow advance. The kill to come shimmered in Hansen's mind.

"I can't bring back the ones you starved to death," Hansen said. He spoke with the care of a man talking in a foreign language. All the animal parts of his brain were concerned with the animal processes of staying alive in combat; only the deeply-buried intellect formed words. "Worked to death. Killed."

Race and Julia stood against the wall, hugging one another for support. Neither woman looked capable of casting a shadow. They watched the battle with a hungry avidity, their eyes as bright as hawks'.

The probability generator had disintegrated when its integrity was broken. Its remnants lay on the floor like colored sand. Venkatna's boots streaked the granules as he backed between the benches on which the Searchers had lain.

Hansen feinted left, struck with his right. Venkatna threw himself backward from another crash and blue corona. Clerestory windows popped with the transient currents surging through them.

"But I'll send you the same place, Venkatna," Hansen promised softly. "Or a worse one."

"*Watch*—" Race warned in a shrill voice.

In Hansen's mind: *the emperor dived toward his opponent. Venkatna's body was a spearshaft and the arc from his right glove the spear's cutting head.*

In Hansen's mind.

Hansen leaped into the air as Venkatna dived forward. He didn't bother to block the emperor's thrust. Venkatna's weapon blasted a trench half a meter deep in the stone floor.

Hansen's boots crashed down on the emperor's back. His arc chopped. His gauntlet blazed in direct contact with its target. The flooring shuddered again as it drank the residual impact of Hansen's weapon.

The helmet of the Emperor Venkatna rolled away from the remainder of the battlesuit. It came to rest against the fungus-tinted cheek of his empress. The slug that smashed Esme's body had spared as much of her head as survived decay.

Hansen rose from the corpse of his opponent. The air shimmered like stress cracks deep within black ice. A pair of dragonflies appeared before Race and Julia.

"Bless you, Lord Hansen!" the emaciated women whispered. They threw themselves aboard their mounts.

Air popped in the place they had been. Freed by Venkatna's death, the Searchers rode home through the Matrix.

The doorway to the audience hall had been blasted ten meters wide and as high as the ceiling vaults. The armored carcases of at least a score of Venkatna's troops lay beyond in desperate profusion. It would be difficult to count the dead with certainty, because of the number of lopped limbs and torsos.

Body cavities still steamed from the arcs that had seared them open. Blazing draperies and lathes from the plaster work softened the carnage with gray smoke.

Only one member of Hansen's Blue Group remained: Shill, still upright though his bumblebee battle colors were blistered in a dozen places by cuts that missed lethality by a hair.

He turned and saluted Hansen with his arc. "Until the Final Day, milord," he cried.

Even as his armored soul vanished back to North's round of death and slaughter, Shill added, "We did 'em up proper this time! Didn't we, buddy?"

Hansen was almost too exhausted to stand. His arms throbbed from the oven heat of his gauntlets. His lungs felt as though they had been torn out and used to scour paving-stones.

But that was all right, that would pass.

Not even gods could bring the dead to life.

Swearing through his tears, Nils Hansen hurled himself into the icy Matrix, on his way to an empty home.

≡ 50 ≡

SABURO'S GIANT HOG, saddled and caparisoned in cloth-of-gold, snuffed its broad snout along the gravel beach. The beast was two and a half meters at the shoulder. Sparrow's dog eyed it watchfully.

Miyoko led the party which had already carried Mala and Olrun to the palace in pomp and splendor. Gulls screamed above the surf, recalling the unaccustomed display to one another.

Saburo remained, and the smith who served him.

"I, ah . . . ," said the slim god. For all Saburo's power, his nervousness quivered like a flame in dry twigs.

Sparrow stood stolidly. The cat's cradle of crystal and metal spun between the smith's index fingers, wrapped in a soft purple haze.

"You did perfectly, Master Sparrow," Saburo resumed. "I—your wishes will of course be fulfilled, whatever they may be . . . within reason."

Sparrow smiled. "The princess will need a new maid," he said. "I intend to marry the current one, if she'll have me. As I think she will."

"What?" said Saburo. "Oh. Well, of course. I've—you know, I've always wished you might find some companionship among my other servants. I—I rather feared you might be lonely, to tell the truth."

The sea breeze ruffled the god's robes of layered gossamer. The undermost was the same hue as the gold saddle-blanket, and had the same metallic sheen.

The hog had found something dead at the tide line a few hundred meters down the strand. It snorted and began to bolt the carrion while gulls complained above.

"I'm not lonely," said Sparrow. "I have my work. But Olrun is a . . . worthy person. And I hope I prove worthy of her."

For the first time in Saburo's recollection, he saw what he read as softness on Sparrow's visage.

"Yes," said Saburo. He had given the maid no more notice than he had the gulls overhead. "She, ah, seemed very suitable." With his face and tone carefully blank, the god went on, "I notice that she didn't appear to have waded through mud, the way . . . ?"

The smith nodded. "I thought that I'd better keep my attention on the princess, not the skimmer controls. Mala and I walked. The others—"

The shadow of a laugh tinged Sparrow's voice, though nothing showed on his face. His toes rubbed the flank of his dog, leaving streaks of dry mud against the animal's clean black hide.

"—rode, since we had a vehicle for them."

"I," said his master, "see."

Saburo spent indeterminate moments staring at the water. The sea was gray almost to the horizon, where it changed to deep mauve.

"I was startled when the railgun projectile disrupted my sand table," Saburo said with consummate care. His eyes were focused on the horizon. "As soon as I—looked into the matter, though, I realized that it resulted from Commissioner Hansen's sense of humor. Reckless humor, I must say. But no harm done."

Sparrow shrugged. "Lord Hansen isn't reckless, milord," he said mildly. "He always thinks through his actions. As Lord North thinks through his actions . . . and I do also, milord, sometimes."

He waited for Saburo to turn and face him before adding, "Only we act anyway, after we've thought matters through.

And no doubt that will some day cost us our lives, the three of us."

Saburo blinked. The remainder of his face was tight as he listened to a servant refer to himself on terms of equality with two gods. After a moment, Saburo shaped his mouth into a minute smile and said, "Yes, of course."

He glanced down the beach. The giant pig was half a kilometer away, scavenging the edge of the surf. Saburo frowned and pointed. A blue spark snapped from his finger. The animal lurched up on its hindquarters like a dog which has run full-tilt to the end of its chain. It turned and galloped back, huffing and pounding the shingle with its cloven hooves.

"There's one other thing, Master Sparrow," Saburo said. His manner was no longer hesitant, and his voice rang like thunder on the hilltops. "Though I took you into my service because of your ability to create things, I'm still amazed at the quality of the illusion you were able to project in the Princess Mala's bower."

"Illusion, milord?" the smith said. His eyes had been checking for the dog's location as the giant hog rushed toward them, but now his attention was back on Saburo.

"Yes," said the slim god. "The illusion that you had created a device to modify event waves."

A tick of Saburo's eyebrow indicated the ovoid rotating slowly between Sparrow's fingers. "That would constitute . . . godlike . . . powers. Which of course could not be permitted."

Saburo's huge mount braked to a halt, hunching its hindquarters beneath it and gouging trenches in the strand with all four hooves. Loose gravel hopped and danced. Some of it ricocheted from Sparrow's legs. The dog barked in sharp fury from behind her master.

None of the flying stones touched Saburo, though some of them rebounded from a hair's breadth short of his perfectly-shaded garments.

"I see," said Sparrow neutrally.

"There's not a problem with me, of course," Saburo continued. "But if anything of the sort should happen again, one of my colleagues might—misunderstand. And act hastily."

All the while the two men spoke, a freak of the weather

caused a tiny breeze to course from the general vicinity of the device in Sparrow's hands. The wind had scoured the smith's legs clean of the mud which caked them.

Sparrow eyed his legs critically, then hung the probability generator on his belt. He reached down absently to polish his leg brace with the callused fingers of his right hand.

Gulls screamed above the surf, and the giant hog drew in snorting breaths to recover from its gallop. Sparrow's dog rubbed back and forth against her master's thighs, whining softly.

"Things like that happen," the smith said. "I couldn't prevent King Hermann from crippling me, either. Though it might have been as well for him if he hadn't."

Sparrow straightened.

Saburo gave a quick nod. "So long as we understand each other," he said. He paused, no longer imperious, and added, "Captain North is quite ruthless, you know."

Sparrow smiled. "Yes, milord," he said. "As is Lord Hansen. And I would not have brought your bride to you if I were not ruthless as well."

"You are indeed a perfect servant," the god said in a voice without any emotional loading whatsoever.

He cleared his throat. "Ah . . . ," he said. "We should be getting back. I, ah, appreciate your . . ."

The dog skipped from the shelter of her master. She made short rushes in the direction of the giant pig, now that the huge beast stood cowed and blowing.

"Shall I take you to the palace myself?" Saburo asked, changing the subject brightly.

"Thank you, milord," said Sparrow. "But my dragonfly is here—"

He gestured curtly towards the spindle-legged vehicle at the edge of the high-tide line.

"—and anyway," Sparrow continued, "I think I'll walk along the beach for a while. It feels good to walk, sometimes."

He nodded, then turned and strode away at a moderate pace. Gravel crunched beneath his ponderous steps. There was nothing in front of him but weed and spume kicked onto the tumbled stones by the waves.

After a moment, the dog noticed her master's absence and gamboled after him. She barked each time her high-flung forefeet hit the strand again.

Saburo mounted his squatting hog and took its reins in his hand. The beast rose expectantly, but Saburo waited until Sparrow was almost out of sight before he wrenched his mount and himself into the Matrix.

Sunlight on the crippled smith and his crippled dog turned their leg braces into jeweled adornments.

≡ 51 ≡

NORTH ROSE IN the center of his hall, shuddering like a man dragged from drowning in the frozen waters of the Matrix.

In his own form, he was a tall, craggy man with a gray beard and one eye as gray as sea ice. There were old scars on his body, lines and puckers and a dent the size of a maul's head in the side of his left thigh.

"Welcome home, Third," said Dowson's brain in a wash of tawny light. "Were you amused by your expedition with Commissioner Hansen?"

North snorted. He made a gesture with his right hand. Loose velvet garments clothed him, very different from the Consensus Exploration Authority coveralls which he ordinarily wore in private.

"As interesting as that?" Dowson gibed. The shower of light that brought his words was as pale as dry sand. A listener who knew Dowson as well as North did could hear the regret of a disembodied brain for the days in which it could act as well as be.

North barked out a harsh, false laugh. "I'll tell you this about our kommissar," he said. "In the old days, I'd have given him a job as scout for just as long as he lasted."

He laughed again. "Which wouldn't be long at all."

Thoughts with the sheen of hydrated turquoise scaled from the pillar before Dowson's tank. "When you look to *your* end on the Final Day," the brain noted, "as Commissioner Hansen does not . . . do you not see him still fighting as the hordes sweep you under? *I* see that, Captain."

"Oh, I never said he couldn't fight," North said. His tone was so coolly unemotional that a listener could almost ignore the fact that he was changing the subject.

North stretched high in the air. The garment's loose sleeves piled on his shoulders while his scarred, knobby arms wavered above them. "That's all he knows how to do, though, the commissioner. He brought down Keep Starnes, all right, but he got nothing at all out of APEX."

North dropped his heels to the floor and lowered his arms again. "Nothing!" he repeated forcefully toward the floating brain. "It was just an excuse for him to kill. He hasn't learned that we *gods* don't need excuses to do as we wish."

Dowson's laughter was as cold as the horizon-blue light that carried it in an expanding sphere across the hall. The lower edge sparkled and vanished as it rubbed against the floor, blocks of dense white laid in intricate marquetry with blocks of void in which distant galaxies gleamed.

"I don't think Hansen will ever learn that lesson," Dowson said, drawing out the final word into a mental sneer. "But as for what he learned from APEX—"

"Nothing!" snapped North. "APEX *had* no data on how I took Northworld out of the universe of the Consensus."

"That isn't what Commissioner Hansen asked while you were coupled to the Fleet Battle Director," Dowson explained. "He asked APEX to determine what *you* knew about how Northworld was removed from the universe of the Consensus."

North made a minuscule gesture. At the end of it, he was dressed again in gray coveralls with an equipment belt and a command helmet—the utility uniform he wore when he first arrived on the planet to determine why the original exploration unit had disappeared.

"He knows that you didn't steal Northworld at all, Captain," the brain continued in a shower of faded rose. "That you accepted the powers you had been given, but that you don't have the least idea yourself of who gave them to you."

"Do you know, Dowson?" North demanded. His voice was edged steel. North had never needed rank insignia to convey his authority.

"Karring did at the end, I think," Dowson replied/half-replied. "The Fleet Battle Director was the correct tool to correlate external data with what *Third* knew and to synthesize an answer. And I suspect Commissioner Hansen—"

From the pillar shimmered icy laughter the color of rotted bronze.

"—has guessed the answer as well. Did you think the Consensus of Worlds had chosen a mere gunman as their investigator, Captain North?"

For a time without measure, the tall man stared at the brain in the tank before him. At last North began to laugh—booming, godlike mirth that echoed from the mighty vaults of his palace.

≡ 52 ≡

REACTION HIT HOME fully when Nils Hansen climbed out of his battlesuit and stood in his undergarments in the dwelling he had created for himself.

He began to tremble. When he realized that he might vomit, he tried to reach the bathroom off the main hall. Spasms caught him too soon, doubling him up on the pale, resilient flooring.

Outside the clear panels which encircled the room, morning breezes combed a landscape of grassland and brush. The boulder-huge lumps silhouetted on the eastern horizon were a herd of titanotheres.

After a few minutes, Hansen started to get to his feet. His stomach lurched again sourly, but he managed to wait the moment out. There was nothing else in his guts to lose, anyway.

The synthetic floor purred as it cleaned itself, sucking in all traces of vomit through micropores in its surface. Hansen's idea of a palace was a utilitarian structure which took care of itself and which never intruded on its master's existence the way a human servant might do.

Hansen didn't want humans watching him puke his guts up because he wasn't perfect, even though he was a god. . . .

"Sometimes I live in the country . . . ," Hansen sang in a monotone as he looked down at his garments. His shirt of gray homespun was black with sweat, and he'd managed somehow to tear the right sleeve half loose from the body as well.

And the vomit.

He loosed the gold-clasped belt a woman had given him, then pulled the shirt over his head and tossed it away. The floor would take care of it and of the breeches of naturally-black wool. They'd been well-made garments at the start of the battle. Hours of sweat and straining had felted the fabric and left it reeking like a goat in rut.

"Sometimes I live in the town," Hansen sang as he stepped the rest of the way into the shower. His presence summoned a firm spray of water, two degrees above blood temperature, without need for a command.

The filth would wash away quickly. Fatigue would pass in time. Both his arms were bright red and tingling at the water's touch, but Hansen hadn't done himself permanent injury by loading his arc gauntlets so heavily for so long. . . .

"Sometimes I take a great notion . . . ," Hansen gurgled as he closed his eyes and opened his mouth to water that could not sluice the bile from his soul.

He had watched through North's screen as Krita's battlesuit lost its luster in a cyan fireball. That memory would never heal. Nils Hansen had enough deaths in his soul to be quite sure of that.

" . . . to jump in the river and drown," chorused a woman in a throaty contralto; an attractive voice, but untrained and off-key.

Hansen's eyes opened. Krita stood outside the bathroom. She looked thin and worn. A patch of skin had rubbed from the edge of her right wrist, and the hair on the crown of her head was kinked and discolored.

She was all the beauty in the world.

"What . . . ?" Hansen said. He gestured, shutting off the water that had almost choked him.

"The door was open," Krita said. She crooked him a tired smile. Her suede singlet was polished smooth where it rubbed the inside of her battlesuit. "My lord North brought me here. After the battle."

"But you were . . . ?"

Hansen reached a hand out and drew the woman to him. She came willingly. Her normally-taut body was almost boneless in its present exhaustion.

"Not killed," she murmured into Hansen's shoulder. Her burned hair stank and cracked away as he nuzzled her. "His arc, my lord North's, it tore the top off my helmet. But not *me*."

Hansen began to laugh in a complex of emotions which he couldn't have untangled himself.

"He told me to say to you . . . ," Krita continued. She paused, desperate to get the quote precisely correct, despite her fatigue. "He said, 'You aren't the only one who could handle a weapon. . . . ' He called you 'Kommissar.' And he said—"

She raised her eyes to Hansen's and gave a half sob, half chuckle. "My lord North said that good Searchers were too valuable to waste; and that anyway, you might appreciate the favor. Was he right, my lord?"

Hansen was crying. He kissed her. Her mouth was as soft as a ripe peach.

Krita giggled in relief. "Do you mind company when you shower, my love?" she murmured.

"I don't mind you," Hansen said. The water sluiced down, and outside the sun rose in a crimson, purple splendor.

AUTHOR'S NOTE

Two of the finest and most evocative of the poems of The Elder Edda, and a tale from The Younger Edda whose poetic form has not survived, became the core of *Justice*. These are:

1. The *Grottasongr,* in which Othin gives King Frothi, a ruler who has imposed absolute peace on his kingdom, a mill which will grind out exactly what the king asks for;

2. The *Skirnismal,* in which the human servant—and friend—of the god Frey goes to fetch his master a wife from Giantland; and

3. The journey of Thor to the hall of the Giant Geirroth, for sports that the giant and his daughters plan to end with Thor's death.

The *Grottasongr* appears to have been put in its present form around the middle of the tenth century. The poet knew and probably survived the unification of Norway by Harald the Fairhaired, who died in A.D. 933.

It appears to me beyond question that when the poet spoke of the Peace of Frothi, he had in mind (rather than some soft, modern vision) the iron-shod peace that Harald imposed on the squabbling petty kings who were his neighbors. Therefore, I've based the background of the novel on the techniques which King Harald used in cold fact.

Reinhard Heydrich employed similar methods when he governed Czechoslovakia on behalf of Hitler. The technique works perfectly—if the person wielding power is both smart and absolutely ruthless. Harald differed from his red-handed fellow Vikings only because he was smarter than the rest of them.

Despite modern impressions to the contrary, there was a highly-developed legal system in Dark Age Scandinavia, from which these Edda tales spring. Courts, compromise, and the reduction of injuries to money payments were the tools of the Law.

But that was the Law. Laws are made by society and applied by society. It's the Law that puts a killer back on the street because he was of unsound mind when he raped and slowly murdered the child selling Girl Scout cookies. Unlike our own civilized place and time, the Vikings also had a system of Justice.

Justice carried a sword.

Dave Drake
Chapel Hill, N.C.